CW00521295

# ONE SMALL VICTORY

MARYANN MILLER

Copyright (C) 2019 Maryann Miller

Layout design and Copyright (C) 2019 by Next Chapter

Published 2021 by Next Chapter

Edited by Emily Fuggetta

Cover art by Cover Mint

Back cover texture by David M. Schrader, used under license
from Shutterstock.com

This book is a work of fiction. Names, characters, places, and incidents are the product of the author's imagination or are used fictitiously. Any resemblance to actual events, locales, or persons, living or dead, is purely coincidental.

All rights reserved. No part of this book may be reproduced or transmitted in any form or by any means, electronic or mechanical, including photocopying, recording, or by any information storage and retrieval system, without the author's permission.

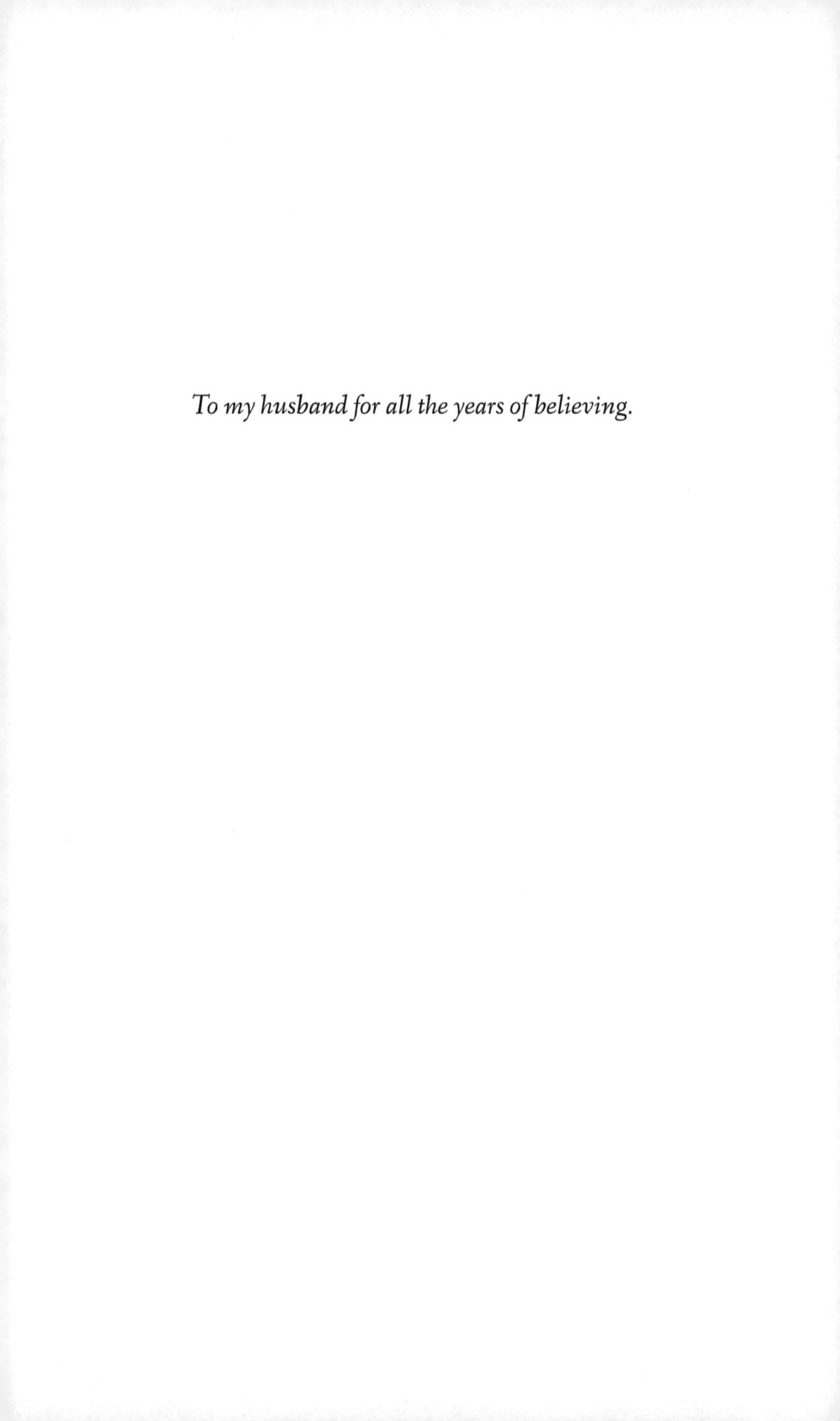

*To my husband for all the years of believing.*

# ACKNOWLEDGMENTS

I want to thank the officers at the Little Elm, Texas, Police Department for their willingness to share information and expertise. If I got something wrong in the writing, the blame is mine, not theirs. I also want to thank my son, David Miller, who is the best research assistant a person could ask for and learned all there is to know about guns working in the armory for the Marines. Semper Fi.

# PRAISE FOR MARYANN MILLER

**"*One Small Victory* is great Romantic Suspense and a read you won't want to miss."** Victoria Kennedy, Midwest Book Reviews

**"*One Small Victory* is not for the faint of heart, but it is an excellent, well-crafted novel. The tension is all pervasive, and heat, rage, sorrow, despair, and all-enveloping terror fill every page."** Carolyn Crisher for Romance Reviews Today

**"The resolution of these {personal} threads is most satisfying, in that they aren't neatly resolved, much like real life. The undercover side of *One Small Victory* is exciting and fast paced."** Reviewed by Larry W. Chavis for Crime & Suspense

**"*One Small Victory* is an engrossing suspense thriller with a hint of romance that is intelligently kept very minimal and mostly off page."** Harriet Klausner for Amazon.com ***** FIVE STARS

**"*One Small Victory* is an amazing, heart pounding, emotional tale about one mother's love of her children, and the steps she takes to protect them from harm."** Jennifer Lawrence for Amazon.com **** FOUR STARS

**"A compelling read of a grieving mother's crusade to rid the streets of her home town of drugs, and those who lure our children into addiction."** Laura Castoro, author of *Icing on the Cake* & *Love on the Line*

***"One Small Victory*** **is one huge win for author Maryann Miller and her readers. This is a novel that rings sadly true as readers follow a mother's journey from the depths of grief and loss through menacing territory ruled by street gangs and drug lords. Miller's done a masterful job of creating interesting, sometimes quirky but always believable characters and in weaving a story sure to be a favorite among lovers of mysteries and countless other genres**." Paula Stallings Yost, Editor/Author, *What Wildness is This: Women Write About the Southwest,* Editor, StoryCircleBookReviews,

**"*One Small Victory* is a riveting journey through fear, love, and a woman's determination to make things better."**

Slim Randles, author of *Sun Dog Days, Raven's Prey* and the syndicated humor column, *Home Country.*

**"While the war on drugs may not be winnable, there are occasionally small victories. Not bad."** Jack Quick for Bookbith.com

**"The writing is eloquent, and the story is well plotted, and I would recommend this book to anybody who is interested in crime novels and human drama."** BCF Book Reviews

# PROLOGUE

THE CAR HURTLED through the darkness, and the wind whipped through the open windows, a cool lash against warm skin. Mike braced his feet on the floor and fought a rising sense of panic. *How fast are we going?* He snuck a look at the speedometer. *Holy shit!* The needle inched toward a hundred, and Brad showed no sign of slowing. *Do I dare ask him to stop acting like Mario fucking Andretti?*

Mike took a deep breath. "Aren't you afraid of getting stopped?"

Brad glanced over with a cocky grin. "Are you?"

"No big deal, man. Just thought you might want to hang on to your license."

Mike wished he had the guts to say aloud the thoughts that whirled through his head. He was scared. And he wished Brad would slow down.

"You need to chill out." Brad took the joint out of his mouth and offered it to Mike. "This is excellent shit."

Mike pushed his friend's arm away.

"Hey, what's the deal?" Brad took an angry toke. "You weren't passing it up last year."

"I only did it so you'd get off my ass." Mike paused to gauge Brad's reaction. "Besides, the thrill escaped me."

"That's 'cause you never gave it a chance." Brad took another long drag. "You got to build yourself wings before you can fly."

"Just remember this isn't a fucking airplane."

Brad laughed, and Mike couldn't resist the urge to join him. That was the deal with Brad. Life was just one big joke—his reasoning for doing dope in the first place. Why shouldn't they have a little harmless fun before they had to settle down to serious living? So Mike had let him talk him into trying the grass at Dempsy's party last summer.

After the first hit, Mike had waited for some effect, but nothing happened. So Brad told him to take another. Deeper. Hold it longer. That time, Mike thought he'd cough a lung out before he got around to enjoying the benefits of the grass.

Most of the time, Mike didn't care that Brad continued to use dope. It was his life and his business. But now, as Brad's red Trans Am screamed along the narrow country highway with Mike clinging white-knuckled to the 'aw-shit' handle, it wasn't just Brad's business.

The tires screeched as the car careened around a tight corner. The stench of burnt rubber blew in the open windows, and icy fingers of fear crawled up Mike's spine. "Why don't you ease up," he said.

"On what?"

"The gas and the goods." Maybe if it sounded like a joke Brad would take it better.

"I got it under control."

Mike wanted to believe him. They were friends. Brad

wouldn't do anything to hurt him. And there was hardly any traffic way out here in nothing-land. What could happen?

"Hey, what's the record on that?"

Mike looked out the front window to see a tight curve looming at the farthest reach of the headlights. "I don't know."

"Didn't Butcher do it at fifty?"

"Something like that."

"Bet I can beat it."

Panic stabbed Mike's stomach, and he glanced quickly at his friend. "Come on, Brad. Don't even try."

"What? You scared?"

Mike gripped the door handle as the car barreled into the curve. Even without his hands on the wheel, he felt the car slide as the rear end lost traction. He didn't know whether to pray or to scream.

At the precise moment Mike thought they'd careen off the edge of the road, the front wheels grabbed the asphalt. The car blasted out of the curve like a cannonball. Brad looked over with a triumphant grin. "See. I told you. Fifty-five."

Before Mike had a chance to let out a breath of relief, a violent thump threw the car out of control. His head banged against the window with a painful thud as the vehicle slewed back and forth. A sense of dread buffeted him like a blast of frigid air as he watched his friend fight to stay on the road.

"What was that?" Brad asked.

It wasn't a question that needed an answer, and Mike watched the muscles in Brad's arms strain as they struggled to control the steering wheel. What the hell had they hit? He braced one hand on the dash and the other on the seat and twisted to look out the back window. Darkness swallowed the world. Then he heard his friend shout.

"Oh, shit!"

That's when the car went airborne.

It seemed to float, and for a fraction of a second Mike found it almost a pleasant feeling. Brad was right. They were flying, and it was fuckin' awesome.

Then the thrill ended in a powerful impact amid a horrible explosion. A cacophony of high-pitched screams surrounded Mike as glass shattered and metal ground against metal. He recognized one of the screams as his own. Then a terrible weight pushed into his chest...harder...and harder...and harder.

*God, it hurts!*

The weight closed in on him. He couldn't breathe. He tried to reach over to Brad, but his arm wouldn't move.

Nothing moved, except the pieces of metal twisting and gouging at him. *Make it stop!*

Suddenly, everything was still. Blessedly still, and Mike was glad it was over. Then a great wall of blackness rose before him.

It moved slowly at first, then gained momentum as it enveloped the twisted interior of the car. It reached up to dissolve the shattered windshield and snuff out the pale moonlight.

In the dark void, Mike felt, rather than saw, the liquid blackness crawl up his mangled body until it covered him like a heavy blanket.

*Oh, my God!*

*MOMMIEEE...*

# ONE

LIFE CAN CHANGE in just an instant. That thought wove its way in and around her mind as Jenny fingered the clothes jammed along the wooden rod in the closet. His funny T-shirts promoting the likes of Prince and "The Simpsons." His one good shirt, only worn under duress. His leather jacket that still carried a faint aroma reminiscent of saddles and horses.

Sometime soon she'd have to clean out the closet. Isn't that what usually happens?

Tears burned her eyes, and she turned away. She didn't know what was supposed to happen. No one had ever told her. And a multitude of questions swam through her mind like restless minnows in a pond.

There were books on choosing a college. Books on how to plan a wedding or how to help your child find a job. But no one had ever written one on what to do when your son dies.

In that moment of truth, the weight of the pain overcame her. It was like being smothered under a huge quilt. Gasping for breath between sobs, Jenny ran from the room, slamming the door.

Her chest heaving, Jenny stopped halfway down the hall.

*I've got to get control.* Viciously, she wiped the trail of tears from her cheeks, then ran her fingers through the tumble of hair that persisted in falling across her forehead.

The door to Scott's room opened, and he cautiously poked his head out. "You okay, Mom?"

Jenny nodded, not trusting her voice to words.

Her younger son stepped into the hall, all angles and oversized joints common to fifteen-year-old boys. In a flash, she saw Michael as he'd been at that age, muscles just starting to form under the softness of childhood skin, a rakish smile on a face squaring away to that of a man, a tousle of dark brown hair so much like her own.

The pain of remembering was like being gut-shot, and she crumpled like a doe in hunting season.

Scott closed the distance quickly, and his arms went around her in an awkward hold that was as much embrace as support.

Silent messages of mutual reassurance passed between them like fragments of electrical current. Jenny could smell the muskiness of night sweat on his shirt and heard the muted thump of his heart. And for a fraction of a second, all was okay in the comfort of their embrace.

Then Jenny pulled away to see a mirror image of her own pain reflected in the murky depths of her son's eyes. They were so dark they were nearly black and defined the adage, "windows to the soul."

Scott wouldn't like it if he knew she could see so much. *He thinks he's such an expert at hiding beneath layers of loud music or sullen remoteness. But he's always there, just waiting to be discovered.*

She wanted to say something. Ease his pain. But he broke contact before she could formulate appropriate words.

Again, Jenny didn't know what to do. She was the mother.

She was supposed to know. She was supposed to take care of this child. That child. If only she hadn't let Michael go camping that weekend. If only. God, how perfect the world would be if we could go back and change things.

The agony of loss cut so deep she turned away from Scott for a moment to gulp in air. Was it always going to be so hard? And who was supposed to take care of her while she was trying to take care of what was left of her family?

She felt a light touch on her arm. "It'll be okay, Mom."

God. She wanted to scream. It was not going to be okay. Nothing was okay. But she had to pretend. If not for herself, for Scott. She forced the anger into a far corner of her heart.

"Did I wake you?" she asked.

"No." He shrugged. "Couldn't sleep."

"I couldn't either." She tried a tentative smile, and her emotional burden shifted ever so slightly.

She reached up and touched Scott's face, feeling the soft stubble of immature beard. "You need a shave," she said. But the message was, 'We'll be okay.'

Though Scott pulled away, his eyes said, 'Thank you.'

"Jenny?" a voice called from down the hall.

Giving him one more brief smile, she hurried into the living room and almost collided with Carol.

"There you are."

The naked anguish on her friend's face scraped against Jenny's emotions like a file. "Where else would I be?"

The slight woman froze, her brown eyes wide and pain-filled, and Jenny immediately regretted snapping. She seemed to have so little control over her reactions since The Phone Call last night. *That's what it'll always be,* she thought in some weird twist of mind. The Phone Call. Forever in capital letters.

The words had played endlessly in her mind ever since.

"Mrs. Jasik... Your son Michael has been in an accident... He's been taken to North Texas Medical Center..."

They wouldn't tell her over the phone whether he was okay or not, but somewhere deep inside she'd known. A mother always knows. She'd pushed her ailing Ford Taurus toward the hospital while the awful dread grew from a kernel of apprehension into a grotesque monster that gnawed on her heart.

By the time she'd arrived at the ER, some coping instinct had mercifully kicked in, and she'd numbly received the news that Michael was dead. Nothing else was clear in her mind or memory. She didn't know how her mother had known to come. Or who she was supposed to call about arrangements and when. Or was someone supposed to call her?

"Oh, God..." Carol's voice brought Jenny back to the present. "I'd do anything..."

"I know." Jenny kept her voice soft in an attempt to hold her friend's emotions at bay. Grief hung like a pall throughout the house, crowding out any other feeling, and Jenny was sure one more tear would break her fragile hold on sanity.

Carol wiped the smear of moisture from her face. "I hope you don't mind that I just walked in?"

"Of course not. *Mi casa* your *casa*."

Carol forced a small smile. "Someday we're going to have to learn that other Spanish word."

Jenny tried to match the smile but was afraid her face would crack under the effort.

"Some of the neighbors have called...to help. Bring food. Whatever..." Carol seemed to have trouble finishing.

Jenny's instincts rebelled. Not now. She couldn't see people. Talk to people. Not until she figured out how she was expected to act. Thank God, Mitchell hadn't asked too many questions when she'd called to tell him the shop would be closed today. After she'd told him why, there was an abrupt silence on the other end of the phone. Then a cough and his voice assuring her that he would help in any way. She knew she could count on him and Jeffrey, didn't she?

Jenny looked at her watch. Just after eight-thirty. "Later," she said. "Could they come later? I'm just not..."

"Sure." Carol hesitated a moment. "You want anything? Or I could just go. Or I could fix some coffee."

Jenny rubbed her throbbing temples. It was too much. Too fast.

Almost as if she sensed this, Carol asked, "You want me to leave?"

Jenny shook her head. "I just need to be alone for a moment."

"Okay." Carol touched Jenny's shoulder in a small gesture of understanding. "I'll go see if the kids want anything."

The slight woman strode toward the hallway, purpose straightening her spine.

*If only it could be that easy for me. Find something to do and everything'll be okay.* Jenny looked around the living room. The laundry she hadn't finished folding was strewn in a jumbled mess across the overstuffed sofa. The coffee table overflowed with a scattering of magazines and notebook paper from someone's forgotten homework. A week's worth of newspapers made a haphazard pile on the floor next to the recliner.

If people were coming over, she should try for some semblance of order. She picked up the newspapers and, for one crazy moment, had no idea of what to do with them.

The shrill ring of the phone made her heart thump and her arms weak. She dropped the papers and stood inert; amazed that the simple act of answering her own phone terrified her. She stared at the instrument on the little side-table. *It isn't a monster. Just go pick up the receiver.*

On the sixth ring, she did.

"Mrs. Jasik?" a pleasant male voice inquired. "This is Fred Hobkins with Canfield & Sons Funeral Services. The hospital called us."

In the midst of all the horror that had been last night, Jenny vaguely recalled the decisions she'd been asked to make when she couldn't even think. She'd told the nurse who was filling out the paperwork to just pick a funeral parlor and have them contact her. But she didn't expect the call so soon.

"First," the man said, "let me offer my sincere condolences for your loss."

Jenny assumed she was to insert some word of thanks into his silence, but she'd rather scream. She clamped her lips against the urge.

"Unfortunately, we do need to take care of some details." Again he paused, and Jenny knew she should say something. Anything. But her mouth refused to obey. She heard him clear his throat, then speak again. "I wondered when would be a good time to come over and make arrangements."

"I don't know." Her throat was so tight she could hardly push the words out.

"Well," Hobkins continued in that soft, well-modulated tone. "There's never a good time. Perhaps we could try in, say, an hour?"

"Fine."

Jenny replaced the receiver and stood immobile. *God. How am I going to do this?*

Carol walked in, one arm draped over a still drowsy Alicia. Scott trailed behind.

"It was a man from the funeral parlor," Jenny said in response to the question on her friend's face.

"Oh, Mommy!" Alicia broke from Carol's side and ran to her mother's arms. Jenny held her tight, burying her face in her daughter's long hair that carried the sweet little-girl smell of sleep.

"It's okay," Jenny murmured. "We're going to get through this."

"Is he coming over?" Carol asked.

Jenny looked over the top of Alicia's head and nodded. "In about an hour."

"Well, you, uh, go get yourself ready," Carol said. "I'll fix something for the kids to eat."

Jenny released her daughter and wiped the tears from the girl's flushed cheeks. "You okay?"

Alicia gave a slight nod, belying the sadness brimming in her amber eyes. Such a unique color. In Jenny's estimation the only good thing that her ex-husband had left her. *That's not true. He left you three children, and like it or not, there's a piece of him in each of them.*

Jenny gave Alicia a kiss. "You go on with Aunt Carol. I'll be out in a jiff."

Carol put her arm around the girl and reached for Scott, but he pulled back from the contact. Jenny understood. Touching might break the fragile wall of strength.

In her room, Jenny was struck by the absurdity of what she was doing. Choosing an outfit to meet with the man who would bury her son. Does one dress up or down for an occasion like this? Make-up? Jewelry?

Sudden, manic laughter overtook her.

"You're crazy," she told her ravaged reflection in the mirror. "Fuckin' certifiable."

Jenny's laughter turned to tears as she remembered yelling at Michael to watch his mouth the first time he'd said that.

It had happened last fall, a month after his eighteenth birthday, and Michael had been testing new waters. It was like he was saying, 'I'm an adult now. Let's see how much I can get away with.' He'd told her about a goofy old man who'd yelled and screamed about his pizza order getting screwed up. "He was the one who was screwed up," Michael had said. "He was crazy. Fuckin' certifiable."

Jenny could still feel the hesitation before Michael said the last two words, could still see the question in his eyes. 'Am I going to get away with this?'

And she could still remember the immediate regret at reacting too much like a mother, not realizing what it meant for him.

"Mom! I'm not a kid anymore," Michael had protested, the force of his words stopping her mother instinct long enough to see that he was right.

With another stab of agony, Jenny realized it wasn't just her child she'd lost last night. She'd lost his whole future. There would be no daughter-in-law from him. Or grandchildren.

She sank to the edge of her bed, the pain threatening to drag her into the dark abyss. Her blood pounded so loud in her ears it took a minute to realize someone was knocking on the door.

"Mom?" Scott's voice called from the hallway. "Can I come in?"

Jenny took a deep breath, then rose and opened the door.

"I was wondering...uh,.." Scott's eyes had difficulty resting on hers. "Has Dad called back yet?"

She shook her head.

"Well, uh...do you want me to call him?"

Again, she shook her head. "It's something I should do. I'll try again as soon as I'm finished here."

Scott hesitated a moment more, then backed out of the doorway. Jenny quickly closed the door. Better that he not see the flush of anger that warmed her cheeks. She'd tried to call Ralph last night, sometime during those hours of agony between leaving the hospital and finally collapsing for a brief period of fitful sleep, but there'd been no answer.

Last night she'd been too numb to care. It was just so typical. He had never been there for her or the kids. Not while they were married, and not in the years since he'd left. Most of the time she just accepted it and tried to ease the disappointment for the kids as much as possible, but even though little was said, the message was clear. Ralph wasn't involved with the kids. Not like a father should be.

His excuse for missing Michael's first football game had been a project for work. The excuses were always something to do with work. He justified his decisions with the standard, "This is what the man does. He provides for the family." But she'd always sensed that he welcomed the excuse for not being there because even when he was home, he really wasn't.

And Jenny often wondered why it had taken her so long to see that. It wasn't until after Alicia was born that she faced it squarely. After she'd been home for a week with their baby, she had to ask him if he wanted to hold his daughter.

So, it wasn't such a big shock to either of them when their marriage ended in divorce court. It was particularly painful for the kids for the first year, but life became easier after he moved to California. Then she didn't have to deal with the shattered hopes that this year he would show up for a birthday, or Christmas, or just because he missed seeing the kids. Distance became an acceptable excuse for his absence because the truth was too harsh to face.

But the truth was like a kick in the gut this morning.

"You stupid, sorry, son of a bitch," Jenny said, running a brush through her dark hair with quick, angry strokes. "Why should I care how you find out? I should just clip the obituary and send it to you."

It gave her a perverse rush of pleasure to consider doing

that, but she wouldn't. She couldn't. Out of respect for the fact that he was Michael's father, she would call again.

Jenny crossed the room and picked up her cell that she'd dropped on her bedside table. Still no answer after ten rings, and she started to worry. Maybe it wasn't even his number anymore. He had a penchant for moving and not getting around to giving them the new number for weeks. She could try him at work later, but she wasn't even sure that number was current.

Longevity, either professional or personal, was never one of his strong suits.

She slammed the phone down. "Couldn't you be there for me? Just once?"

# TWO

LIEUTENANT STEVE MORRITY pulled the report from his printer, the force of his anger almost causing it to rip. The emotion was a holdover from last night when he'd been called to an accident scene after drugs had been found. Two young men. Kids really. One dead and the other barely hanging on. When was the nightmare ever going to end?

"You talked to the parents yet?"

The question belonged to Linda Winfield, who stood in the open doorway of Steve's office. He was always surprised at how unlike a cop she looked. Tall and lithe, with a face that could have been carved out of fine porcelain, she should have been a model or an actress.

Today, that perfection was ravaged.

The residual effects of last night's ordeal of extricating what was left of two victims from a tangle of wreckage were evident in the grim set of her mouth and the tightness around her blue eyes. It brought to mind painful pictures of his first accident scene as a rookie patrol officer ten years ago. A mangled car. A young mother almost cut in half by the dashboard. The husband in the driver's seat, flattened like some bloody paper doll. And the baby in back... God, he didn't want to remember the baby in back.

He shook his head to chase away the images and asked, "What brings you in on your day off?"

Linda shrugged and stepped into the office. "Couldn't get it out of my mind."

Steve understood. He'd noticed the signs of distress last night after the winch had pulled the car out of the culvert and they'd had their first glimpse of the horror inside. But she'd appeared to steel herself and concentrate on the details of the job. Her ability to flip that switch had impressed him. There were times he still had difficulty doing that, and when he did, the emotions always caught up with him later. He wished he could tell her it would get easier.

Horrible, bloody accidents with bodies as twisted and bent as the steel that trapped them were the hardest, especially when they involved kids. And Steve could never decide if the deaths were more senseless when it was just a case of recklessness, as they'd first assumed last night, or when the accident was tied to booze or dope.

"Can I do anything?" Linda asked, leaning a blue-jeaned hip against his cluttered desk.

"You want to follow up with the driver? Go by the hospital and find out if he's able to talk?"

Linda nodded.

"Then you could check with McKinney and Lewisville. See if they have anything on him. Check the sheets on the Jasik kid, too."

"Was the Brennan boy dealing?"

"Possibly. There'd been some suspicion when he was in school. But if he was, he was slick enough not to get caught. Then he disappeared for a while. Franks has been watching him since he came back but hasn't been able to get anything on him."

"You think the other boy was doing it, too?"

Steve shrugged. "Won't know 'til we get the results of the tox screen."

Linda slid off the desk and rolled her shoulders. Steve heard a vertebra snap. He eyed her. "You sure you want to do this?" he asked. "You look like you need the closest bed."

"I tried that." A flicker of a smile touched her face then was gone. "It didn't work."

He laughed and waved her off, turning back to the mess littering his desk. He had to get the paperwork in gear for the toxicology lab in Dallas. Put a hold on the body at the hospital morgue. Make sure all the reports were signed.

The endless paperwork. Should have been a freakin' office clerk.

---

Dressed in her good tan slacks and a silk blouse the color of cream, Jenny opened her bedroom door and heard snatches of conversation punctuated with the clatter of dishes drifting from the kitchen. People, possibly lots of people, had arrived. She winced and considered closing the door and never coming out again. Then some long-forgotten sense of propriety told her she shouldn't be rude.

When she stepped into the kitchen, the first person she saw was her mother. Time warped for one brief flash, and Jenny was a child rushing to the comfort of her mother's arms. The older woman held her and crooned, "There, there. It'll be okay."

Jenny allowed herself to be the child for a moment, savoring the security of being taken care of. Then she pulled back and looked at Helen, struck by how much the woman had aged in the past twelve hours. Anxiety deepened the furrows on her forehead, and her hazel eyes were dull and lifeless.

"You okay, Mom?"

Her mother bit her bottom lip and nodded.

A touch on Jenny's arm drew her attention, and she turned to see her neighbor, Millie, so impeccably proper in her hat and gloves. Today's black hat was topped with a small sprig of red silk roses, perhaps chosen to reflect the dignity of the occasion.

"I'm not going to bother you now," Millie said. "Just wanted to bring something by. There's nothing else we can do."

That simple statement spoke volumes, and Jenny was grateful for the kindness. It broke a chink out of the wall of reserve she'd been trying to erect. The wall was a necessary part of survival for a time, but she knew the danger of building it too thick. It would be too easy to block out more than she'd intended.

Her impulse was to hug Millie, but the older woman had her own wall of reserve. In the six years Jenny had known her, Millie had always been friendly but had avoided intimacy at any level, so Jenny kept her distance as they moved toward the entryway.

"Don't be afraid to call if you need anything," Millie said.

"Thank you."

Jenny closed the door and then walked back to the kitchen. "Where's Alicia?" she asked Carol, who was busy washing dishes.

"She went to get dressed before the man from the funeral parlor gets here."

"I don't think I want to stay for that," Helen said, picking up her black leather purse from the table. "I'll come back later and see if Alicia would like to come to my house for a while. Keep me company."

For an instant, Jenny wanted to revert to childhood again. Then she could run away with her mother and wouldn't have to do this. Not that she blamed her mother for leaving. Jenny took a deep breath, remembering that lost look of pain her mother had worn last year when they'd buried Dad. She couldn't ask her to replay that scene again so soon.

She kissed Helen's cheek, which felt cool to the touch of her lips. "That's okay. I'll call you later."

---

Fred Hobkins was a tall, thin man who carried an air of consolation along with a cashmere coat and a briefcase. Jenny found his gentle manner and soft-spoken voice comforting as he greeted her and wondered briefly if that was something he'd learned at mortuary school. Are there classes in being soothing and sincere?

Jenny took his hat and coat and hung them on the coat tree in the foyer. Then she led him toward the living room, using the mundane task to chase that crazy question away. Would she ever get control of her mind again? She motioned for him to sit on the straight-back occasional chair where he could use the corner of the coffee table for the folder he pulled out of the leather case. She sat on the sofa, clutching a blue throw-pillow to quiet her nervous hands. Alicia, wearing a dress for the first time in months, sat beside her, and Scott slumped at the other end of the couch.

Other than running a brush through his hair, that was so pale it was almost white, she couldn't see that Scott had done anything special for this moment. He still wore his gray warm-ups and the black Nike T-shirt he'd put on earlier. Jenny tried to catch his eye, to offer some gesture that would connect them, but he kept his gaze averted.

She turned to face Hobkins when he cleared his throat.

"We can be ready for the family viewing tomorrow afternoon," he said. "Then it's up to you."

"What is?" Jenny asked, her voice coming out in a croak.

"Whether you want an open casket for public viewing." He paused as if choosing his words with care. "It is possible... considering that there were no injuries above the neck."

The picture that Jenny had successfully kept at bay for the past few hours flashed vividly into her consciousness; Michael lying cold and dead on the gurney. Her first thought had been that they were wrong. He couldn't be dead. His face looked so complete. So whole. Surely he was just asleep. But then her eyes were drawn to the horror that had been his chest.

Without warning, the dark abyss yawned before her, and she fought to stay out of its control.

"This is a breakdown of our various costs," Hobkins said, his voice like a lifeline. He slid a paper across the coffee table while she took a deep, ragged breath, her mind again going down a crazy path. Did he learn this in school, too? Deflecting the Outburst 101.

"These are some of our more popular caskets," he continued, pulling a brochure out of the folder. "You don't have to decide now. Let your family look them over, and we can settle it after we talk about a few other things."

Jenny picked up the booklet and offered it to Scott. "You want to look at this?"

He turned away so quickly she only caught a glimpse of a pained expression.

"I will," Alicia said.

Jenny looked at her daughter. "You sure?"

"Uh huh."

"Now." Hobkins settled back in the chair. "Have you given

any thought to the service? What you'd like? What you think he would have wanted?"

Jenny shrugged and looked from Scott to Alicia, then back to Hobkins. "It's not, uh–"

"Flowers," Scott interrupted, his voice gruff with emotion. "He definitely wouldn't want flowers."

When Jenny glanced at him, Scott softened his tone. "At Grandpa's funeral. He said they were a waste. And the smell made him want to puke."

Hobkins cleared his throat. "Flowers are optional, of course. Although people might send them. That's something we can't control."

Jenny nodded, wondering why Michael had never told her he hated flowers. Then she had to smile. Of course. He wouldn't have said that. The selling of flowers had put the meals on the table for the past six years.

If Hobkins noticed the smile, he didn't let on. He continued in his soft, soothing voice. "What about the service itself? Do you belong to a church?"

"Not formally," she said. "Sometimes we went to that little Catholic church, but..."

"Michael liked that other church on Main Street," Alicia offered. "The one that has the sign out front with the messages. He thought that was cool."

Jenny bit hard on her lower lip. *How could I not know this about my own son?*

"That would be Calvary Baptist," Hobkins said, and the interruption to her self-damning thoughts again came like a life saver. "We've worked with Pastor Poole before. I'm sure he'd be willing to let you have the service there. Or we could have it at our facility with him presiding."

Jenny focused on a small acne scar on the man's cheek, trying to still the whirl in her head. So many decisions. So many emotions. There was no way she trusted herself to decide anything.

"We'll have to think about that, too," she said.

"That will be fine." Hobkins shuffled a paper to the bottom of the stack. "Do you have family coming from out of town?"

She nodded. "Uh, my brother. He's in Ohio, and, uh, Michael's father from California."

"Have they been notified?"

Jenny paused to consider how to answer, and Scott nudged her. Looking at him, she knew the question he was silently asking. "Yes, I tried again," she whispered, hoping Hobkins didn't pick up on the tension.

What could she say if he did? She didn't want to explain the whole sordid mess of her life for the past six years. That wouldn't serve any useful purpose. But to simply say she hadn't talked to her ex-husband yet left the subject open for too many interpretations. None of which made her look good.

Hobkins leaned forward again. "Three days is pretty common," he said. "But we can wait longer."

"Three days will be sufficient," Jenny said. "Everyone who wants to be here will make it by then."

# THREE

"WHAT'S SO DAMN important you had to get me out of a meeting?"

Jenny faltered at the force of Ralph's antagonism coming across a thin wire of communication like some insidious emotional cancer. She gripped her phone until her fingers burned. "Your son."

"If there's some kind of trouble, we can discuss it–"

"Ralph, will you please just listen." Jenny hesitated, some inner core of compassion trying to keep her voice gentle.

"I have half a mind to–"

"Ralph, it's Michael–"

"What fool thing did you let him do now?"

Again, a deep stab of pain, but Jenny fought the urge to attack him with angry words. She could never be that cruel. "Please, Ralph. Just let me... He's..." She paused again, finding the word so incredibly hard to say. "...dead."

There was a moment of silence until she heard a quick intake of breath. She sat on the edge of her bed to give him time.

"Oh, my God," Ralph said, his anguish becoming a part of hers over the miles that separated them. "When did it happen?"

"Last night. It was–"

"Last night? And you just now got around to calling me?"

"Don't yell. I tried to call before. You weren't home all night." She stopped before adding the familiar old refrain, 'Where were you, Ralph?' But he picked up the melody line anyway.

"What I do is my business."

Jenny took a deep breath and let it out in a slow hiss. "Could we please not fight? Not now."

In the long silence that followed, she got up and paced the small confines of her room. Then she heard him exhale in a long sigh.

"Are you coming?" she asked.

Again, silence. Into the void she offered a gesture of peace. "If you come, we can just be two parents who've shared and lost a son. We can put everything else on hold."

Still no words from him, and she felt another flicker of compassion. Some part of him had to care, had to be hurting. "Just call me, okay? Let me know when you're coming."

She pushed the disconnect button and leaned her forehead against the wall. *I can't do this. How am I supposed to make all these decisions? Handle all these details? I just want to go someplace and die.*

Her inclination was to slide down the wall and huddle in the corner, but she pulled away from the temptation. *Go outside*, some inner voice told her. *Nothing is ever so terrible outside.*

Stepping off the back porch, Jenny was struck by a brilliance of light that made everything sharp and crystal clear. The huge expanse of sky was a rich, deep blue with only an occasional wisp of white, backlit by the sun. The air was crisp, fresh, incredibly alive.

The voice had been right. Despair could not live long in such a setting.

Jenny walked down the sidewalk toward a weathered lawn chair under the sprawling elm tree that had started dropping leaves in random piles of yellow and brown. She had to step with care over the gaping cracks in the pavement. She'd wanted to get the walkway fixed for as long as she'd owned the house, but somehow life's essentials always bumped it to the bottom of her list.

A sense of rightness settled on her as she sat down, the warmth of the sun touching her cheek like a caress. Then a flutter of movement caught her eye, and she turned to see a Monarch butterfly sailing in lazy circles on the wind. The brilliance of orange and brown against the fading grass was striking, and Jenny was caught up in the butterfly's dance. It lit briefly on the edge of her watering can, opening its wings in an innocent display of beauty, then lifted again to find another morsel of nectar in the bed of wildflowers along the fence.

As the butterfly soared, Jenny could almost feel some part of her spirit lifting with it. Butterflies always made her feel that way. As if, like Peter Pan, all she had to do was believe and she could fly with them.

When she was twelve, she'd told her friend Angie that. The other girl had laughed. Told Jenny that was the dumbest thing she'd ever heard.

Jenny smiled at the memory. Their friendship had almost ended when she wouldn't help catch butterflies for a collection. The idea of drowning the poor creatures in alcohol had been more than she could stand. Angie had argued back that butterflies didn't live long anyway, but that hadn't swayed Jenny. No matter how short the life span was, the creatures deserved every minute of it.

So did Michael.

The thought caught her off guard and cast a shadow on the moment as effectively as the cloud that brushed across the sun. She didn't want to think about the injustice of it all. That only made her furious, and she wasn't sure if the fury was harder to bear than the pain.

The back door opened with a loud bang, and she glanced over to see Scott step out.

"Phone for you," he said.

Jenny reached for the handset for their landline, but he held back. "Did you talk to Dad?" he asked.

She nodded.

"Is he coming?"

Jenny went out on a limb. "Yes."

To avoid any more questions, she took the phone and hurried past him into the house.

---

Steve stepped back from the sheer force of this woman standing before him demanding answers. A cop's worst nightmare. The mother of the deceased.

Trudy, the dispatcher, had buzzed him when the woman stormed in, and he'd come into the hall to face what was obviously barely controlled anger.

"Mrs. Jasik. Please–"

"No I won't, please." Fury smoldered in the woman's deep brown eyes. "I demand to know what's going on."

"You want me to call the Chief?" Trudy asked, already reaching a finely manicured hand toward the phone on her desk.

Steve shook his head and turned to the woman who clutched a large leather purse to her chest like body armor. "If you'll come down to my office, I'll explain."

She stood rigid, and Steve recognized the stance of anger. He reached out and touched her arm. "It would be better than trying to handle it here."

He watched her glance around the room, taking note of the patrol officers who had been drawn to the commotion and stood in doorways. Then she shifted her gaze to Trudy, who still had her hand on the phone.

Finally, she faced him again. "Yes," she said. "Perhaps you're right."

At her compliance, Steve felt the tension dissipate. There was a rustle of movement as the other officers returned to their desks, and he gestured for the woman to follow him. He led her down the hall, their footsteps muffled in the soft carpeting. In his office, he indicated she should sit in the chair in front of his desk. "Something to drink? Coffee?"

"No." She didn't sit. "I want to know why my son's body hasn't been released to the funeral parlor."

"It's a matter of routine–"

"Don't try to smother me in the party line." He watched her reach up to sweep a cascade of auburn hair off her forehead before she continued. "Mr. Hobkins called. Told me arrangements would have to be delayed. There's some kind of official interference."

Steve bit back a sharp reply. Getting defensive about what she considered 'interference' wouldn't help. He gestured again for her to sit, and this time she did.

"Mrs. Jasik, I'm sorry you found out this way." He stretched the moment by pouring a cup of coffee from the pot on top of his filing cabinet. Then he sat down at his desk and faced her.

"I should have contacted you myself. I just thought I had a little more time."

"That's no excuse."

"You're right. It's just an explanation." He kept his gaze steady. "And I do regret making this more difficult for you."

"Okay." She let the large purse drop into her lap. "So just tell me why?"

"We're investigating the circumstances of the accident."

"What circumstances?" Alarm widened eyes that were almost as dark as her hair.

"Drugs were found in the car." Steve paused and grasped his coffee cup with both hands. "We have to determine if your son was using them."

"No. Not Michael."

Steve chose his words with care, not wanting to set her off again. "Most parents don't know if their kids are doing drugs."

"I know!" Ire seemed to stiffen her spine again. "Maybe he tried it. I don't know. Lots of people try it. But he didn't do drugs."

"I hope you're right." Steve paused to give her a moment. "But we can't ignore the facts. Drugs were found in the car, and the Brennan boy's blood tests showed he was under the influence. We have to consider the possibility he wasn't the only one."

Jenny wanted to scream that he was wrong, but some rational part of her mind recognized the detective's position. After twenty years on the force in Houston, her Uncle Sid had told her that a good cop believes what is seen, not what family members say. So she swallowed the urge to lash out in blind defense of her son and sat mute.

"I don't like to do this, Mrs. Jasik. But the questions have to be asked."

"I know."

"What do you know about the Brennan boy?"

"Not much. They've been friends through most of high school, but he was always a little reserved with me."

"Did you ever suspect he was doing drugs?"

"I'm sure he wasn't. I mean—"

"The tests are conclusive, Mrs. Jasik."

"Oh." Jenny cast her mind back to the times she'd been around Brad, searching for some clue, some sign that he might have been taking something. Not that she'd recognize the signs. She still thought of a 'joint' as a place. She sighed. "I'm probably not the best judge of who's into drugs."

"That's fine." The detective took a swallow of coffee, then set his mug on a stack of papers on his desk. "Have you noticed anything different about him recently?"

"He hasn't been around for a while. The boys drifted apart toward the end of senior year." Her voice faltered. "I think Michael said Brad left town after graduation. I didn't even know he was back until he picked Michael up the other day."

"Where were they going?"

"Turner Falls. They were supposed to camp all weekend."

She watched the detective note her responses in a steno-type notebook. Then he closed it and looked at her with some unrecognizable emotion stirring in his eyes.

*They really are the most remarkable eyes.* That thought caught her up short. *My God, woman, you are nuts.*

She shifted her gaze and shrugged. "I wish I knew more."

"That's okay." He paused for a moment, and she glanced back in time to see him drain his coffee. "When we get the test results, I'll let you know."

"How long?"

"I'll push it through as fast as I can. Hopefully, not more than a day."

Jenny nodded, hefted her purse over her shoulder and

started to rise. Then some impulse made her turn back. "Tell me about the accident." Her voice was soft but steady.

"Perhaps it would be better–"

"No. I don't think so." Jenny sank back into the chair. "It's still so unreal." She looked away, then back. "Maybe because I want it to be. I don't know."

Again, she paused and looked down at her hands that were tightly clasped in her lap. Then she let her eyes drift back to the detective. "I don't even know where...it happened."

"Out on 720. West of town."

Jenny took a moment to consider her next question. "Were they speeding?"

"It appears so."

Jenny listened as the detective described the distance from where the car hit the deer and where it impacted on the concrete drainage pipe in the culvert and tried not to picture what it must have been like for Michael.

The detective finished the narrative with, "To have sailed that far, they had to have been going at a pretty good rate of speed."

"I see." She dipped her head and took a deep breath. The explanation was so crisp. So clinical. But maybe that was better than trying to put any kind of words to what her son might have suffered.

She bit her lower lip hard to fight off a wave of tears.

"I know it doesn't make it any easier," the detective said. "But it was quick."

Jenny nodded and took another deep, shuddering breath. Then she met his gaze. "Thank you."

---

Through the large window at the front of the station, Steve watched Jenny Jasik cross the parking lot to an aging Ford Taurus that had a prominent dent in the left rear quarter panel. Briefly, he allowed the speculation of what it must be like to lose a child to cross his mind. Then he wondered what it would take to ease the sharp lines of pain he'd seen in the woman's face.

Not for the first time in his career, he thanked the alignment of the stars — or whatever was responsible for his good luck — that he'd never had to experience this kind of loss firsthand. Not that it was so easy secondhand.

He stayed at the window for a few minutes after the car pulled out of the lot, then wiped a hand across the stubble of his beard in an attempt to dispel the depressing mood before heading down the hall toward the break room. There he found Chief Gonzalez plowing his way through a huge chunk of chocolate cake and working a crossword puzzle. Bastard always did them in ink.

Steve sat down opposite the lanky man and reached for a jar of fat-free, unsalted peanuts. Bastard could also eat like a freakin' farmer and never gain an ounce.

Once, as a joke, a few of the guys had posted a notice on the bulletin board that said tall, skinny Mexicans shouldn't eat so many sweets in front of short, fat Anglos. The Chief posted a response pretty much dictating that short, fat Anglos should get their asses back to work.

They'd decided not to say anything about the crossword puzzles.

Without looking up, Gonzalez asked, "What's on your mind, Lieutenant?"

"Going to the lab in Dallas."

Gonzalez sat back in his chair and looked at Steve. "Why you?"

"So I can ride their ass 'til they finish the tests."

"What's the hurry?"

"We need to let this mother bury her son."

Steve grabbed another handful of nuts and waited for the Chief's response. He was a man long on procedure and short on emotion. Procedure said a patrol officer could run errands. A detective had to put his or her time to better use. But Gonzalez also believed in victim's rights. It could go either way.

Gonzalez rubbed slender fingers across his chin, then went back to his puzzle. "Don't make it a habit," he finally said.

# FOUR

JENNY only half listened to the buzz of conversation drift around the room. It was one of those odd periods of numbness when she felt distanced. This wasn't her living room, her friends, her mother. They all belonged to someone else, and she was watching some bizarre form of reality TV.

Earlier, she'd been relieved when Lt. Morrity called to tell her the serum tests were negative. So now the three-day countdown could begin. He'd been kind enough to tell her again that he was sorry he couldn't rely on her word as proof about the drugs. The kindness had been a comfort.

It was also comforting to know she hadn't been wrong about Michael. Not that being wrong would have changed anything. Even if Michael had been taking drugs, the accident still wasn't his fault. Brad was the one who had been driving too fast.

Out of nowhere an almost uncontrollable surge of anger hit her. How dare he? Was he so stupid he didn't realize? Or didn't he care?

She considered going to the hospital and confronting Brad's

parents. Did they know what their son and his foolishness had done?

Then she realized she was being unfair. Of course, they knew. What parent wouldn't? Even as their own son hovered in that murky place between life and death, they had to have a painful awareness of the one who hadn't made it. They didn't need her reminder.

Noticing the drink she clutched in sweaty hands, Jenny took a swallow of lukewarm cola and tried to focus on what people were saying. Most of the comments seemed to center on how unfortunate it was that drugs had invaded the security of their little rural community. How unfortunate that the lives of young people were often so difficult that they turned to drugs. How unfortunate it was that it was ruining so many futures.

"It's not unfortunate." Anger put a strident edge in Jenny's voice. "It's a crime. Anyone who deals in drugs ought to be shot."

Stunned silence followed the outburst as gazes shifted to anywhere but at her. Then her mother cleared her throat. "We all realize that, dear. There's no need to shout."

"I'm sorry." Jenny stemmed the force of the emotion and focused on the startled expression on Carol's face. "It's just that everybody just sits around and talks about it. But nothing is done."

"What do you suggest, Jen?" her friend asked. "Arm ourselves with Uzis and blow them all away? Wonder Women of the New Millennium?"

Jenny laughed as an unflattering image flashed through her mind. "I'm not sure about the steel bra, but maybe the gun's not a bad idea."

"Jenny! Surely, you're not serious." Helen's voice cracked in alarm.

"Of course not." Jenny smiled. "We're just talking here, right?"

Jenny wasn't sure how she got through the next couple of days before the funeral. It helped when Mitchell made her laugh by saying she was hurting her own business by not having flowers for the viewing. And oddly enough, it helped when Ralph showed up and the other kids clung to him for a little while. She hadn't realized how much their needs had drained her.

Now, she stood beside the grave as the workers prepared to lower the casket. The strength seeped from her legs, and she wanted to slither into the hole with her son. How could she go on without him?

Ralph touched her hand, and the contact kept her upright. A light breeze brushed across her face, and she became aware of muffled sobs beside her. Alicia. The girl had buried her head in Jenny's side. *When had that happened? And I didn't even feel it?* Jenny wrapped an arm around her daughter and tried to be strong for her.

---

Scott watched the casket holding his brother's body slowly descend into the large, dark hole. He could smell the dank, sour odor of the dirt that ringed the grave, and it made his stomach roil. He wanted to scream. He wanted to throw himself on the bronze surface of the casket. He wanted to pummel his brother's lifeless body. And all of those urges felt so horribly wrong. How could he be this...angry?

He glanced at his mother, who had one arm around his sister. His mother kept her face forward, a solitary tear trickling down her cheek. She did nothing to acknowledge the tear. Almost as if she had gone into some deep inner place and there was no awareness of the outside. This was a demeanor Scott had seen a lot of recently, and he wondered when he was going to get his mother back.

His father stood on the other side of his mother, hands clasped behind his back. His suit coat was unbuttoned, allowing the wind to lift the end of a Mickey Mouse tie. Scott vaguely remembered sending that to him for Christmas a few years ago. Did he think he'd get points for wearing it? His dad turned as if sensing that he was being watched.

Scott wanted to feel some emotion beyond indifference toward the man. He'd at least had the decency to show up for the funeral. But even his little smile of encouragement failed to stir a shred of affection. How could they have become such strangers in just a few short years?

Last night at the funeral home, his father had said Scott could call on him anytime. "I know I haven't been a great father. Hell, I haven't even been a good father. But I do care. And I will help you if you ever need it."

If the little speech was supposed to be reassuring, it had had the opposite effect. Scott had employed every ounce of restraint he had to keep from striking out. If the fucker really cared, he wouldn't have been gone all this time.

Another surge of anger swept over him, and he had a hard time separating the anger he was feeling toward his dad and that which he held for his brother.

And both of them felt so wrong.

Caitlin slipped her hand into his, and the cool touch of her skin was soothing. He squeezed her hand, and she returned the pressure. He could almost feel the ugly emotions drain out of him in response to her comfort. His was glad his mother allowed Caitlin to be up here with family. It's not like she had any right to be. They weren't engaged or anything. Weren't even an item. Not yet, anyway. The friendship was too new for anything like that. But he felt good around her, and he needed that goodness right now.

His whole life had been shattered, and he was still waiting for all the pieces to fall.

---

The scene was so much like the one a few days ago, Jenny wondered for a moment if she was in some weird time warp. They were all gathered in her living room again. Her Mom. Carol. Mitchell and Jeffrey. And dear, sweet Millie. All of the people who had been in and out of her house a hundred times since that first awful day.

Now it was the second worst day of her life, and she noted the differences. Her brother, Jim, stood talking to their mother. He'd come alone. Anna, only a few weeks from delivering their third child, wasn't able to make the trip. Complications had her in bed for the duration.

Caitlin hovered with Scott and Alicia in a far corner. Perhaps they all felt a little awkward in the presence of so many adults. Or was there some level of comfort that drew them together?

Ralph stood alone in the doorway between the living room and the kitchen, looking uncomfortable in this home they had not shared. She'd moved up here from Plano after their divorce, seeking the slower pace of small-town living. He'd moved to California the following year without having set foot in the new house.

The fact that he'd never seen it was the strongest evidence of his lack of interest in the kids and their lives.

Earlier, their home had been jammed with after-the-funeral well-wishers, most of whom had stayed briefly then left as if eager to escape. Many of the visitors had brought more food, and she wondered how she was ever supposed to know whom to thank for all this kindness.

She tried to smile and act the hostess when anyone stared at her too long, and she knew she'd scream if one more person said how sorry he or she was. If she just kept busy, she wouldn't have to think about what they'd done just a few short hours ago. And if she ate, even though her stomach rebelled at the thought, nobody would want to hug her when she had a plate of food.

So that's how she got through the last couple of hours, until more people started drifting off.

Jim embraced their mother, then strode toward Jenny. He took the plate from her hands and set it on the sideboard, then pulled her close. Even though he was younger, he'd always played the older brother role, and she'd learned to count on him for comfort and protection when needed. And oh, how she needed it now. She leaned into his strength for a long moment, savoring the warm, masculine smell of his cologne and the feel of strong muscles as he wrapped his arms around her.

"I've got to go, little Sis."

Jenny stepped back. "I'm so glad you came."

"Me, too." Emotion clouded his face, and he glanced away.

"Want me to drive you to the airport?"

He shook his head. "I'm hitching a ride with your ex."

"Really?" Jenny couldn't hide her surprise.

Jim chuckled. "Yeah. Figured that would give me an hour or so to rip him a new one."

"You wouldn't—"

"Naw. Not that I don't want to. Never did get to tell the bastard what I thought of him."

Jenny smoothed the lapels of his coat. "Give Anna my love."

"Will do."

"And call me when the baby comes."

"Of course."

Jenny watched him walk toward Ralph, who was now apparently saying goodbye to the kids. She thought about following. Common courtesy would prompt her to see any guest to the door, but she just didn't know how much longer she could keep up this façade of civility.

As if sensing her reluctance, Ralph merely waved at her before heading toward the door with Jim. Alicia tagged along as if sensing someone had to play hostess.

A little while later, Mitchell left with Jeffrey after assuring Jenny that he would cover the store for as long as she needed him to. The reassurance was a small bit of comfort on this horrible day, and she smiled her thanks.

Finally, Jenny was alone. She stood in the middle of the room, wondering what she was supposed to do now. One of the grief brochures Hobkins had given her had said that the funeral was supposed to bring closure. That often it marked a turning toward regaining life.

She hadn't felt anything close to closure this afternoon.

# FIVE

JENNY PULLED up in front of the white frame house and turned off the engine. It seemed like years since she'd been here, not just a few weeks, and she saw the old Victorian structure with a mixture of familiarity and surprise at details forgotten, much like a soldier might view his home after a tour of duty. The sign still needed a fresh coat of paint. And the name she'd thought was so clever seven years ago struck her as silly today. A TOUCH OF JOY/Flowers for All Occasions.

She was so glad that Scott had stood firm about no flowers at the funeral parlor. It was hard enough coming back to work without having her business be a constant reminder. Although maybe the reminder would be good. For the past two weeks she'd alternated between moments of such clarity the pain had cut deep and total disorientation where she felt almost nothing. Sometimes she even had trouble remembering what the funeral had been like. And she was still waiting for that turning point.

Ralph had surprised her a week after the funeral by calling, and his voice had not seemed heavy with grief anymore. Had he found the corner and turned it? Or was the ease of conversation just because they had both avoided any mention of Michael?

The biggest surprise of his call was his request to talk to the kids. He actually spent more than two minutes talking to each of them, and she wondered if losing Michael had made Ralph realize some things. She certainly hoped so. The kids needed a father. *God knows I haven't done such a hot job trying to carry the load alone. Maybe that's why—*

Jenny tore herself away from the thought and opened her car door. Go to work and don't try to figure out the 'why.'

Pushing through the front door, she had a moment of disorientation as if she were stepping into the store for the first time. Even the bell announcing her arrival seemed alien. She hardly had time to consider why that was happening before Mitchell looked up from the papers strewn across the front counter. He rushed over to crush her against his six-foot frame. "Jen. How are you?"

"I'll be better when you let me breathe."

"Oh. Sorry." He stepped back and considered her with his pale green eyes. "The funeral was lovely."

"Yes. Yes, it was." Jenny swallowed the sudden lump.

Mitchell touched her arm gently. "You shouldn't be here."

The sentiment almost undid her. She forced a smile and tried for a joke. "I own this place in case you forgot."

Mitchell smiled, too, and it was like a light came on in a dark room.

*There. You can do this. All you have to do is pretend things are normal and everyone will think they are.*

Mitchell walked back to where he'd been working. Jenny hung her denim jacket on the coat tree by the door and followed him behind the counter that spanned the front of the room. Before the conversion into a retail space, this had been the parlor of the stately old house. The large kitchen and dining room directly behind it provided the main work area.

The counter had once been the bar at The Broken Spoke — a now defunct country joint that used to book some incredible local bands. The deep mahogany had been restored and polished to a rich shine that was almost mirror-perfect.

"What do we have so far today?" Jenny asked, picking up a stack of order forms and leafing through them.

"An anniversary bouquet. Three gifts for the hospital and two funeral arrangements."

Jenny didn't miss the quick glance he shot her beneath the straggles of blonde hair that washed over his broad forehead.

"It's okay," she said. "I'm not going to break every time somebody says 'funeral.'"

The words rang with bravery, and she wished she were as sure of them on the inside.

"Still. Maybe you should take a few more days." Mitchell picked up a yellow carnation and slipped it into the arrangement he'd been working on when she'd walked in. Even though he pretended concentration, Jenny felt his eyes on her.

"I'll be fine." She grabbed an apron and tied it. "But I'll work on the hospital gifts."

He glanced up, and she flashed him a quick smile.

"Gotcha."

By noon several more orders had come in, and Mitchell ran to make the hospital deliveries. Jenny finished the anniversary flowers and prioritized the new orders. If Mitchell made it back within an hour, they'd be able to get everything done by three. But first, lunch.

She went into the back room and grabbed her bag and a cola out of the old refrigerator, kicking the door closed with her toe. There was a state-of-the-art refrigeration system for the flowers, but the food was housed in a broken-down Kenmore that groaned with the effort to keep the interior temperature below 45 degrees. The incongruity made Jenny smile. Maybe Marie Antoinette should have said, "Let them eat roses."

Clearing a space on the card table, Jenny unwrapped her PB and J sandwich. It had been a year since she'd trusted anything else to the venerable old refrigerator.

As she ate, she went through the accounts-receivable ledger and noticed that several old accounts had been brought up to date. She wondered what Mitchell had done. Threatened a few limbs? A picture of the man threatening anything was impossible to conjure. If he ever killed anyone, it would be with kindness. And again, for the millionth time since he'd come to work for her, Jenny wondered why the nicest, most sensitive men had to be gay.

If she could find someone like him who also liked a good heterosexual romp, she might even cast caution aside and go play. It had been a long time. Partly because she'd been too hurt when Ralph left and partly because she didn't have time to breathe when the kids were younger and she was drowning in their needs. The time to find and engage a partner in any kind of bedroom activity had simply been non-existent.

"But just don't let it atrophy," Carol had cautioned during one late-night pajama party — which they both had agreed was better than the ones of high school because they could have beer with their pizza. "There might actually come a time when you want to use it."

"Fat chance."

And here today, surrounded by symbols of love and romance, she had the same thought. She'd probably win the lottery before she ever met a man who could ease her out of her fears and love her for all her peculiarities, not in spite of them.

When the front bells clattered, Jenny glanced at her watch, surprised to see that she'd been lost in that reverie for almost a half-hour. She must have had some kind of guilty expression because Mitchell laughed at her. "You look like Jeffrey when I catch him taking the last Oreo."

---

The afternoon was so perfect, Jenny wished she could bottle it and save it for the heart of the winter. A light breeze chased gold and brown leaves down the sidewalk, and the sun rendered a stand of yellow mums so spectacular the sight almost took her breath away. She was glad that Mitchell had literally pushed her out the door and told her to "Go smell the leaves."

Yet a part of her that was still melancholy ached with the knowledge that Michael would never see a glorious day like this again. She wished it wasn't this way. That everything wasn't measured by loss. *Will there ever be a day that I won't think of something in terms of Michael?*

She rounded the corner and saw the high school down at the end of the block, kids streaming out the front doors like horses being turned out of a stable. When she realized she was looking for Michael, she forced herself to repeat mentally, "He isn't here."

Watching a small group of boys break off from the crowd, Jenny paused and turned to follow them with her gaze as they approached two older boys. Something in their manner held her curiosity as they paused briefly. She wasn't sure, but it looked like one of the older boys passed something to one of the others.

"Mom! What're you doing here?"

Jenny turned to see Scott. She put a hand to her chest to see if her heart was actually pressing through her breastbone. "You scared me to death."

"That answer is non-responsive."

She had to turn her face to hide the smile. He was always so good at turning her parenting techniques back on her.

"I thought I'd walk you home."

"Mother!"

"Okay, I'll stay behind you. Nobody has to know."

He shrugged and started to move down the sidewalk. Jenny touched his arm. "Who are those guys?"

"What guys?"

"There." She pointed to the small cluster of kids. "Those two bigger kids don't look like students."

Scott grabbed her elbow and tried to propel her along. "You don't want to know."

"But I do." She pulled out of his grasp and stood still. He took a few steps away, then turned back. The look on his face made it obvious that the only reason he was stopping was to avoid the embarrassment of her calling after him.

"Okay." He shifted his bookbag and tugged at his denim jacket, then glanced quickly around. "They're dealers."

"What? Like in drugs?"

Scott grabbed her arm again. "Why don't you shout it? I'm not sure they heard you."

"Don't get smart." Jenny tried to pull out of his grasp, but he held her tightly and forced her to match his steps.

"Let's go," he said. "You can smack me when we get home."

She shot another look over her shoulder as Scott pulled her along. The men were watching, and a shudder passed through her, caused by an emotion she couldn't quite put a name to. Revulsion? Apprehension? Both?

She leaned closer to her son. "Does this go on all the time?"

"Only on school days."

That comment stopped her so abruptly he lost the hold he

had on her arm. "This is routine? Why don't the police do something?"

"They try. Patrols come by a lot. But they have a good early-warning system?"

"I'm lost. Who has a warning system?"

"Mom. This isn't the time to make you street smart. Let's go home."

"Do you ever...?"

His look could have withered weeds.

"They say the parents are the last to know."

Scott glanced away. "Is that what they told you about Michael?"

"This isn't about Michael. It's about you." Jenny tugged on his sleeve. "I know it's hard to resist all this. The pressure. And I suspect that Michael tried it with Brad. So I just want to be sure about you."

"I haven't. I won't. Ever." He held eye contact, and for a moment his stance was so much like Michael's when he'd been making a point, Jenny was afraid she'd lose it right there in the middle of the street.

She took a breath to steady herself. "Be careful of absolutes. They tend to come back and bite you in the ass."

The touch of humor worked. Strength returned to her knees, and the tightness around Scott's mouth eased into a brief smile. "I'm pretty safe on this one," he said.

# SIX

"I WANT to join this task force." Jenny dropped the newspaper on top of an open folder on Steve's desk.

"Wha—"

"This." Jenny pointed to a headline CITY LAUNCHES DRUG TASK FORCE.

Steve glanced at the paper then raised his eyes to meet hers. They appeared to burn with intensity. "You can't."

"Why not? Aren't the police always complaining about lack of cooperation from the public?"

Steve regarded her, noting the defiant tilt of her chin. "This isn't what we're looking for."

"I've been watching them for two weeks." Jenny threw a notebook down on top of the paper. It opened to reveal a page dotted with scribbles of numbers and notations. "They're out there like the fuckin' ice-cream man."

Jenny didn't realize how her voice had risen until Trudy popped her head in. "You okay in here, Steve?"

He held Jenny's gaze. "We okay?"

She released a deep breath and nodded. He waved the

other woman off and motioned to a chair. After Jenny perched on the edge of it, he rocked back in his and regarded her. "Do you have any idea what you're asking?"

"No." She let a smile touch the corner of her mouth.

The smile looked good, and that realization startled him. Not that he was immune to a pretty woman, but this...

"Civilians have no place in this kind of operation." He tapped the news story with the tip of his pencil.

"I'm not just any civilian. I'm a woman with a great deal of emotion-driven energy. You ever see what a bit of anxiety can do when it comes to cleaning a house?"

He leaned back in his chair and studied her. Jenny wasn't sure if he was considering her request or trying to sort out her example. Finally, he sighed. "I hardly think—"

"Are you the final authority, or is there someone else I can talk to?"

The interruption seemed to rattle him and he glanced around quickly as if looking for backup. When he faced her again, he tapped his cheek with the end of his pen. "You're not going away, are you?"

"No." Again she allowed a small smile.

Steve sighed and stood up. "Come on."

Grabbing her notebook and the newspaper, Jenny followed him out of the office. They went down the hall and paused in front of a closed door. Steve knocked, then opened it when a voice inside said, "Yo."

The Hispanic man behind a large, pristine desk looked at Steve, then at Jenny, then back to Steve. He raised one bushy eyebrow in question.

"Mrs. Jasik, this is Chief Gonzales."

"It's Ms. Jasik." She stepped forward and offered a hand. "But you can call me Jenny."

Gonzales sent another questioning look around her, and

she turned to see Steve leaning against the wall with an impassive expression. He spoke to the Chief with a brief nod in her direction. "Ms. Jasik is the one who lost her son in that accident a while back."

"Oh." Gonzales spoke softly and gave her a look that she interpreted as sympathetic. "My sincere condolences."

"Thank you."

He continued to look at her as if waiting for her to get to the point of this impromptu meeting.

"She wants to join the task force," Steve said.

"Oh." This time the intonation was different, and Gonzales wiped at his stubble of beard.

"I told her we don't use civilians," Steve continued.

"That's right."

In the face of his steady gaze, a wave of uncertainty washed over Jenny. What the hell did she think she was doing? Extreme frustration had driven her to the station this morning, but did she really think they'd accept her? It wasn't like she was brimming with qualifications. A florist? A mother? A woman?

But even as the mental debate raged, Jenny's heart told her she couldn't back off without a bit of a fight. Scrapping was second nature to her. Anyone who wondered just had to ask Ralph. For all his faults, she was big enough to admit that she didn't always make it easy to live with her.

"This is highly unorthodox," Gonzales said.

Jenny resisted the urge to say, "Sure. Sorry I bothered you." She forced herself not to fidget under the force of his gaze.

Gonzales leaned back and cradled his head in his hands. "What makes you think you can do this?"

"Determination." It was the first and only thing that came to mind.

"Determination's good," Steve said.

"I was thinking in terms of practical experience," Gonzales said. "Something that would catch my eye on a resume."

Jenny stifled a laugh. *I can arrange a mean centerpiece.*

Gonzales released his hands and sat forward. He studied her for a long moment, then sighed. "Tell you what. Pass the fitness test, and I'll consider your request."

Fitness test? A picture of Marine boot camp training flashed through her mind. How the hell could she pass a fitness test? Was this the moment she should say, 'Thank you very much' and take her leave? "What exactly do I have to do?"

The man seemed as surprised by her question as she was. "A modified form of our cadet requirements."

"Which are?"

"Run a mile without passing out. Twenty-five sit-ups. Twenty-five push-ups. A few more things I can't recall. It's been a while since I looked at the training manual."

Jenny kept her feet planted firmly in place despite her inclination to run like hell. She couldn't even remember the last time she'd done a sit-up. "How long do I have to get ready?"

Gonzales seemed to consider her slight frame for a second longer than necessary. "Four weeks."

Driving home, Jenny's mind whirled with the effort of trying to sort out the complications she'd never considered before making that brash decision to storm the police station.

Not the least of which was keeping everything a secret.

Gonzales had explained that the only way they could make this happen — if she passed the physical challenge — was to run her as a confidential informant. That meant not telling anyone. "Not your kids. Not your mother. Not even your dog can know where you go or what you do."

That had struck her as funny at the station, but now as she approached her driveway, anxiety tore through her. Her whole relationship with the kids had been built on honesty. How could she lie to them? And hide things from her mother, or Carol? There was a good reason Jenny never played poker.

After the car rolled to a stop in front of the house, Jenny killed the engine and sat for a moment. Through her open window she heard the chatter of a blue jay that was worrying a robin in the elm tree. As she watched the birds, she couldn't help but notice that the branches of the tree dipped dangerously close to the roof. Pretty soon they'd be scraping across the shingles. Something else to fix. Maybe she should just forget this nonsense and take care of her house. Take care of the family that she had left. Forget the drugs and forget—

No. She couldn't just forget. Otherwise there would be no way to make any sense of Michael's death. And somehow there was this burning need for reason, for order, for retribution.

---

The pain in her side finally brought Jenny to a halt, and she bent over to get her breath. Good thing she'd toted deliveries around for all these years. No upper-arm wobble for her. But the stamina could use work. She jogged a few blocks and broke out in a huff.

Surprisingly, Carol had outdistanced her. Who would've thought short and a little pudgy would beat skinny as a rail?

Her friend now came back with a broad grin. "I still have it."

"What?"

"How quickly you forget. High school track? Who beat you then?"

"Bite me." Jenny headed down the street at a slow lope that Carol easily matched.

"Tell me again why we're doing this?"

"So we can enjoy our old age together."

"Who says I want to spend it with you?"

Jenny managed a semblance of a laugh in between huffs. That had been an ongoing joke with them for years. Carol had lost her husband to cancer two years after Ralph had run off. Neither of them had been able to decide which loss was worse, finally deciding that it didn't have to be a contest. But what they both agreed on was a real reluctance to make that kind of emotional commitment again. Maybe it was enough to have one good friend and plenty of extended family to love and be loved by.

It had seemed to be a good philosophy until some other basic human needs, the kind that could only be met by someone of the opposite sex, had clamored for attention.

While Jenny had been too busy with kids and eking out survival to tend to those needs, Carol had the means and the opportunity to seek out someone new. Six months ago, George had entered her life, complete with the family she and Barry had never been able to have. Granted, they were only every-other-weekend kids, but it was better than the nothing Carol had had previously. And it looked like the relationship was going to last.

Jenny was happy for her friend. Glad to see the dreamy smiles and hear the contented sighs when she talked about George and his two kids. But a little part of her couldn't help but be envious. Oh, that old green snake.

She shook off the thoughts and coaxed her trembling leg muscles into action. She only had a week left. No time for loafing.

---

"Did you see the morning paper?" Mitchell asked as Jenny walked in the door.

"No." She hung up her coat and joined him behind the counter where he had the local rag spread out.

The headline he pointed out read: SECOND ACCIDENT VICTIM DIES. It took a moment for Jenny to realize the story referred to Michael's accident.

"Nineteen-year-old Bradley Brennan died at..." the story began, and that's as far as Jenny got before her eyes blurred and her chest constricted.

She took a deep breath and the tightness eased.

"I'm sorry," Mitchell said. "Maybe I shouldn't have—"

"That's okay." Jenny took another deep breath and forced a small smile. "I needed to know."

"Were they close?"

"Yes. For a while. I'm not sure about just before..." Even after all these weeks, she still had trouble with some of the words. And she was currently having trouble with some of her feelings. The first she recognized was sadness that another boy had died, but a little glimmer of satisfaction snuck up out of nowhere and made her want to throw up. How could she be so callous? His death wouldn't give Michael life.

She remembered her initial sense of injustice that Brad had lived and her son hadn't, but she was certain she was the only one who felt that way. Even Scott in the midst of the worst of his anger hadn't voiced that vile thought.

"The funeral's day after tomorrow," Mitchell said, and Jenny welcomed his intrusion. "I could watch the store if you want to go."

She paused before responding, trying to determine if she could even face another funeral, then almost laughed when she remembered that she hadn't exactly faced Michael's. And the Brennans had been kind enough to make an appearance. Their presence in the far back of the church she could remember. She could at least be as gracious.

"That would be nice," she said.

Mitchell nodded and started to turn away. Jenny touched his arm. She'd been looking for just the right opportunity to talk to him. If she made the task force...no, make that when she made the task force, she'd need him to cover for her. "I might need you to hold the fort now and then over the next few weeks."

"Oh?" The single word was pregnant with curiosity that Mitchell was obviously too polite to voice aloud, but Jenny ignored the inferred invitation to explain. What was she going to tell him? That she needed time off to learn how to make drug deals?

"It won't be often," she said. "And I can let you leave early sometimes to make up for it."

"Sure. I can be flexible."

"I appreciate it. But you should check with Jeffrey. Make sure he doesn't mind. I feel like I've taken quite a bit of advantage already."

"No problem. And we could use the extra money."

# SEVEN

JENNY'S MUSCLES turned to Jell-O. She felt the quiver and knew her arms were about to give out. She struggled to hold but knew there was no way she was going to push her weight up one more time. *Damn. I was so close.*

Steve stood on the other side of the mat but didn't say anything when her arms collapsed and she fell flat on her face. He threw her a towel. "Come on."

Wiping the sweat off her face, Jenny followed him out of the gym. "Twenty-two was pretty good, wasn't it?"

"Come to the Chief's office as soon as you're changed."

She waved an acknowledgement before stepping into the locker room and closing the door. She quickly mopped the rest of the perspiration from her body with the towel, and then pulled her sweats on over her workout clothes. She wasn't comfortable using the big open showers.

After putting her hair in some semblance of order, Jenny went through the door that led to a long hall back to the office area of the station. She stopped at the door to Gonzales's office and knocked. His distinctive voice told her to come in, so she pushed the door open and stepped through. Steve was leaning against the wall beside the desk. Gonzales motioned her to close the door. "Steve was waiting for you before he gave his report."

Jenny nodded, afraid if she opened her mouth she'd whimper.

Gonzales turned to face Steve.

"She passed."

Jenny almost fainted. That was not what she expected to hear. Obviously, Gonzales didn't either. He looked at her, dark eyes wide with surprise. "She did?"

Steve stepped over and passed a sheet of paper to his boss, avoiding eye contact with her as he stepped near. "Got the results right here."

Gonzales studied the paper for a moment, then shook his head. "Now what the hell are we supposed to do?"

Steve stepped back from the desk. "We sign her up."

"She's a civilian for Pete's sake. We can't sign her up."

"A deal's a deal."

Gonzales huffed, and his face turned an alarming shade of crimson. He turned to her. "Uh, give us a few minutes. Tracy can get you coffee."

Jenny stepped out but stayed by the door. She could hear Gonzales clearly. "What the hell? Never thought she'd actually do it."

*Did that mean he was just stringing me along*? That thought made her want to storm back in the room and confront him, but practicality held her back. Venting her anger would probably destroy any chance she had — slim as it was. She put her ear to the door, trying to make out what Steve was saying, but his response was muffled.

She had to step back when Gonzales shouted again. "Christ, it's my ass if she screws up and gets injured. Or worse."

Again, she couldn't hear what Steve said, and for the next few minutes both voices were muffled. A short, scrawny officer in blues stepped out of the break room, stopped and stared at her. "Can I help you?"

She motioned to the door. "Just waiting for Steve."

Wariness controlled his expression, and he made no move to leave. "I can show you to his office."

"No need." Jenny turned and walked down the hall, her back itching with the feeling that the officer was watching her very intently. The door to Steve's office was open and she stepped in, nodding to the officer who still had not moved.

The perpetual coffee pot on the tall filing cabinet was half full of what looked like sludge, but it was better than nothing. She found a Styrofoam cup and poured the dark liquid that flowed like two-year-old motor oil. She doctored it with two creamer packets, and that made it almost drinkable.

Fifteen minutes later, she was contemplating another cup of the coffee. Just to keep her hands busy so they didn't respond to the temptation to read some of the case files strewn on Steve's desk. The Wanted posters tacked to a bulletin board had only provided five minutes of interest.

Her stomach was given a reprieve when Steve stepped through the doorway. She looked at him, letting her expression ask the question.

"Come on. The Chief wants to talk to you."

She tossed her empty cup in an overflowing trashcan and followed Steve back down the hall. He opened the door to the Chief's office, and Jenny walked in. Gonzales still sat behind his desk, and he motioned her to sit in the chair facing him. Steve pulled up another visitor chair and sat beside her.

"You have to sign this waiver." Gonzales slid a document across to Jenny. "You're still a civilian, and the department can't be held responsible."

Her heart skipped a beat. "You mean I'm in?"

Gonzales nodded toward Steve. "You've got quite an advocate."

Jenny shot Steve a quick glance and noted the little smile that softened the hard planes of his face. She whispered a thank you, then picked up the paper. It had a bold heading:

CONFIDENTIAL INFORMANT

"It's not too late," Gonzales said. "You can still back out."

His tone made the statement sound like a plea, and she glanced at him, realizing it would probably be easier for him if she did.

*Too bad, Chief. You're stuck with me.*

She scanned the document. It had general wordage to the effect that should she be injured or killed while acting in a limited capacity for the Little Oaks Police Department, there would be no compensation. Short, sweet, and to the point.

Jenny put the paper back on the desk. "Where do I sign?"

"Right here." Gonzales pointed to a line at the bottom of the page.

"May I borrow your pen?"

After the slightest hesitation, Gonzales pulled a thin silver pen out of the inside pocket of his jacket and handed it across to her.

As Jenny scrawled her name in the space, he kept up a running commentary. "You call in every day. Even if you don't think you have anything important to report. Despite what it says on this paper, we are responsible for you. It doesn't look good if people die on our watch."

"I'll be your contact," Steve said, handing her a piece of paper. "Here's my cell number. Use it to set up a time and place for a meet or a secure phone call. When we do meet, it will be out of this area. A different place each time."

"Pretty cloak-and-dagger kind of stuff."

"It's essential. We're dealing with the worst of the bad boys."

The seriousness on his face kept her from a flip comment about chewing the paper after she memorized the number. And she wasn't quite sure why her mind was going in silly directions. Maybe to keep from latching on to just how dangerous this could be? She'd been so busy just getting in shape; the effort had crowded out any scary thought that dared raise a monster head. But she couldn't ignore the reality today, and a tight fist of panic squeezed her stomach. *What on earth have I done?*

An instinct for self-preservation tempted her to back out of the room with some lame apology for wasting their time. But the desire to squash the drug-dealing vermin held her resolute.

"When do I start?" she asked.

"After I show you what you're facing." Steve took her arm and led her to a conference room that had several long tables with a multitude of chairs. "This is our version of a roll-call room."

He disappeared for a moment, then returned with coffee in two heavy, ceramic mugs. "Got this fresh from the break room."

"Good. I'm not sure I could stomach another cup from your office."

Steve set the mugs down, then motioned for her to sit across from him.

"I saw you at the funeral yesterday," he said as he spread a folder on the scarred surface of the table.

"You were there?"

"Yeah." He grinned. "Way in the back on the other side. Made it easier to slip out when I wanted to."

Jenny flushed at his obvious reference to her early escape. "It was just too—"

"I know." His smile vanished. "It was nice of you to show up at all."

"It was the right thing to do."

His expression turned so serious for a moment that Jenny wondered if her comment had come across too pompous. But then he gave her a slight nod and touched her hand lightly. "Yes, it was," he said.

She shifted slightly and motioned to the folder. "Maybe we should get started."

"Yeah. Right."

Later, driving home, Jenny's mind swam in a jumbled sea of all the information she'd tried to assimilate in the past hour and a half. That big beautiful ranch just outside of town that she'd always admired so much — Steve said it was the headquarters of a Cuban man who controlled the drug business in North Texas, Oklahoma, and part of New Mexico. And here she'd been naïve enough to think that the price of cattle must have taken an upswing to support a spread like that.

She also realized how incredibly naïve she was about the whole drug scene. Steve had bandied terms about — mule, runner, dealer, distributor, and main man. Other than mule, the rest sounded like they could be applied to any legitimate business. When she'd voiced this thought, Steve had assured her that except for the product and some of the means, the drug trade was very much like a legal enterprise.

Her first challenge would be to make a connection with the street dealers. She'd have no trouble locating them. God knows she'd seen them often enough around town. But she'd have to actually approach them and convince them she was a customer. Not something she felt adequately prepared to pull off, but then Steve had said they'd meet with someone from the DEA tomorrow. Maybe she could learn how to be a druggie in one easy lesson.

---

The back door banged open and Alicia bounded in. She bounded everywhere. "Mom. You're home."

"Yep."

"Something smells yummy."

"Chili."

"Real chili?" Alicia shrugged out of her red warm-up jacket and hung it on a peg. "Not out of the can?"

"Real chili." Jenny scrounged through the cabinet and found a box of Jiffy cornbread mix. Maybe it wasn't too old to rise to the occasion.

Scott lumbered in and dropped an overflowing book bag on the table.

"Guess what," Alicia said. "Mom's cooking. Real food."

"That's nice," Scott said to his sister, then looked at Jenny. "Trying to fatten yourself back up?"

"I was never fat."

"Oops. Sorry. Didn't mean to insult." Scott opened the refrigerator and grabbed a carton of juice.

"But I am glad you noticed the new, improved version of me."

"How could I not? You were out running all the time." Scott started to drink from the carton, and Jenny gave him a stern look. He took a glass out of the cabinet. "Is that over now?"

"Is what over?" Jenny dumped the cornbread mix in a bowl and grabbed milk and eggs from the refrigerator.

"Frozen dinners." There was just a hint of an edge in

Scott's voice, and Jenny gave him a searching look. "And you missed two of my soccer games."

"I like frozen dinners."

Jenny had to smile at her daughter's comment. Dear Alicia. Always the peacemaker. How she must hate the extra layer of tension that had lived in this house in recent weeks. Has it only been weeks? It feels like years.

Pausing in the stirring, Jenny looked pointedly at her son. "I'm sorry I missed the games."

"Yeah. Whatever."

His tone invited an argument, and Jenny took a deep breath to avoid a sharp retort. *You're the adult here. Act like it.*

She crossed the distance to him and touched his cheek lightly. "You know I'd give anything to make our life normal again. But I don't seem to know what that is anymore. We're all getting through this the best way we can. You're moody and sullen. Alicia escapes into her imagination. And I choose to be active. So, no. It's not over. And I don't know when it will be."

Jenny hoped for some small concession from Scott, but he stood as if made from wood. Neither moving into her offer of comfort nor out of it. She consoled herself by relishing the latter.

# EIGHT

IT WAS MORE like winter than autumn, and Jenny pulled her leather jacket tighter against the cool night air that left a trail of goose bumps where it touched her bare midriff. *Should've worn a turtleneck.*

Not only would that be helpful now, but a decent shirt might have gotten her out the door without the silent accusation from Scott as he checked out the little jersey tube-top she wore and the gold chains that currently lay like thin strips of ice across her upper chest. He hadn't said anything since the little spat the other day, but body language spoke loud and clear. Most of the time she could almost see the questions spinning through his mind. Then again, she had a few of her own.

When this whole mess started, she hadn't anticipated ending up looking and feeling like a hooker to play the role of a drug user. But Steve, along with Burroughs from the DEA, had spent an afternoon coaching her on how to be "Connie, who's just looking for a little fun," and the image included a wardrobe straight from a brothel. Frank Burroughs had worked Vice in

Baltimore for ten years before applying to the DEA. She figured she could trust him to make her come across convincingly, even if the part felt so alien.

So here she was now, dressed like a tart and ready to make her first approach to the pushers. She was proud of herself for using the right term. Thanks to the in-depth briefings with Burroughs that had followed up on what Steve had told her, she knew the chain of command from pusher up the line to the main man. Jenny had almost laughed when Steve had first used that term. She remembered it from high school, but it used to mean something totally different. Or was that main squeeze?

Recognizing the mental stalling tactic, Jenny shook the thoughts aside. *Concentrate on what you're here for.*

Earlier, she'd parked her car three blocks off Main Street and walked to the edge of the Dairy Queen parking lot. Another piece of insider knowledge from Burroughs. "Always have a get-away route, and don't let them see what you're driving."

Now she watched the same three men who'd been plying their trade by the school; but tonight, it was a drive-thru business. Two men in a small, black compact car indistinct in the shadows, one outside, a tall, lanky black man who looked barely out of his teens. He wore a fleece parka with a large front pocket. Cars pulled up and a flurry of movement had money exchanged for little plastic bags. Jenny knew they were probably Baggies. She couldn't even count how many peanut butter and jelly sandwiches she'd packed in those over the years. How did something so innocent become a carrier of such horrible destruction?

While she stood trying to talk her legs into carrying her toward the pushers, a boy about fourteen sidled along the building then hustled toward the car. He didn't run. The action was more like a fly moving from one piece of garbage to another. From her intense two-day course in drug use and addiction, Jenny recognized the nervous jangle of movements as signs of someone desperately in need of a fix.

Only the imperative of not breaking her cover kept her from doing a 'mom' thing and dragging the boy home by his ear.

She turned away so she wouldn't have to watch him make his score, then dipped into her well of resolve and stepped out of the shadows on the side of the building.

She wasn't worried about the pushers recognizing her. They weren't the type to frequent a florist shop. But the lack of recognition could be a detriment, as well. She had a big hurdle to overcome because they didn't know her. They would be cautious about someone new.

She approached the tall black man who lounged against the rear fender. When she got close enough that he could see her clearly, she flashed the money just like Steve had taught her. "For it to ring true," he'd said, "it has to look like you've done this a million times."

They'd decided on this approach after realizing that she had no hope of connecting to local parties. The kids wouldn't accept her at theirs, and there was too much risk at the adult parties. Someone there might recognize her.

The man eyed her carefully. "Lookin' for something?"

"About a nickel's worth."

"What you talking about?"

The question caught her off guard. This wasn't going the way they'd rehearsed. She quickly sifted through a variety of responses, knowing only one thing; she couldn't say the word drugs.

She decided on bravado, despite the fact that she didn't feel very brave. "Listen. The longer we stand out here jawing the more we both risk."

The Hispanic man in the passenger seat leaned out his window and scrutinized her for a moment. "Buzz off, lady."

Then he motioned to the driver, who started the engine. The black man jumped in the back seat, and Jenny smelled their exhaust before her mind accepted the fact that she'd failed.

*Great. Now what am I supposed to do?*

The one thing she knew she couldn't do was stand out here and be conspicuous. She pulled her jacket closed against the chill wind and headed back to her car. Maybe it wouldn't feel so much like a complete fiasco after a hot bath and a call to Steve.

Alicia was already asleep when Jenny got home, so she slipped quietly went into the girl's room to kiss her goodnight and remind herself again why she was doing this. Then she went back out to the living room where Scott was watching TV. He'd barely acknowledged that she'd come home early and still kept his attention on the program.

"Everything okay, Scott?"

"Sure."

"Did you finish your homework?"

"Didn't have any."

Jenny fought the urge to question the veracity of that, but things were so rocky between them, maybe she should show some trust. One of his major beefs was always that she didn't trust him.

"I'm going to take a shower. Then we could do something if you want."

"No. Thanks. I'm on my way to bed as soon as this is over."

His indifference created a pain deep inside, and she longed for one those rare moments of closeness that had become even rarer of late. *But you can't force it. You know that.*

Letting out her frustration in a deep sigh, she turned and headed for her bedroom. After a quick shower, she wrapped a towel around her head, slipped into her fluffy robe and called Steve on his cell phone.

"Problem?" he asked.

"You could say that." Jenny sat in the little chair in the corner of her bedroom. She'd put it there next to a bookcase, hoping for hours to spend reading, but that hadn't happened. Life kept interfering.

"Wait. I'll go to a secure landline and call you right back."

A few minutes later, her phone rang.

"What happened?" Steve asked without any preliminary small talk.

"The dealers drove off."

"Don't worry. We told you it was going to take a while for them to accept you."

There was a pause and a rustle of movement, and Jenny wondered where he was and what he was doing. Then she had this sudden awareness of being naked beneath her robe, sitting in her bedroom and talking to this man who was starting to make her feel things she hadn't in years.

She stood up.

"Was there something else?" he asked.

"Uh, no. I just wanted you to know."

"Listen. Just keep going back until they let you make a buy. Trust me. They won't put you off for long."

Jenny felt marginally better after they hung up. She dried her hair, put on some sweats and a t-shirt and crawled into bed, even though she wasn't particularly sleepy. A new Laura Lippman novel was on her nightstand, and she picked it up.

After reading a few pages, Jenny realized that she kept losing track of the story, which wasn't fair to the author. She rested the book on her stomach and thought about what she was doing. Who was she to think she could pull this off? She was no superhero. She was a middle-aged mother whose biggest challenge up to this point had been surviving her bad choice in men.

# NINE

JENNY just barely remembered the parent/teacher conference in time. She had fifteen minutes to get there and could forget about a shower first. If only she'd remembered earlier, it would have been the perfect excuse to put off a major cleanup of the flower cooler.

She washed the big chunks of grime off, then locked the doors and headed for her car. She wouldn't have to contact the kids. Scott would remember she had the conference. It was for him, and they'd argued last week about her need to go. She was sure she should; he wasn't. He said the failing notice from his biology teacher was taken care of. He'd pulled his grade up. Everything was fine. But Jenny knew it wasn't fine. And she should have questioned him that first time he said he didn't have homework.

But then, wasn't everything a lot clearer with hindsight? Long before the current mess of her life, Jenny had learned that it was better not to beat herself up for past mistakes. Not a damn thing she could do about them in the present.

She pulled into the school parking lot, locked her car, and

headed for the red-brick building. She was supposed to meet the teacher in the lab.

For being such a small community, Little Oak High School had a state-of-the-art biology lab, much better than the one in the school Jenny had attended in Dallas. Walking in, she couldn't miss the strong aroma common to all labs: formaldehyde. She also took note of the three people sitting at a table near Mr. Taylor's desk. So, it wasn't just a conference with him. She recognized the other teachers. Both had taught Michael, and she'd had conferences with them in the past.

"Ms. Jasik, thank you for coming." Taylor stood in that ungainly stance often used by very tall men and motioned her to an empty chair. "You know Brenda Ames with the English Department and Sylvia Comstat, our History teacher. And please call me Gordon."

Jenny nodded to the pert, young blonde and the older woman who had an incredible cascade of auburn curls. Then she perched on the edge of the seat and willed herself not to brush at her rumpled clothes. The teachers looked better at the end of their day than she ever did even at the beginning of hers. *They must think I'm a moron coming in looking like a slob.*

Obviously, they didn't, as they all gave her bright smiles and didn't glance once at the bleached-out spot on her jeans.

After greetings were exchanged, Gordon sat back down. "I asked them here today because we've all been concerned about Scott's lack of attention to schoolwork."

His pause was met with more eager smiles from the other teachers and a sense of impending dread from Jenny. She didn't know if this was an opening for her to offer a comment, but what could she say?

Brenda Ames cleared her throat. "It's not that he's doing horribly. And we're certainly cognizant of his recent loss."

Another pause, and again Jenny couldn't find an appropriate response. She nodded, and Brenda continued. "We noticed that he seemed to be rebounding from his grief up until a few weeks ago. Then everything seemed to bottom out. Has something else happened at home that we should be mindful of?"

Jenny had to fight to stifle a laugh, and perhaps Gordon mistook that effort for a sign of distress. "Are you okay?" he asked. "Can I get you anything?"

"I'm fine. Just a little fall allergy problem."

"If you're not feeling well, we can reschedule," the history teacher said.

"No problem." Jenny turned to Gordon. "Scott said he's worked to bring his biology grade up."

"Yes. Yes, he has made some effort." Gordon leaned back in his chair, tipping it on two legs the way Jenny had always yelled at the boys not to do. But perhaps it would be best not to reprimand the man who held Scott's scientific future in his hands.

"Well, I'm not sure what to say. Of course, I'll talk to Scott. But I really don't know why he's fallen so far behind. He's home most nights studying—" Jenny stopped abruptly when she realized she really had no way of verifying that. She'd been out most nights the past week trying to do a drug deal. Did she dare share that little tidbit of information with this august gathering?

Another urge to laugh nearly overcame her, and again she turned it into a cough. She glanced over at the biology teacher. "Perhaps I could take a glass of water."

Gordon rose, unfolding his long body in small increments, and went out into the hall. Brenda leaned forward with an earnest expression and touched Jenny's leg. "You know, we were ever so sorry about Michael."

Jenny nodded, staying rigid lest the surge of grief rise too far and spill over if she slumped. Luckily, Gordon reappeared with a paper cup of water before she had to respond.

"Has Scott talked to you about how things are going with the school counselor?" Sylvia asked.

"No." Jenny took another sip of water. "I know he's seen her a few times. But he's very private about those things."

"Well, we'd certainly like to do all that we can to help," Gordon said. "But there is only so much the school can offer. Perhaps it would help for him to see the counselor more frequently."

"I'll talk to him about that." With a sudden clarity, Jenny realized that the cause of the problem lay solidly at her feet. She'd been out almost every night the past week. But what was she to do? She could hardly quit when they'd barely just begun.

She set the cup on the table and stood up. "We'll also work out something to make sure he does his homework."

"We appreciate that, Ms. Jasik." Gordon rose and towered over her. "We'll keep you advised of his progress."

---

After pulling into her driveway and turning off the ignition, Jenny sat and listened to the soft metallic ticks as the engine cooled. All the way home she'd wrestled with the problems with Scott. If this whole silly quest was responsible, should she just abandon it?

She hated to even consider that. Could she live with herself if she gave up something this important? But can you live with losing another son in the process?

Jenny got out of the car and slammed the door. Damn that voice of reason.

Stepping in the back door, she could see Scott in the kitchen by the microwave. He turned when he heard the door close. "Didn't expect you so early." He pulled the burrito out, then turned again and stood perfectly still. "You forgot the conference."

There was a note of anger and accusation in the last statement that rankled. "No. I did not forget the conference." She hung her jacket on a peg in the narrow entry and walked into the kitchen. "It was just very short and to the point."

"And the verdict was?"

His attitude chased any thought of being reasonable from Jenny's mind. "That you'd better knuckle down and do your homework."

"And who's going to tend to Alicia? You're never home to do that."

Her hand stung even before Jenny realized she'd slapped him. He stared at her, shock widening his eyes, and she reached out to try to touch the red spot on his cheek. "Oh, Scott, I'm so sorry."

He pulled back as if she was going to hit him again. "'Sorry' don't cut it."

His words tore at her as he stormed out of the kitchen, almost colliding with Alicia, who turned frightened eyes to her. "Mommy. What's wrong?"

Jenny reached for her daughter and held her close, murmuring softly into her hair. "Nothing, sweetie. Nothing's wrong."

"Then why were you and Scott yelling?"

"I don't know. I think we're both just tired. Let things get out of control."

"I know. I bet it's his hormones."

Shocked, Jenny pushed away to look her daughter in the eye. "What do you know about hormones? And where did you learn it?"

"Mom. You signed the paper for sex education, remember?"

"Oh. Right."

Was not remembering just another sign that her whole life was deteriorating while she was out chasing scumbags?

"What are you learning in sex education?"

"That the hormones control everything. And when they're very busy, we might act strange."

"Oh, baby." Jenny wrapped her arms around her daughter, amusement clashing with this horrible feeling of having royally screwed up with Scott. It's not like she'd never lost it before with one of the kids. They'd all become accustomed to a rare bout of unreasonable anger, but things were different now. They were all so much more fragile since Michael's death. And she'd give anything to be able to take that slap back.

---

Jenny spent the next evening at home, trying to repair some of the damage with Scott, but he was not receptive. After dinner he went to his room on the pretext of having homework to do. How could she argue with that? Instead, she cleaned the kitchen, played a game with Alicia, and did two loads of laundry. Then she fell into bed exhausted.

The following night, she hit the streets again wearing her skimpy outfit that made her feel like a slut. But at least it was warmer tonight, so she wasn't freezing her ass off. The little black car was in the far corner of the Dairy Queen parking lot, and business was brisk enough they could have been running a blue-light special.

Tonight's the night. Jenny had decided that when she left home. She'd already been out here three nights a week for the past two weeks, and she had to make some kind of move to set things in motion or this would take months.

She couldn't risk months.

Trying to maintain a casual air of confidence, she crossed the scarred asphalt and sidled up to the car, nodding briefly to the black man who leaned against a rear fender. It could have been an instant replay of every other night as she flashed her money and the Hispanic man looked her over. He didn't say anything, and she was afraid if she didn't do or say something to convince him otherwise, he'd take off again.

"You know, I've been eating your exhaust for two weeks now." She tried a nonchalant smile. "Getting awful tired of it."

Dark eyes continued to study her without blinking. She put one hand on her hip. "So maybe I should just take my business back to Dallas. Although I've always liked the motto 'Shop at Home.'"

Jenny heard a quick intake of breath and glanced at the thin black kid. His expression seemed to be wary, and he fiddled with a dreadlock that had come loose from a bandana that bundled the rest of his hair like a bunch of curly sausages.

She turned back to the Hispanic man. He took so long to respond, she wondered if she'd blown it. Sweat pooled in the middle of her back, and the muscles in her face strained to hold the smile.

After what seemed like hours, he finally nodded at the kid. "Give her the stuff."

The kid came instantly alert. "You sure, Boss?"

"Hell. She ain't no narc."

"How you know that?"

"Look at her. She's a skank. Couldn't bench-press a twig."

Pride made Jenny want to argue her case, but expediency won out. If this was what it would take for them to accept her, she'd keep her mouth shut.

The kid palmed her money, dug into the fold of the oversized parka, and passed a bag over. Jenny shuddered when her hands touched it, barely resisting an urge to look over her shoulder to see who was watching. It didn't take much to transport her back to childhood fears of her mother's eagle eyes.

There was a moment of awkwardness as Jenny tried to figure out what to do next. Did one say "thank you" when completing a drug deal? That wasn't something that Steve or Burroughs had covered, and the kid just stood there with a closed expression. He probably wasn't going to say, "Have a nice day."

Jenny dropped the bag in her pocket and turned away. It was an incredibly vulnerable feeling to have her back to them, but no shout stopped her, so she assumed her actions had been appropriate. Walking back toward the building, she put a little sashay into her step, forcing herself not to hurry.

It was only when she'd regained the shadows that she released the breath that had been threatening to burst her lungs for the past three minutes. *Is it always going to be this hard?*

As her breathing returned to something close to normal, Jenny wasn't sure if she wanted it to get easier or not. Her impulse now was to race home, strip off these nasty clothes, and stand in a shower for at least three hours.

She resisted that impulse. She'd worked too hard to get to this point to throw it all away. Feigning a nonchalance she didn't feel, she leaned against the building and pulled the makings of a cigarette out of her purse. She'd practiced this one day last week, flashing back to an early adolescent indiscretion as she locked herself in her bedroom with plenty of Lysol spray on hand. The practice served her well now. She rolled the cigarette with a few efficient moves. After lighting it, she cupped it and toked on it the way Burroughs had demonstrated.

Considering how hard she'd worked to quit smoking two years ago, she wasn't thrilled with this part of the charade, but Steve had emphasized it was important to be seen doing this. And from a distance — if they were watching her — the pushers wouldn't know she was smoking regular tobacco.

# TEN

"YOU'VE CHANGED, JENNY."

"No I haven't."

Carol put her hamburger down and gave Jenny a hard look. "You can't bullshit me."

Jenny looked around the small café that was comfortably full at the tail end of the lunch rush. Anywhere but at her friend. The silence at their table thundered in contrast to the chitchat and bursts of laughter from a nearby table of ladies with name badges that proclaimed they worked at J.C. Penny.

Finally, Jenny sighed and made eye contact. "Everything's changed since Michael died."

"It's more than that." Carol paused to sip her Coke. "You had the time after the funeral when you were quiet... sad... remote. Then that frenzy of physical fitness. But now..."

She paused again as if searching for the words. "It's like you're unavailable. For me. For your kids. For anybody."

"I'm available. I'm here." Jenny tried for a smile.

Carol glared. "It took a week to set this lunch date. We used to get together on an hour's notice. And how many of Scott's soccer games have you made?"

Jenny lost her smile. "Maybe you'd understand if you'd lost a child."

The pain that washed across the other woman's face twisted her normally pleasant image into a grotesque mask of anger and pain, and Jenny realized that of all the things she could have said to her friend, this was the worst. How could she have been so thoughtless?

"I can't believe you said that." Carol took a deep breath, held it for a moment, then let it out in a loud whoosh. "You never used to be cruel."

"I'm—"

"No. This is beyond apologies." Carol stood, her chair scraping across the wooden floor with a screech. "When the real Jenny Jasik shows up, have her call me."

After slapping a ten-dollar bill on the table, Carol slung her leather bag over her shoulder and walked out.

*Of all the—* Jenny shoved her plate, nearly toppling the bottle of catsup to the floor. *What kind of friend simply stomps off like that?*

*The kind who's been left in the dark*, another voice in her head answered. *The kind who deserves some explanation, not a verbal injury.*

It was more than the stares of other customers that made Jenny blush as she grabbed the check and stood. She left Carol's money on the table. The thought of touching it made her skin crawl, almost like she would be some kind of Judas if she took it. It wasn't exactly blood money, unless it did symbolize the death of the friendship, but it was tainted with her friend's anger, and that was reason enough to walk away from it.

Not for the first time, regret reared its ugly head and

sneered at her. *See what you've done? Something more important than revenge is at stake here.*

*It's not my fault. None of this would be happening if Michael hadn't—*

That terrible thought faltered Jenny's step, and she would have fallen if not for the back of the chair she grabbed. The blonde woman who occupied the chair turned, her expression of annoyance turning quickly to concern. "Are you all right?"

"I'm fine." The words soured in Jenny's mouth as she made her way to the cashier. What a crock of shit.

The transaction of paying and receiving the change barely registered. It was almost as if she'd been transported in some emotional time machine. Maybe Carol was right. Maybe the real Jenny Jasik was someplace else and an imposter had invaded her body, like a remake of the old *Quantum Leap* television show.

Jenny pushed the door open and stepped outside, hoping for some emotional relief, but it didn't happen.

The sun was like an assault, and the breeze was more a slap than a caress. Was she being punished? For what? For risking everything for some kind of revenge? For that awful thought about Michael?

Anguish slammed her against the front of the building, where she leaned for support until her legs might find strength again. How could she be angry with him? It wasn't like he'd chosen to die. Closing her eyes, she took several deep breaths, trying to tame the beasts of anger, shame, and guilt. *Oh, God. Please tell me I haven't made a huge mistake.*

"Jenny?" The voice and the touch jerked her from the misery. She opened her eyes to see the same look of concern on Mitchell's face as the blonde woman in the restaurant had worn. For a moment, she wondered why he was there, then remembered he had a delivery scheduled about this time; a birthday arrangement to a woman in the real estate office two doors down.

He kept his hand on her arm to steady her. "Lunch didn't agree with you?"

Jenny let the humor calm the storm of emotions. "It's just been a rough time."

"Well. If I can be so indelicate, it shows."

A gentle squeeze offered the comfort his words were missing, and Jenny smiled.

"Wish I could help. But short of taking over the whole store, I don't know what there is."

"You've done plenty. And I do appreciate you covering for me as much as you have."

"No problem." He started to walk toward the van parked at the curb, then turned back. "Will you be in later? We've got that big Homecoming order."

"Just give me a few minutes to clear my head."

"Live dangerously. Take a half-hour."

Jenny had to stifle a manic surge of laughter. Live dangerously? If only Mitchell knew. If only she could tell him. Carol. Someone. Guarding the secret was proving to be as difficult as living the secret.

---

Scott sat on the empty bleachers and watched the football team practice. Michael used to tease him about not trying out for the team, but Scott hadn't wanted to walk in the shadow of a star running back. God knows there was plenty of his brother's legacy that he couldn't avoid at school; honor student in history and math and a technical wizard in the drama department.

If he ever decided to give up soccer, maybe he'd try basketball. Michael had never played.

It felt weird to still feel so competitive. But then everything felt weird. He thought that life would get better as time went on. That's what Ms. Kotcher, the school counselor, had said on one of the mandatory visits, that there would come a time when he wouldn't think about his brother every second of every day. Even though he didn't care for her cloying sweetness, he figured she spoke with some authority, but things hadn't gotten better.

The hole in his life was still a huge, open sore that bled anew every time his mother went out. It was bizarre. She'd never done this before — leaving them at night. She'd always said the family was too important for her to go out. So why now? Was family only important as long as Michael was alive? *Do we not fuckin' matter?*

What would Ms. Kotcher say if he asked her that question at their next session? A bit bizarre, but that's how he felt, and he couldn't stem his feelings. Sure, his mother had stayed home one night after their last big fight. And as much as he wanted to dis her for just going through the motions to placate him, it had felt good to just chill out, the three of them watching a movie and eating every snack in the house. He'd even let his guard down long enough to hope that maybe she'd stay home the next night, too. *Ha. What a sap you are.*

The clatter of footsteps on the metal bleachers drew his attention, and he turned to see Caitlin hurrying toward him. She wore a light, quilted jacket and clutched an armful of books to her chest. Just seeing her wide smile lifted the blanket of gloom. He could've sworn the sun even brightened.

"Guess what?" She plopped down beside him. "I got the coolest dress for Homecoming. Mom and I went to the mall in Frisco last night. Lord and Taylor was having this awesome sale. And I got, like, this two-hundred-dollar dress for half that."

Scott smiled at her excitement, but the reminder of Homecoming made him wonder if his mother would remember to make the flower thing he was supposed to give to Caitlin. She'd said she would. She'd even seemed pleased that Scott had a date, but that was before the fight; before he'd gotten this feeling that he couldn't count on his mother anymore.

"What's wrong?"

The question startled him. He hadn't realized he'd gone into the black hole again.

"Sorry." He reached out to run his fingers through the strands of her hair that lay like an auburn shawl across her shoulders. "Tell me. Is this dress sexy?"

She ducked her head, but not before he saw a new touch of red on her cheeks. "Wait and see."

He pulled her close, and she seemed content to lean against his shoulder in silence. There were times they didn't talk much. Partly because he didn't know what to say, and he was sure she felt the same way. It was like some incredible awkwardness seized them both, but he also kept silent because he couldn't imagine saying some of the things that went through his mind. She'd dump him for sure.

# ELEVEN

THE MOON SCUTTLED BEHIND a bank of clouds, and Jenny hoped the rain would hold off until she got home again. It wouldn't do to catch pneumonia in the middle of her superhero act. She could see Chico leaning against the side of Whipple's Laundromat, long ago boarded up and left to deteriorate along with this whole section on the outskirts of downtown. Small-town slums.

He'd taken to meeting with her here since she'd increased the amounts she bought. Maybe the Dairy Queen parking lot was too open for the big buys. He'd also given her a card with a cell phone number she could call when she needed more stuff. She hoped that meant he trusted her enough for the next step in the game.

Drawing closer, she noted that he was alone. That was odd. She'd never seen him without his shadow before. She knew that boy's name, too, Leon. Was he waiting in a darkened doorway down the street? Was she walking into what fiction writers referred to as "a drug bust gone bad"?

"Yo, Mamma. Wassup?" A smile flashed white against the amber tones of Chico's face.

She controlled a shudder of panic and returned his smile the best she could. "Where's your friend?"

"Takin' care of some bidness."

Jenny didn't want to even consider what that 'bidness' might be. Certainly nothing as innocent as picking up a few groceries at Tom Thumb or paying the electric bill.

"I got a little business of my own needs taken care of." She handed him a ten-dollar bill, making sure he saw her hands shaking.

"Make it look good," Steve had said. "You've got to convince him that you're up against it."

Tonight, she didn't even have to pretend to be nervous. She was never going to get used to doing this.

Chico slipped her the baggie, and she stuffed it in her jacket pocket. Now is the time. Ask him. And remember to sound desperate.

Remembering what that boy had looked like a few weeks ago, Jenny mimicked his fly-on-speed movements and looked up.

"Money's getting a little tight, Chico." Jenny paused, glad that a sudden case of jitters put a tremor in her voice, adding authenticity to the improv. "Maybe I could move a little stuff for you. Help pay my way."

He regarded her with cold, unreadable eyes. "We're good here."

The line in the sand was clear, but maybe it wasn't too deep to cross over.

"I know some folks in Dallas. Said they'd like to do business with a friend." Jenny held his gaze, hoping the lie rang true. "Don't push," Steve had warned. "Just let the request lay there."

So she did.

Chico fished a toothpick out of the breast pocket of his leather jacket and stuck it in the corner of his mouth. "It ain't like buying a fuckin' franchise, lady."

Jenny hesitated for just a fraction of a second, then realized she shouldn't back down. Steve hadn't told her what to do if Chico was resistant, but some instinct told her he wouldn't expect her to meekly accept his first response.

"You know what, Chico. I'm trying to be nice here. Not cut you out of the picture. But you keep treating me like I'm stupid, I'll have to try someone else."

She turned her head slightly, hoping he'd say something before it became imperative that she actually leave.

Chico took what seemed like forever to respond as he played the toothpick back and forth in his mouth. Finally, he tucked it in one corner. "I gotta talk to my man about it."

"Sure. I understand. I'll—" She clamped her lips over the torrent of words that rode her relief that he hadn't said no.

"I'll get back to you."

Jenny nodded, then turned and walked the three blocks to where she'd parked her car. It felt a little strange to be happy that she was now going to be a drug dealer. But it meant she was one step closer to ending this whole mess.

That thought buoyed her spirits as she got in the car and headed for home. Maybe she'd get lucky on two counts and catch Scott before he shut himself in his room for the night.

---

The living room was dark when Jenny walked in. Damn! She went down the hall and stopped by Scott's room, where the latest offering from-Nine-Inch Nails blasted from behind his closed door. The bass rumbled the floorboards under her feet.

She tested the doorknob. Locked. She debated the wisdom of knocking. Not a good idea. Even if he could hear her over the squeal of guitars being tormented, interrupting would not be a good idea. Even in the best of circumstances, Scott did not like to be disturbed, and this could hardly be considered the best of circumstances.

The only positive thing Jenny had seen recently was that his grades were improving, but their relationship was in the toilet. Homecoming had bordered on disaster. No, he did not want to start the evening by bringing Caitlin over for dinner first. And did she absolutely have take pictures? He could give her one that the photographer took at the dance.

He'd finally agreed to a half-hour at home to indulge his mother's need for pictures, but his mood that night was dark. Jenny saw a frown of concern cross Caitlin's face, but Scott had hustled her out before she could voice that concern.

Since then, he'd shown the good grace to acknowledge Jenny's gift of the mum for Homecoming, but otherwise had barely spoken to her during the past week. He didn't need words, however, to make his point. His resentment came across loud and clear. Despite the icy silences, there was no way she could miss how much he hated being left with Alicia so often.

Jenny tried to limit her demands to two or three nights a week, but that consideration failed to register with Scott. And in her heart of hearts, she knew it was about more than having to watch his sister. He just hid his real feelings under his surly attitude. She'd learned to recognize that when Michael was fifteen and fought that same tension between the independent man who was emerging and the child who was afraid to let go of the security of dependence. Yet who could blame them. It was easier to let someone else tell you what you could do and what you shouldn't.

Jenny could feel the pull of that same desire. If her mother knew what was going on, she'd tell Jenny to quit this very instant, and being a dutiful daughter, she'd have to obey Mom, right?

Stepping away from Scott's door, she walked further down the hall. Alicia's room was accessible, and Jenny slipped in, thankful that the years with two teenage brothers had given her daughter the ability to sleep deeply in spite of thunderous music or the clomping of heavy footsteps in the hall.

A shaft of moonlight shone through the slats of the blinds, casting zebra-like stripes across the bed. Alicia lay in a tangle of blankets and stuffed animals, and Jenny watched the light play on her daughter's face. Two things consciously registered: how serene Alicia looked and the realization that the threat of rain must have moved off.

On another level, there was a subtle emotional shift that Jenny was barely conscious of until resolve replaced doubt. One of the reports she'd read during her crash course in drug dealing indicated that consumers were getting younger and younger. How soon before the sales pitch was given to Alicia and her friends?

Jenny was willing to do whatever it took to ward off that threat to safety and sanity.

---

Chico pulled off Highway 720 into the gravel drive. It led to the house that sat on a bluff a good half-mile from the road. Shit, it wasn't a house. It was a mansion. Chico couldn't wait until he could afford something worth even a fraction of what this place cost. He could have a family. Retire from the business. Be respectable. Maybe even join the church. With little *tsks* of admonition, his mother continually warned him about the consequence of abandoning the faith. "You do not want to burn in the fires of damnation."

A chuckle erupted. Hell? Sometimes he felt like he was already there. The Boss was crazy and was getting crazier by the day. Frank had speculated that the Boss was dipping into the goods, but Chico figured the crazy came from another kind of dipping. He'd seen his uncle go loco after too many trips to town to visit certain señoritas at the tavern. The place had not been a fine example of good sanitation, and God knows what else the girls had shared besides lice. The Cuban was known to run pretty hot with the ladies and hadn't always been rich enough to afford the quality he bought now.

Whatever the reason, the Boss's unpredictable behavior had everyone on edge. Chico would rather have dealt with the woman without running it by him, but Frank didn't want to make an independent decision. When he thought about it, Chico couldn't blame Frank. People had died for independent thinking.

Pulling his little black Kia behind the classic Rolls White Cloud, Chico stilled the engine. Maybe in his future life he could afford decent wheels, too.

Before he'd had a chance to step out of the car, two men appeared on the wide wrap-around porch that had pillars supporting an upper balcony. The men wore dark suits, shoes shined to a blinding luster, and Ray-Ban shades. Despite the wardrobe nod to respectability, there was nothing respectable about these two. Chico was well acquainted with their Havana reputation, which boiled down to "don't fuck with us."

He didn't even bother to greet them as they flanked him up the steps and across the porch to the door. The courtesy would have been wasted. Instead, he followed them silently as they opened the sculpted-wood double doors.

Inside, they continued to guide him through the large entry

where their leather heels clicked across the Terrazzo floor in a staccato rhythm. Original Picasso and Monet pieces graced the walls with the same abundance that some people hang posters. The men paused at the doorway to a room that opened on the left and motioned for Chico to enter.

Even though he'd seen it before, the sheer magnitude and opulence of the room still filled him with amazement. His family home in Mexico could have fit in there with space left over. Windows filled one entire wall with lace curtains that swayed in a light breeze. Ornate vases and sculptures sat on pedestals placed precisely around the room like museum displays.

A large teak table dominated the center of a Persian rug that seemed to stretch for miles. The table was empty. The Boss sat at a smaller table in front of a wall of bookcases. He appeared to be contemplating a move on a marble chess set. Lazano, a rotund man in his early thirties, occupied the chair on the other side. Chico remembered meeting the man once before. He was on the same level as Frank and ran the Denton area. It was also rumored that Lazano thought a shared heritage gave him an advantage with the Boss and guaranteed his swift ascent up the corporate ladder.

Solly, who filled a role Chico had never quite been able to put a name to, stood to one side of the table. Hands clasped behind his back, Solly balanced his large frame with his feet slightly apart, his pale, almost albino-white face impassive. But Chico knew the man was anything but impassive. The bulk inside the finely tailored suit was not fat, and the ice-blue eyes missed nothing. Anybody who made the wrong move toward the Cuban might never move again.

Chico kept that in mind as he took a few steps forward. "You wanted to see me, Boss."

The man didn't take his eyes from the board. "First I take this guy out. Then we talk."

Solly gave the other muscle the briefest of nods, and they retreated to the doorway, where they assumed statue-like stances. Chico stayed where he was and watched the men at the table. The Boss moved his knight and flashed a triumphant smile at his opponent. "Check."

Lazano stared at the arrangement of chess pieces for a moment, then reached out. Chico had no idea what the man might do. This was one game he knew nothing about. But he was fascinated with the play of emotions on the man's face as he looked at the Cuban, looked at the board, then looked at the Cuban again.

Chico didn't have to know the details of the game to recognize the body language of two bullies playing double-dare. Tension crackled between them, and he saw beads of sweat pop out like blisters on the fat man's forehead. Behind him, Chico sensed a stir of apprehension in the two goons.

Lazano finally picked up his bishop and started to place it on a square. His hand hovered for a moment, and then he moved the piece in another direction in one swift action. "Checkmate."

As the word reverberated in the sudden stillness, Chico instinctively took a step backward. The Cuban erupted out of his chair, upending the table and sending the chess pieces tumbling across the white carpeting like miniature acrobats. Lazano appeared frozen in place as the Boss pulled a Walther P5 out of his waistband and shoved the barrel deep into a pudgy cheek. "Don't. You. Ever. Fucking. Do. That. Again."

Chico held his breath, sure that if someone made the wrong move or the wrong sound, Lazano's brains would join the chess pieces on the floor.

After what seemed like hours, the Boss pulled back and

tucked the gun away. He patted Lazano on the cheek. "Now be a good boy and clean up this mess."

Lazano gave a brief nod, and the Boss turned to Chico. "Why do some hombres figure the rules don't apply to them?"

"I don't know, Boss. Rules are rules."

"Good answer." The Cuban walked over to a portable bar and poured a drink. "What about this broad Frank tol' me about?"

"She says she can move some stuff."

"Not in our territory."

Chico shook his head. "I was clear on that."

"What's her story? She just show up out of the clear blue, or what?"

"She's been buying for a while. No hassles. No problems."

"So. You're going to speak for her?"

Chico swallowed hard. If anything went wrong, it'd be his ass. It'd be safer not to risk his position, and possibly his life, but he hated to pass up the opportunity to add to his stable of pushers. He wasn't going to get rich if he didn't expand.

"We'll start slow. I'll watch her."

"You do that."

The icy tone that underscored the words sent a ripple of shivers up Chico's back. He'd have to make double sure this bitch didn't screw him over.

# TWELVE

WALKING into the entrance of the Harvey Hotel, Jenny glanced at the beautiful sculpture to her left and regretted wearing jeans. The setting was definitely more upscale than Randy's steakhouse, and she could have at least worn jeans with neat creases. But at least she wasn't decked out in leather and chains. She was beginning to hate that costume.

Steve had suggested meeting here because the hotel had several conventions booked, and they could blend into the crowds. Nobody would pay any attention to one more couple having drinks in the lounge. He'd said the lounge was right across from the registration desk, and she spotted it right away. She also saw him sitting at a table at the far wall. He looked comfortably casual in Chinos and a Polo shirt and had a glass of something amber resting on the small table in front of him.

A few other couples sat at various tables scattered throughout the room, with a few singles on stools at the bar. The hum of conversations battled with some country tune on the radio, and a thin layer of smoke battled with the ventilation system.

Jenny wound her way around tables to reach the corner and took a seat across from Steve. "Sorry I'm late. Should have allowed more time to find the place."

"No problem. I've only been here a few minutes." Steve motioned to the young, blonde waitress who stepped over.

"What can I get you?"

What Jenny really wanted was an ice-cold beer, preferably a longneck, but the setting seemed to call for something a bit more genteel. "Amaretto and coke."

The girl looked to Steve. "Ready for another?"

"I'm good."

After the girl walked back to the bar, he gave Jenny a searching look. "You okay?"

Jenny broke eye contact, trying to guess how he'd pegged her nervousness that quickly. Maybe because he's a cop. She almost laughed. Talk about putting her brain on hold.

"It's just been a little rough."

"Oh?"

Jenny held her response until the waitress set her drink down and moved off. "Not with the...uh, business. That's going fine. Although I feel a little slimier every time I meet with them."

Steve smiled, an action that softened the rough planes of his face and made him almost... attractive? *That is not the kind of thinking you need to be doing right now, girl.*

"When I worked narcotics in Dallas, I showered so much I was afraid I'd lose a layer of skin."

The humor provided a welcome diversion, and Jenny smiled back.

Steve took a swallow of his drink, then glanced at her. "So, what's wrong?"

His quiet attention was inviting. With all avenues of verbal intimacy cut off, sometimes she felt like she would explode if she couldn't unload some of the feelings that needed to be shared. But this was professional. She shouldn't even consider confiding in him the way she'd confide in Carol or her mother.

"Just the strain of living this double life." Jenny was careful to keep her tone light. "The kids give me flack. My mom gets pushy about my carousing."

"You want to pull out?"

She shook her head quickly. That was the only thing she was sure about in this whole mess. She did not want to quit. "I can handle the family," she said. "And I think the bad guys are going to let me move to the next level."

"I thought the timeline had that happening a few weeks from now?"

"The moment seemed right. I seized it."

Steve signaled the waitress for another round, and Jenny recognized it as a stalling action. Did he want to yell at her the way Ralph used to for doing something he considered stupid and rash?

She sighed. *Don't go there, girl. You've come a long way since that period of extreme doubt.* "It was a good call."

He rubbed the back of his neck. "I can't begin to list the risks of going too fast with this."

"I know. But I also know the huge risk of discovery if this drags on." Jenny leaned closer and lowered her voice as if even talking about it made her more vulnerable. "It's not like we're working in some metropolis. Somebody could blow my cover any time."

The waitress appeared with the drinks, and Jenny realized she hadn't even touched the first one. She sat back and watched Steve over the rim of her glass as she took a swallow. He seemed to be conducting an internal debate, a frown pulling his eyebrows together so they appeared to be one continuous brown line. At least he didn't look angry. Thoughtful she could take. Anger she still cowered from.

Finally, he set his glass down on the table and met her gaze. "I'm not going to debate the merits of a mother's instincts as compared to those of a cop. Hell, my mother would kill me if I even insinuated mine were better than hers. But let's keep a perspective here. I wouldn't feel confident in your arena, so you shouldn't be overconfident in mine."

"Point taken. I won't push about this."

"Good."

They sat in silence for a moment, other conversations humming around them. Jenny watched Steve sip his drink and look around the room, eyes resting briefly on each person. She wondered if he was mentally checking them against wanted posters.

"Do you have a family?" Where had that come from? Jenny touched a finger to her lips, wishing she could rewind this scene and edit that question out. "I am so sorry. I had no—"

"That's okay." He leaned back in his chair, and a hint of amusement crinkled the corners of his eyes. "Just takes a sec to adjust to the sudden conversation shift."

Jenny covered her nervousness by folding her napkin into a neat little square. "That was a stupid question. Please don't feel compelled—"

Steve touched her hand to stop her restless fingers. "No worries. I'm not easily compelled to do anything."

Again, his humor eased her discomfort, and she realized that she harbored a wish that the answer to her question was 'no.' But then what? You going to ask him if he wants to move in?

That thought spurred another surge of nervousness, and Jenny grabbed her leather purse. "I should go. Spend some time with my kids."

"And leave the question unanswered?"

The smile lines deepened around his eyes, and she noticed how dark they were in the subdued lighting. Like languid pools... *Okay. I am definitely going to have to quit with the romance novels.* She glanced away, hoping to keep her unprofessional thoughts from showing.

"I've never had the pleasure of a family," Steve said.

Something about the way he phrased that drew her curiosity. "Oh?"

Now he seemed to have difficulty meeting her gaze, and Jenny wondered what could be causing his discomfort. Not that it was any of her business. But this was very different from the air of confidence he normally wore like a comfortable old jacket.

"Not that I haven't probably messed up a couple of opportunities," Steve said, the attempt at humor sounding a bit forced this time. "But...I don't know." He shrugged. "I think I've been running a bit scared since..."

Not sure how she should respond to his frankness or his hesitation, Jenny used her napkin to wipe condensation off the side of her glass.

He sighed. "I should just shut up so you can go."

"That's okay. I mean. I've got time. You can talk if you want. Or not." *Way to go. Smother him with words.*

"You don't want to hear the whole boring saga of Steve Morrity." He hesitated a moment, then emptied his glass in one large swallow.

Jenny waited. Maybe he just had to work up the courage to talk about whatever it was that had him running scared. But he surprised her by dropping a couple of bills on the table and standing. "It would look better if we left together."

"Oh, sure." Jenny pushed back her chair, wondering what was propelling him out the door so fast.

Stepping out of the air-conditioned building, the heat was like a rude slap. What had happened to autumn? This was like August at its worst. But why should she be surprised? Nothing seemed to be happening in anything close to a prescribed manner, including this meeting with Steve. What had ever possessed her to ask such a personal question?

Stopping at her car, she glanced two rows over, where he was unlocking a blue Maxima so crusted with street dust it looked like it hadn't been washed in years. She watched him open the door and slide in, glad for the moment to be distanced from him. It made it easier to think. It also made it easier to remember in which compartment of her life he belonged.

The sun ricocheted off the windshield of an SUV that pulled in, momentarily blinding Jenny. When her vision cleared, she saw his car heading out of the parking lot.

He didn't look back.

---

Steve walked into the station and was hailed by Linda. "The Chief wants us in the conference room ASAP. Some of the task force is there, too."

"Did he say why?"

"No." She looked at him appraisingly. "You got anything you want to tell me before we go in?"

"Why does it always have to be something I did?"

"Now that's a dumb question." Linda smiled to soften the indictment.

Steve led the way down the hall and pushed open the door to the conference room, holding it for Linda to enter. Gonzales sat at the head of the table, Sheriff Tubbs to his right, and the DEA guy, Burroughs, to his left. Gonzales wore a scowl with his three-piece suit. Burroughs looked like he'd gotten his crimson shirt and white blazer from the *Miami Vice* wardrobe department. Tubbs had his usual khaki uniform with the usual sweat stains seeping out from under his arms. Never failed – summer or winter, the man oozed like he had an internal sprinkling system.

"What's up with our girl?" Gonzales asked without preamble.

"Okay if I sit?" Steve asked.

The Chief made a vague gesture. Steve made a big show of pulling a chair out for Linda, then sat down.

"Last time I was this uncomfortable I was under the screws of Internal Affairs." Steve leaned his chair back on two legs and regarded the trio of men facing him.

"You been keeping close tabs on this Jasik woman?" The question came from Burroughs.

"Yeah."

"You didn't let her do anything stupid, did you?" This again from the Fed.

Steve glanced at Gonzales, who nodded, apparently happy to let the DEA guy have center stage for a while. Steve would rather the questions come from his boss. Then he might be more inclined to answer – and to keep said answers civil. He also wished that Jenny had not jumped the timeframe. Obviously, that action had caused some trouble, but he wasn't going to take full responsibility.

"If there's some problem, it doesn't all fall on me. If I recall, the bulk of the orientation was done by you."

Burroughs's face started to turn red, almost as if his shirt were bleeding color.

"No need to get testy, here." Gonzales leaned forward, insinuating himself into the direct line of sight between the two men. He kept his attention on Steve. "Something appears to be heating up out at the ranch. Burroughs spotted all kinds of activity out there. Including a visit by a local distributor. What's his name?"

The question was directed to the Fed, who answered in a tight voice. "Chico."

Gonzales turned back to Steve. "The usual pattern is that Chico doesn't go to the ranch. His boss, Frank, handles that contact. Therefore, Burroughs had to wonder what happened to send Chico to the main man. And is that something connected to our lady?"

"Okay. It could be." Steve filled them in on what Jenny had told him. "But taking that step may not be a bad thing. She's had damn good instincts in dealing with these people."

"Not if she spooked them."

"I don't think she did. I think she just upped the ante."

The words were delivered with a confidence Steve was not so sure he felt deep inside. He was risking a lot with this endorsement, and he hoped he wouldn't regret it. Jenny had appeared to be wound as tight as a fiddle string earlier. Had she held something back?

"If I can be so bold as to jump into the middle of this swamp of testosterone," Linda said, "I think Steve's right. The Jasik woman is smart and savvy. And she's put too much into this to do something stupid and blow it."

Tubbs gave a derisive snort, and Linda shot him a frigid look along with her question. "What?"

"Never should'a let a civilian get this deep."

Steve enjoyed watching Tubbs squirm under Linda's glare and had to hide a smile when she came back at him. "Would you still be thinking that way if the civilian was a man?"

"Of course."

The response was just a bit too slow and a bit too loud to ring true, but before Linda could counter, Gonzales slapped the table. "That's enough. I want to hear this kind of sniping I'll go home to my kids."

His tone, more than his words, commanded everyone's attention, and quiet reigned until he turned to Burroughs. "Where to from here?"

"We let it play out. But I would caution the woman to step carefully."

"Already taken care of," Steve said, keeping his tone neutral lest he incite more wrath.

"Fine." Gonzales held each of them in his gaze for a moment. "What's done is done. We can't change that. So let's put judgments and tempers on ice for a while. Morrity, I want you on top of this woman at all times."

At another snort from Tubbs, Gonzales looked like a pressure cooker getting ready to blow. The other man held up a placating hand. "Sorry. Couldn't help the image that came to mind."

Linda shot him a withering look, and this time Steve had to turn his face to hide the smile as Tubbs protested. "What? Just trying to have a little fun. Lower the temperature in here."

"We're done." Gonzales stood and shoved his chair up to the table. "Everyone report in as usual."

# THIRTEEN

JENNY WALKED into the living room, where she could hear the TV blaring. Scott, wearing dark blue flannels and a Longhorn sweatshirt, was sprawled on the floor, engrossed in the latest offering from MTV. She cleared her throat and he looked up, slowly checking out her outfit that consisted primarily of leather and chains.

"Halloween's over," he said.

"Very funny."

She watched her son try to smile, but the underlying seriousness she'd sensed in him these past weeks overrode the banter.

"Going out again?" he asked. "It's the third time this week."

Jenny flashed a smile that she hoped would soften the rough edge of his attitude. "That's supposed to be my line."

"Nice try, Mom. But jokes aren't cutting it." He sat up to face her. "What's been going on with you lately?"

"Watch the tone of voice, Buster."

"Maybe I'm entitled to a tone of voice."

The little-boy hurt that was barely concealed behind the

bluster clutched at Jenny's heart. If only she could tell him. She knew he'd understand. Even support her. He had this grand sense of justice, just like she did. And if she could let him in on the secret, they could tilt at windmills together. Although, remembering that awful sense of evil she felt every time she met with Chico and his minions, she was sure that was a windmill she wanted to keep Scott far, far away from.

"I know this has been hard. I'll make it up to you."

"Fine. We make an appointment or what?"

He turned back to the TV, and Jenny stood for a moment. The words had cut deep, and she was torn between a desire to make things right with her son and the need to finish what she'd started. *Oh, hell.* She dug her car keys out of her pocket.

"Alicia's in her room studying. Y'all can have ice cream later."

Keeping his attention on the TV, Scott waved a hand in a brusque acknowledgement.

It almost broke her heart to walk out, but she knew she had to. She could always hope that he'd just get over it. *Yeah. That'll happen about the time I win the lottery.*

A prickle of unease stayed with her as she started her usual prowl, and later she would wonder if that had somehow influenced what happened that night. Had she emitted some odor of fear or weakness?

Everything was fine at first. Chico was at his favorite spot by the old laundromat, and Leon was with him. Business as usual. Maybe he'd even have an answer for her tonight. But as Jenny drew close, she realized it wasn't the same kid with Chico. It wasn't a kid at all. The feral eyes that studied her were set deep in the face of a man a good ten years older than Leon. That face had been ravaged by a sharp instrument that had left an ugly rope of a scar down the length of one cheek and across the jaw line.

Jenny swallowed a gulp of panic as the weight of the man's scrutiny washed over her. *Who the hell is this guy, and why is he here?*

Despite jeans and sweatshirt, attire that Jenny had come to recognize as a dealer's uniform, she knew the older man was no lowly dealer. In addition to the menace that seemed to ooze out of his pores, he carried an air of authority that was probably the reason Chico was a little twitchy. He couldn't seem to find a resting place for his eyes, and his greeting was strained.

Another prickle of unease created dampness between Jenny's shoulder blades. "Who's your new friend?" She tried for nonchalant as she nodded toward the man.

"Just a guy."

The other man was so still he could have been a statue. *Doesn't he know you have to blink now and then to lubricate your eyes?*

*Does that even matter now?*

Jenny didn't know if she wanted to laugh or to run. But she finally decided she should take care of what she came for, then get the hell out of Dodge.

"Doing business today, Chico?"

"Let's see your money."

The harsh tone sent another wave of fear skittering down her spine. She swallowed hard and pasted on a smile. "Hey, man, it's me, Connie. Why the attitude?"

Chico shot a quick glance at the other man, then lifted his chin. "You got it or not?"

Jenny fished a couple of bills out of her pocket. "I need a dime."

Rolling forward on the balls of his feet, Chico snatched the money out of her hand, then kept right on walking.

The action stunned her for a moment, and then she whirled. "Hey! Where's the stuff? You can't do that."

"But I did, didn't I?" Chico waved the bills over his shoulder. "Thanks for the tip."

Jenny turned back and again came up against the hard scrutiny of the mystery man. *What the hell is this? Some kind of test? For me or for Chico?*

Frustration dared her to speak. "Don't you ever even move?"

A ghost of a smile touched his granite face. Then he followed Chico down the street, moving so effortlessly his feet seemed to glide along the pavement.

Taking a deep breath to slow her pounding heart, Jenny wondered what the hell she was supposed to do now. Was this some sort of bizarre end to the whole deal? Had they made her? Was she out?

She didn't like that thought. Nor did she like feeling so powerless.

When she reported it to Steve later, he masked any concern in assurances that she hadn't done anything wrong. Maybe it had been some kind of test for Chico. She should be able to go back in a few days and everything would be fine. Meanwhile, he'd check with Burroughs to see what was happening out at the ranch.

After they hung up, Jenny tried to make herself believe what Steve had said, but her gut wasn't buying it. She wasn't so sure it was a test for Chico. It was a test for her, and she was damned if she was going to fail.

---

Jenny pulled into a parking spot in the small strip mall just off highway 380. The marquee boasted: 380 MALL – PIZZA, GUNS, DONUTS. After doing an Internet search for gun shops, she'd called this place because it was far enough away from Little Oak that she felt safe going there. But the man she'd talked to hadn't sounded like he had the kind of wit that could come up with this sign.

Then again, maybe no joke was intended. The stores could simply have been listed with no thought of amusement. Only people like her who were finding ways to avoid the next step would waste their time wondering if one bought a pizza, shot it, then ended up with a donut.

Stepping out of the car, Jenny locked the doors and made her way to the end of the mall, where another sign said: DAVE'S GUNSHOP. Last week's late fall heat wave had mellowed, and a cool breeze tousled her hair. Out here, almost in farm country, the breeze carried a rich odor of earth and animals. Beat the hell out of car exhaust and the other wonderful smells of city life.

Jenny walked into the store, and coming from the brightness outside, it took a moment for her eyes to adjust to the dim interior of the shop. A bell over the door had tinkled when she walked in, and she could hear the soft strains of a classical tune coming from somewhere in the darker recesses of the store. Another incongruity.

"Can I help you?"

The voice belonged to a man who stepped through a doorway behind the counter. Now that she could see, Jenny assumed the doorway led to a back room. She stepped closer and saw that the man was in his late thirties. There was a cautiousness about him that Jenny had come to recognize as a byproduct of military service. Her cousin had looked like that when he'd come back from Iraq.

Of course, the man's close-cropped hair and Semper Fi tattoo on his forearm were pretty good clues that he'd seen a tour or two. He was dressed in jeans and a black t-shirt that boasted: Guns don't kill people. Idiots with guns kill people.

Jenny had to admit he had a point. "I called earlier. About a gun," she said.

"Sure. And you wanted this for...?

"Protection. I'm a single mother. We don't live in a great area."

He seemed to consider her comments, and Jenny wondered if she'd come across too anxious. She reminded herself to take a breath and calm down.

"In that case, you want something with a bit of stopping power." He moved down the glass-topped counter and unlocked a back panel. He pulled out a gun that was dull silver in color. It didn't look like any pistol Jenny had ever seen, but then her experience was limited to cop shows and movies. Somehow being this close gave it a whole new perspective; not one she was sure she liked. What she was sure of was the desire not to be humiliated by Chico again.

"This is a Glock Model 17L," the man said. "Not pretty to look at, but it shoots straight. It's safe and reliable."

After a couple of quick actions that Jenny couldn't quite follow but assumed were meant to ensure the gun was not loaded, he held it out to her. "See how it feels."

Jenny hesitated briefly and then took the weapon. It was surprisingly light, and the grip felt strange. It wasn't the cool feel of metal she'd been expecting.

"It's made of a polymer," the man said as if she'd voiced some question aloud. "But the striations insure a good grip, even if your hand sweats."

And it certainly would. "Could you show me how to use it?"

"Never sell a weapon without a test run." He took the gun, walked around the end of the counter, and motioned her to follow. "Got a range out back."

---

Later, driving back home, Jenny marveled at how well she'd shot. Even the man — she'd finally determined he was the owner, Dave — had been impressed, asking if she was sure she'd never fired a weapon before. Her first few shots had been wild, but after he showed her how to steady the gun by cradling one hand in the other, she hadn't missed the target. No bull's eyes, but then, with a weapon like that she wouldn't need a perfect aim. At least that's what Dave had assured her.

The cost of the gun, ammunition, and a gun safe put a serious dent in her savings. She'd left a two-hundred-dollar deposit and would pay the rest when she picked everything up after the five-day waiting period was over.

She still had to decide how to handle this with the kids. It was a no-brainer that she'd keep the gun in the safe high up on a shelf in her closet, but should she tell them about it? They wouldn't buy her 'single mother' concerns since she'd already spent six years as one without needing a gun. That left her with the question of what possible reason she could give them now. Or would it be better to just keep it hidden until this whole nightmare was over?

Jenny wasn't comfortable with the idea of another secret. Her whole relationship with the kids had been built on honesty and trust. They didn't hide things from each other, certainly not the important things in their lives, but in this case, hiding was her first choice.

# FOURTEEN

JENNY WATCHED Mitchell wrap the roses in green tissue paper for the man who was splurging big time for his anniversary. Three-dozen red roses. *Oh, to be loved like that.* Jenny shook her head. *Get real, girl. You were never destined to be loved like that.*

Putting her mind to something more positive, Jenny realized that it felt incredibly good to have a normal day at work. Maybe she'd even try for a normal day at home later. Surprise the kids with a real dinner again. Even Scott had complained about frozen pizza the other day. That used to be number one on his essential food groups list.

When the door burst open, she was surprised to see the object of her musings walk in. Actually, he stormed in. The man who'd bought the roses quickly skirted around her son and was out the door before it banged shut.

"Scott. What are you doing here?" Jenny glanced at the clock as if for verification that he should still be in school.

"Just what in the hell were you doing the other night?"

His words and tone stunned her into a momentary silence.

This was her son? Yelling at her? Even Mitchell appeared shocked. His face paled before he made a discreet exit to the back room while Jenny struggled for words.

"What are you talking about?"

"I can't believe it." Scott paced as he talked. "Dan said it was you. But I said no. It couldn't be my Mom. Then Tracy overheard us and said she's seen you, too."

"Saw me where?"

"Different places downtown. Talking to a couple of scumbag drug dealers."

Jenny was torn between an impulse to slap him for shouting at her and needing to diffuse this before it escalated beyond control or explanation. Mitchell would have had to go two blocks away not to still be hearing this. How many more lies was she going to have to tell?

"If you'll just calm down, I can—"

"Oh, I can't wait to hear this one."

She covered the distance between them in two quick strides. "Listen, young man. I'm still your mother. And you won't use that tone with me. Not now. Not ever. You got that?"

She was pleased when Scott had the good sense to take a step backward and keep his mouth shut. Now all she needed was to come up with something that would sound plausible to Scott and to Mitchell. There was no doubt in her mind that he was as anxious for an explanation as her son was. Might as well tell the lie now. If she dressed it in enough parental sarcasm, maybe they both would buy it.

"Okay," she said. "You want to know about the other night? Out of the kindness of my heart I'll tell you. Yes, I was downtown. And sometimes I go to the Dairy Queen. Do I talk to any drug dealers? I don't know. I might have. I talk to quite a few people. I don't ask what they do for a living. Does this satisfy your raging curiosity?"

Scott remained silent, but Jenny could see the muscle in his jaw twitch.

"I can take the silence as a yes?" she asked.

She could see a battle raging on his face, but he finally nodded.

"Fine. And the next time you have a question, wait until I get home. You will never, ever, embarrass me like this again."

The force of her words seemed to diffuse whatever internal energy was building in Scott. He let out a breath with an audible whoosh.

"Now go back to school before I get a call from the principal."

Scott went out the door, this time closing it quietly. Jenny turned and almost ran into Mitchell.

He considered her for a moment, eyes wide with curiosity. "Were you really talking to drug dealers?"

"Don't start."

"Whoa." Mitchell held up both hands. "I'm not accusing, or interrogating. But you have to admit that the explanation you just gave your son was a bit lame."

Jenny tried to push past him. "It's none of your business."

"Pardon me?"

Jenny stopped and saw the surprise on his face. "I'm sorry. Didn't mean to be so sharp. It's just—"

"Stop. No more vague responses. Something's going on. I can sense it. Hell, everyone can sense it."

For Mitchell to take that tone with her, Jenny knew he was really upset. She looked away before his anguish prompted some verbal indiscretion.

"You're not going to tell me?"

"I can't." She kept her gaze averted. "I'm sorry. I just can't."

They stood in a frozen tableau for a long moment, then

Mitchell sighed. "I'm only pushing because I'm worried about you."

"I'm okay." She gathered some paperwork from the counter so he wouldn't see the lie in her eyes. "Nothing is going on."

"I hope not. We all care too much to let something happen to you because you are in the wrong place at the wrong time. And if you need help with coping...well, Jeffrey can..."

He let the sentence fade, and the absurdity of what he was suggesting was almost amusing. Yet, the kindness in his tone threatened to undo her, and Jenny struggled to maintain some semblance of composure. She touched the corner of her eye where moisture pooled, then willed the tears to retreat.

"I'll keep that in mind," she said when she was able to force words past the lump in her throat.

"Good. And when you are ready to talk, I'll be here."

The lump grew to the size of a boulder, and Jenny gave a brief nod before skirting around him and heading to the bathroom in back. Inside, she leaned against the door, then slid to the floor. Tears coursed a warm path down her cheeks, but she did manage to still the urge to sob. She'd already caused Mitchell enough grief. He didn't need to hear her cry.

---

Steve looked up in alarm as Gonzales burst into his office waving a piece of paper like it was on fire. "What the hell is this?" Gonzales asked.

"I don't know, Boss. Are we playing some kind of guessing game here?"

"Don't be a wiseass." Gonzales slapped the paper onto Steve's desk. "She's applied for a concealed weapon permit. This is our part of the background check."

"'She' who?" But even as he asked the question a part of him knew the answer.

"Our fuckin' undercover lady."

Steve sat back in his chair, stunned. He knew the Chief was furious. He only said 'fuck' when he was beyond mad.

"We gotta pull her." Gonzales dropped into the chrome and vinyl chair in front of the desk. "A fuckin' gun."

"I think pulling her would be a mistake."

The look Gonzales shot him made Steve wish he could take the words back, but his gut told him he was right. She was in too deep to abort the whole thing now.

"I'll handle it." Steve did his best to sound convincing. "Make sure she doesn't take this any further."

"And you figure she'll just quietly go along?"

"Maybe not quietly. But she'll cooperate. This is too important to her to risk blowing it."

Gonzales snatched the paper and stood up. "Just remember whose ass is on the line if she does something stupid."

Steve nodded and waited until his boss was out the door before releasing a big sigh. Just how much could he risk for this woman? And why did he feel so compelled to back her in the first place?

---

"So, what did she say?" Caitlin lengthened her step to try to keep up with Scott, who was striding down the sidewalk like he was on a forced march.

"Some sarcastic mom thing."

"Wait a minute." Caitlin grabbed the back of Scott's coat. "Will you please stop and talk to me?"

He slowed his steps.

"You don't really think your mom's, like, doing drugs?"

"Why not? Everything else is fucked up in my life."

"I wish you wouldn't say that."

He stopped and faced her. "What? You some kind of prude?"

Almost before the words had spilled out, Scott knew they were wrong. He saw a wince of pain on her face before she turned away. It wasn't the language she'd objected to.

"I didn't mean everything in my life." He tried a light caress across her shoulders, but she shrugged away.

*Damn! Is nothing going to go right?*

"Hey, I'm sorry." He reached for her again, but she took another step away. Then she turned and faced him.

"I know it's been hard. Losing your brother. But it's been months. I just wish we could have one day without you being in some weird mood."

Scott had to bite down hard to stem the anger that rose like bile in his throat. That was totally not fair. They'd had plenty of days... "What about the dinner and dance last week? They were pretty mood-free."

"If you don't count dissing the waiter."

"He brought us cold food."

Caitlin sighed and glanced away again. In the heavy silence between them, Scott became aware of two squirrels chattering in a nearby tree.

"I don't want to fight," Caitlin finally said. "I hate it when we fight."

"Me, too."

This time she didn't move away when he put his arm around her waist. They started walking again, and the squirrels scampered further up the tree as they passed.

"Maybe it didn't really mean anything. What Dan saw," Caitlin said.

"Sure."

Scott knew that wasn't true. But if Caitlin needed to believe it, he'd let her. He wouldn't voice the little fears that assaulted him every time his mother explained what she was doing.

Maybe if he just tried to ignore the whole horrible mess, it would all go away. His mother would go back to her old routine of working and taking care of them. It would be like none of this ever happened.

*Yeah. Right. Except Michael is never coming back.*

He swallowed hard and looked up at the expanse of bright blue sky. The glare was merciless, and he closed his eyes. The darkness was better.

---

Jenny put the handset on the cradle with more force than necessary, glad that the kids weren't home yet. There was no way that conversation could have been quiet. Fury still burned her cheeks, and she paced the kitchen, trying to figure out what to do now.

Steve had been unyielding. No gun. No way. He was sending the paperwork back to the dealer with an explanation that the customer changed her mind.

"Shit. Shit, shit, shit." She jerked the refrigerator open and pulled a cola out.

When she turned around, she saw Alicia in the doorway. "How long have you been there?" Jenny asked.

"I heard you say bad words."

*Shit.*

"I'm sorry, Honey. I've just had a rough day."

"You said we should never say bad words. No matter what."

"You're right. Should I just ground myself to my room?"

The sound of Alicia's laughter was like a balm. Jenny had definitely been missing that lately, and she felt some of the weight of her dilemma lift.

She was about to ask Alicia what she wanted for a snack when the phone rang. She picked up, wondering if it was Steve calling again. Had he changed his mind? "Hello."

"Mom?"

"You were maybe expecting someone else?"

When Scott didn't respond right away, Jenny wondered if there was something wrong, or had the attempt at humor and normal fallen flat? "You okay?"

She heard the distinct sound of a sigh, and it was so much like Ralph's she had a hard time stifling a knee-jerk reaction. Luckily, Scott spoke first. "Can I eat dinner at Caitlin's tonight?"

"It's kind of short notice, isn't it?" Jenny asked. "You sure it's okay with her parents?"

"Mom!"

"Okay, okay. I only worry that they have no clue what it takes to feed a teenage boy. Caitlin looks like she eats less than Jenny Craig."

Another deep sigh from the other end of the line told her that he didn't find that attempt at humor any funnier than the previous one. Ever since that day he'd questioned her at work, their relationship had been like a fresh sore. Easy to irritate and needing a lot of care. Humor was usually a good balm for any difficulty, but of late Scott wasn't accepting any offer of healing.

Jenny felt a tightness in her chest, like someone had reached in and was squeezing her heart. She touched her breastbone lightly. *Just what I need. A freakin' heart attack.* But she knew it wasn't a heart attack, at least not in the strict physical sense. It was an attack of an entirely different kind. And this one wouldn't kill her. It just left her emotions mortally wounded.

"Mom?"

"Sorry. Got distracted there for a moment."

"Is it okay to go with Caitlin?"

Jenny took a deep breath and let it out slowly. "Sure. Mind your manners. And remember to leave something for the dog."

Scott groaned again, but this time there was a little chuckle mingled in. The pain in Jenny's heart eased.

Soon.

Soon it would be okay. She would finish playing Wonder Woman, and then she could explain it all to him. Things would be okay again. They had to be okay again. Jenny didn't think she could bear to lose another son.

# FIFTEEN

"PLEASE DON'T ASK me to explain. I simply can't." Jenny faced her friend across the expanse of fine mahogany. How many times had they sat here in Carol's kitchen sharing a cool drink and whatever was important in their lives? More than Jenny could even count, but never before had she made such a request.

"It's not a cup of sugar you want to borrow, Jen."

"I know." Jenny stirred her tea, using the maneuver to avoid eye contact.

When she'd first gotten the idea to ask Carol about using one of Barry's guns, she'd tried to examine it from every angle. Could she bluff her way through an explanation of why she needed one? Was the friendship still strong enough that Carol would back her on this? They'd survived a lot of ups and downs over the years, but Jenny could still see the hurt and anger that had filled Carol's face the last time they'd been together. She also remembered how many times she'd called to apologize before her friend had finally picked up.

Carol had been chilly then and still was when Jenny had

called earlier today to see if Carol had time for a visit. The chill had started to thaw during the ritual of offering and accepting tea and the initial small talk. Then Jenny had made her request.

"Is it your business?" Carol asked. "You need protection?"

Jenny almost laughed at how close to correct that question was. But it also gave her an easy out. If she said yes, there was no reason for Carol to suspect the business had nothing to do with flowers. "Something like that."

"So why not go the legitimate route?"

"I'm afraid Ralph might find out during the background check." This response was easy. Jenny had anticipated the question when she'd first thought of asking Carol and had rehearsed an explanation that she could give without a flinch of conscience.

Carol dawdled so long over stirring the sugar into her tea, Jenny was afraid her friend was stalling to find some way to say no. Should she argue her case? Beg?

No. In all the years of their friendship, groveling had never appealed to Carol.

Jenny reminded her body to breathe while she waited for Carol to respond. When her friend finally looked up, her expression reflected some kind of inner turmoil. "I need to know something, Jen."

"What?"

"What the hell is going on with you?"

"Nothing."

Carol slapped the table hard enough that the teacups clattered and tea sloshed. "Don't keep lying to me. You can't know how much that hurts."

Jenny did a mental scramble to try to come up with something reasonable to say.

"And don't try the 'I'm just trying to adjust to Michael's

death' line, either," Carol said. "It didn't work before. And I'm less inclined to buy it now."

Jenny leaned forward in her chair. "Could you please just trust me about this?"

Carol started to say something, but Jenny halted her with a raised hand. "Let me have my say. Then you can decide."

Carol nodded.

"Okay. I can't tell you what's been going on. I'm sworn to secrecy. But it's nothing bad, or illegal. And if you loan me the gun, I promise I'm not going to shoot anybody."

"If you don't plan to use it, why do you want it?"

That wasn't a question Jenny had anticipated. She bit her lip, searching for the right response that would appease her friend. "We're the only ones who have to know I won't use it."

Carol wiped at the spilled tea with a paper napkin, appearing to consider Jenny's words while she made small circles on the table. Then she looked at Jenny. "You're not messing with those drug people? Trying to get revenge for Michael?"

Another question Jenny wasn't expecting. Her friend knew her all too well. She took a breath. "No. It's not about revenge."

At least she could be honest about that. She'd spent many an hour mentally asking the same question, wanting to make sure she kept the line between justice and revenge clear. Vindication might be part of it. It seemed to go along with justice. But revenge was not even in the same family.

Carol sighed and wadded up the napkin. "Don't you ever ask for another favor for the rest of your life."

"Does that mean yes?"

"Come on."

Jenny followed her friend into a spacious bedroom that, in addition to the normal trappings, held a huge, teak roll-top desk. Every time she was here, Jenny felt a twinge of jealousy.

This room had to be twice the size of her bedroom. And the adjoining bathroom was big enough to throw a party in.

But it was an awful lot of space to live in alone.

As Carol rummaged in the middle desk drawer for a key, then unlocked one of the side drawers, Jenny cast a quick glance around to see any signs of masculine visitation. Carol had said they were taking it slow, but certainly George had spent a night or two here.

Then Jenny chuckled softly at the ridiculousness of what she was doing. What did she expect to find? A pair of boxer shorts kicked into a corner? Even if George was so compelled, Miss Carol-the neat-freak wouldn't let them stay there for a second past climax.

Okay. That wasn't fair. But they certainly wouldn't be there the next day.

"This is not funny," Carol said, turning with a locked wooden box in her hands.

Jenny didn't even realize her thoughts had given rise to a smile. "I know. Sorry. Mind wandering." She made a vague gesture, hoping her friend wouldn't ask where her mind had wandered to.

Carol gave her a long look, then set the box on the top of the desk and unlocked it. "I sold most of Barry's collection after he died. Didn't see any need for it since I'd never go back to the range without him. But I kept a few pieces that I especially liked."

She lifted out a medium-sized silver gun with an inlaid grip. It was a beautiful gun, although Jenny had some trouble putting those two words together. She'd always hated guns, but she knew that stemmed from fear. Her experience at the gun shop had eased some of that trepidation.

"May I?" Jenny held out her hand, and Carol set the weapon in it. "Is it loaded?"

"No. I didn't keep the guns for protection. Just for sentimentality. You'll have to get ammunition."

That was a kicker. Jenny had no clue how or where to buy bullets. She certainly couldn't go back to Dave's. When Steve had picked up her deposit and returned it to her, he'd made it clear that she was not to go back to the gun shop. And she didn't even know whether she could buy ammunition without risking another background check.

"You can go to any big Wal-Mart," Carol said as if she knew exactly what Jenny was thinking. "Just tell the clerk in sporting goods what kind of gun it is and he'll give you the right bullets."

"Then I guess you'll have to tell me what this is." Jenny hefted the weapon.

"It's a Colt .45 Automatic." Carol reached into the box and pulled out another gun. "And I have this little guy. He's a Walther."

Jenny eyed the small gun and wondered if it could come in handy some time. "Could I borrow both?"

"Oh, my God." Carol slumped against the desk. "You really are doing it."

"Doing what?"

"Going after the drug dealers."

Jenny started to protest, but Carol cut her off with a wave of her hand. "You could maybe fool someone else. But not me. Tell me I'm wrong. I'd love to be wrong."

A host of possibilities swam through her mind as she struggled to hold Carol's gaze. She could tell her friend the truth and swear her to secrecy. But if that didn't work... If Carol told someone else... No. All Steve needed was one more infraction to have an excuse to cut her out of the picture.

"Please, Carol." She touched her lightly on the arm. "Not another word. Not if our friendship means anything to you."

Carol pulled back. "Don't put me on the spot like that."

"Don't put *me* on the spot."

Jenny could feel the tension in her friend as she struggled to come to some decision. God, she hated to do this. And she wouldn't blame Carol one bit if she refused. But she needed that gun. And she'd already said too much.

"Please." The word was a whisper.

Carol didn't respond, and Jenny felt her heart beat almost in perfect rhythm with the loud ticks from the antique clock on Carol's desk. Then a loud chime broke the intense silence, startling them both out of the visual standoff. When the final gong marking the time eddied through the room, Carol handed Jenny the other gun. "Promise you aren't going to do anything stupid or dangerous with this."

"I promise."

Later, in the privacy of her car, Jenny had to laugh at the brazenness of that promise. That was the worst lie she'd ever told her friend. What she had in mind was both stupid and dangerous.

---

The clerk at Wal-Mart didn't even blink when Jenny asked for the ammunition, and the cashier rang it up along with the few groceries like it was nothing out of the ordinary. But she still didn't feel comfortable until she got home and locked the guns in the security box she'd bought along with the ammunition. She stashed the box in her closet, putting it behind a stack of afghans her grandmother had knitted. She fingered the soft wool and had to laugh. What would Grandma think?

For two nights Jenny stayed home. She tried to tell herself she was doing it for the kids. And perhaps that was part of it. But she knew she was primarily driven by fear. The thought of confronting Chico made her legs weak, but she couldn't put it off much longer.

After telling Alicia and Scott that she was going to take a shower, Jenny went to her room and locked the door. Then she pulled the box with the guns from the hiding place in the closet.

She set the box on her bed, unlocked it and took the weapons out. She rested the smaller gun on the floral bedspread and tucked the Colt in the waistband of her pants, just like she'd seen cops do on TV. The hard press of the barrel against her back was uncomfortable, so she reached back to try to adjust it. The reach, the grasp, everything felt awkward. *Hell, if I was ever going to use this, I'd shoot my ass off.*

Then she remembered something the gun shop owner had said during her one and only lesson. "Most people buy a gun without fully realizing that if they have it, they'll probably have to use it."

Pulling the weapon free, Jenny ran her fingers along the smooth surface of the barrel. Could she? Would she?

Still holding the gun, she sat on the edge of her bed and let her mind play with a few scenarios. Someone breaks into the house. He's going after the kids. A no-brainer. *I'd shoot him dead.*

Okay, what about out there? Away from home and away from the kids? If someone threatened her, could she make that split-second decision to take him out first? She truly hoped she never had to make that choice. But she also knew the real possibility of that happening. She wasn't just playing around with some two-bit pusher. Chico had made that clear the night he ripped her off.

Wouldn't do to let them think they'd scared her.

Jenny stood up and slid the gun back into the waistband of

her jeans. This time she put it midway between her spine and her side. She put her jacket on, then practiced reaching for the gun a few times. She got a little quicker with each attempt. Turning into a regular little gunslinger.

After putting the smaller gun back in the security box, Jenny returned the box to the top shelf of her closet. She piled the afghans back in their place, mentally apologizing to her grandmother. Then she turned to look at her reflection in the mirror above her dresser. *Just do it, girl.*

---

Tonight, Jenny found Chico and Leon at the Dairy Queen parking lot.

"Hey, look who's back." Chico leaned out the open window of his Kia and gave Jenny a smile that hung false on his smooth face. "Figured you wouldn't come back."

"What would make you think that?"

The challenge dangled there for a moment while Leon glanced at Chico as if looking for direction on how to respond. The other man kept his gaze on Jenny.

Sweat beaded on her spine as she approached the window, and she fought to keep her expression neutral. She leaned one elbow on the side mirror, bending forward so Chico could get an ample view of what the gap in her tank top displayed. When she saw his eyes move downward, she slid her other hand under the flap of her jacket and pulled out the gun. Before the movement even registered, she had the barrel under his chin.

Jenny let her smile become real when she saw the glint of fear flash in Chico's eyes. Then she caught movement in her peripheral vision. It was Leon, coming fast from his position at the rear fender. "Take another step, and I'll blow his fucking head off."

The man froze.

"Good boy." She kept her gaze on Chico. "Now here's the deal. You give me the stuff I paid for last week, and I don't pull this trigger."

A sheen of sweat emerged on his face, but despite that obvious sign of fear, he stretched the silence until it almost screamed. Jenny fought to keep her hand and her eyes steady as she tried to formulate another threat to forestall the moment when she might have to consider pulling the trigger.

Then Chico called to Leon. "Do what she says."

"We don't bend to no she-rah."

Leon's defiant stance prompted another surge of panic. Jenny swallowed hard, willing him in her mind. *Don't pull the tough-guy routine now. Do what he says.*

"I said give her the stuff."

"And hand it to me real nice," Jenny said, relief fueling her confidence. "Don't want any accidents here."

Leon took a step forward, holding a bag out to her. She took it with her free hand and slipped it into her jacket pocket. Then she pushed the gun harder into Chico's chin. "And I got another tip for you. Don't. You. Ever. Fucking. Do. That. Again."

After giving him a moment to absorb the threat, she stepped back and touched her forehead with the gun barrel as if saluting the men. "Nice doing business with you."

Walking away, she heard Leon ask, "You want I should go after her? Get our goods back?"

"Leave it," Chico said. "That took balls."

# SIXTEEN

DARK CLOUDS ROLLED across the sky, and Jenny hoped the rain would hold off until she made it to her mother's house. Nothing was worse than a drenching on a cold November day.

When Mitchell had offered to stay until closing and encouraged her to leave, she'd thought about going home and making a pot of chili. That might improve things with Scott just a tad. But the many phone calls from her mother that she hadn't returned in the past few weeks tore at her conscience. Her mother wasn't a big proponent of emotional blackmail but wasn't above using it when desperate. Her last message had reeked of desperation.

Pulling her car into the driveway that led to the sprawling ranch house of her childhood, Jenny stilled the engine and let a little bit of peace wash over her. After last night, she desperately needed peace.

This comfortable old house had always been her sanctuary from the horrors of the outside world. Of course, as a child, she'd never imagined horrors like she'd been experiencing in recent history. But the eight-year-old who had lost her first pet had no point of reference beyond the immediate pain. Neither had the twelve-year-old who had been betrayed by her best friend.

Home was where she had found comfort and support. And today, she wished for a little bit of that solace.

If her mother harbored any resentment because of Jenny's neglect, it wasn't apparent in the warm greeting. They went into the kitchen, and the older woman opened the freezer. She pulled out two Dove ice cream bars. "I was just looking for a good excuse to indulge."

"Mother. It's practically freezing outside."

"Then we'll go in by the fire."

Jenny shed her coat, draping it across the back of the wooden chair that matched the deep cherry-wood of the kitchen table. In an ordinary house, the table would be too big for a kitchen, but this was no ordinary house. It had started as a four-room bungalow almost fifty years ago, and as time and money permitted, Jenny's father had added on. The kitchen and dining area pushed out on the west side of the house, with a bath and laundry room tacked on at the end. Three bedrooms and another bath had been added on the east, leaving the original structure to serve as one great living area, open and spacious.

Technically, the house wouldn't win any awards for design, but Jenny had always suspected that design meant less to her mother than function and comfort.

Following Helen into the great room, Jenny could smell the mellow aroma of mesquite burning. As promised, a fire danced in the stone fireplace.

She took the ice cream from her mother, tore the wrapper off, and settled on the large brocade sofa that faced the fireplace. Helen sat on the end of the sofa, taking much more care in opening her ice cream, then faced her daughter. "Have you made any plans for Thanksgiving?"

Jenny almost choked on a piece of the sweet chocolate coating. "Thanksgiving?"

"It's less than two weeks away."

"Oh, my God." For a moment, Jenny was seized with an overwhelming sense of guilt that was replaced quickly with dread. Am I really expected to celebrate this holiday so soon after—

"I'm sure you probably just blanked it out," Helen said, interrupting the thought as if she'd somehow anticipated it. She took a careful bite of ice cream, then continued. "I desperately wanted to ignore every holiday that first year after your father died. Sometimes I still do."

She offered a smile that eased Jenny's discomfort. "But I think Scott and Alicia would benefit from something close to normalcy."

Normal? There could be nothing normal about Thanksgiving without Michael. Who would carve the turkey? Michael had taken great pride in assuming that traditional male—

"Though it might be better to do something different." Again her mother's voice intruded as if she was reading Jenny's mind. "Totally break from tradition?"

"What did you have in mind?"

"Maybe drive into downtown Dallas. Go to a restaurant."

"Are you serious?" Jenny licked at the white stream of ice cream that was sliding down her hand.

"Yes. I think it would be perfect. No cooking. No cleanup. No—"

"Leftovers? That's practically the best part of the dinner."

"Then we'll ask for a doggie bag."

Jenny watched her mother maneuver her ice cream with

much more decorum than she had displayed. No sticky mess down the side of her arm. *How does she do that?*

That's when it hit her. Her mother handled everything in life with more decorum than Jenny could ever hope to have. Helen hadn't blubbered and wailed when she buried her husband, or her grandson. She hadn't alienated friends and family by being an absolute pain in the ass. And she hadn't gone off to play cops and robbers. Or gotten a gun. Or—

*Whoa, girl. You're not your mother. And you don't need to be beating yourself up again.*

Taking a minute to settle her emotions, Jenny ate a couple of bites of ice cream, then faced her mother. "You thinking just family, or your usual entourage?"

"Maybe it's time someone else from church opens their home. I've done it for twenty-five years straight."

Jenny gulped. Put like that it seemed like such a lengthy time. But where had the years gone? It didn't seem that long ago that her mother had brought the first immigrant family to dinner on Thanksgiving. Those annual guests always ended up being people who didn't know English; some of them from Central America and others from third-world countries. All of them without a clue as to what the holiday commemorated. Somehow, despite the language and culture barriers, they'd managed to have great fun and cement relationships that were strong even today between her mother and some of the families.

The government could sure take a few hints from Helen Garrett when it comes to foreign policy and peace talks.

"You think we can get reservations this late in the game?" Jenny tossed her wooden stick into the fire, where it created a small eruption of embers.

"It's not like everybody and their brother will eat out that day. I don't think we have to worry."

"Okay. You make arrangements. I'll start working on the kids."

Driving home later, Jenny wondered if changing the holiday plans would be as easy as it had sounded. Maybe she should have talked to the kids before agreeing to her mother's idea. Scott would certainly have something to say about that one. But then he doesn't really need an excuse, does he?

The harsh scrape of rubber across glass drew her attention, and she flicked the lever to turn off her windshield wipers. She hadn't even noticed that the rain had quit. She also hadn't noticed that daylight was quickly turning to dusk, the headlights of oncoming cars looming out of the grayish darkness like searchlights on wheels.

*You better get a grip, girl, before you become a statistic.*

---

"You did what?"

"What was I supposed to do? He ripped me off. He stalled me on the next step. I had to push a little."

"I said 'no guns.' What part of that wasn't clear?" Steve picked up a rock and threw it into a stand of brush about ten feet from where they sat. Jenny could hear it crackle as it broke through.

She figured the better part of discretion would be to keep her mouth shut until he wasn't quite so angry. She watched the remnants of sun catchers tied to the limbs of a nearby tree dance in the cool afternoon breeze and tried to convince herself she hadn't done anything terribly wrong in ignoring the orders.

Of all the odd places they'd met, this was the weirdest. She'd never even heard of Connemara Conservancy, and she was surprised that Steve had. It was a huge meadow that had been turned into a unique art park where exhibits became one with nature. He didn't seem the type to appreciate art in any form in any place. But he'd assured her that he picked it for privacy. The drug czars might launder some of their profits through fine art, but connoisseurs they were not.

So here they sat in the middle of a stand of trees where the stained-glass pieces decorated the limbs like Christmas ornaments. Steve had told her that the display had been exquisite in the spring when it had first been put up. The summer winds and autumn rains had not been kind to it.

"Do I even want to know where you got the gun?"

"I don't think so." Jenny watched him dig another rock out of the ground and wondered if this was going to be the end of it, after all. Had she passed Chico's weird test only to be shut down by the good guys?

With hindsight, she could see that telling Steve how she'd regained Chico's respect had been a big mistake. But he'd asked, and she just wasn't a good enough liar to adlib a plausible story. For the hundredth time since this conversation started, she wished she'd anticipated the question so she could've scripted a scenario that didn't include the gun.

"Maybe if you tell me you don't have it anymore, I wouldn't have to report anything," Steve said, hefting the rock but not throwing it.

The calm tone of his comment brought a wave of relief, and Jenny wanted to smile at his obvious avoidance of the word 'gun.' What did he think? If he didn't say it, it didn't exist? She leaned back on her elbows and regarded him, stifling the urge to smile. "You know that backing down is not an option."

Still he didn't look at her. "I don't want you to back down. I want you to stop breaking the rules."

"So I should tell you I don't have the gun anymore?"

He transferred the rock to his other hand. "Yes."

"Okay. I don't have it anymore."

He turned to her, a flash of emotion darkening his eyes. "I'm serious, Jenny. This isn't a part you're playing for some fuckin' TV drama."

"I'll try to keep that in mind, Lieutenant." She stood and brushed the dead grass from her jeans.

"Wait."

Jenny sighed but stood rigid.

"Do you have any idea how hard it is to be responsible for you?"

A cloud passed over the sun, and Jenny wasn't sure if her shudder was from the sudden cool shadow or the impact of the question. How was she supposed to answer? She didn't know what it was like for him. Hell. She still wasn't always sure what it was like for her. Only that it still seemed like the right thing to do.

If she was a deeply religious person, she'd believe that God had ordained her to take up this cause. Otherwise Gonzales would have laughed her out of his office when she'd first made her request. And wasn't it within the scope of that mission to use her instincts? They'd always been true to her before.

"Please sit down." Steve tapped her on the leg.

She turned to look at him. "So you can tell me again how much trouble I am?"

"No." The hint of a smile touched his face. "So we can get this operation back on course."

Relief washed through her as she realized that meant he wasn't pulling the plug on the whole deal. She sat down, crossing her legs at the ankles and leaning on her knees.

"Okay," Steve said. "The rip-off was probably some kind of test. And even though I don't approve of your method, I'd venture a guess that you passed. So they may be ready to move to the next step."

"I'm good for that. Then I'll be that much closer to the end of it all."

"Just be careful."

"I will."

"No more gun."

Jenny held up two fingers. "Scout's honor."

"I mean it."

"I do, too."

With a sudden clarity, Jenny realized that she did mean it. Despite the positive outcome, the whole episode with Chico had scared the peewadin' out of her. And all the satisfaction in the world couldn't dispel the feeling of horror at the thought of having to carry that threat to completion.

Steve broke eye contact, digging the heel of his boot into the dirt. Looking for another rock? Jenny sensed a slight edge of tension in him and wondered what had shifted his mood. Maybe she should just go. Leave him to whatever private thoughts he was having. But she hated to head back to the hassles of town and traffic just yet. It was so peaceful out here, especially since the sun had escaped from behind the cloud, casting yellow streaks down to the horizon. The rays warmed her face, reminding her of carefree childhood days romping in a park.

"Katie used to love to come here."

"Oh?"

His comment was from so far out in left field, she had to stretch to grab it. The first thing that popped into her mind was a realization that he hadn't stumbled on this place all by himself. But who was this 'Katie?' He'd said he never had a family. But he could've had a wife without a family.

"A couple of times she helped the artists put up their displays."

"Was...is she your wife?"

"No."

The one-word answer carried a wistful note, and Jenny wondered if he wasn't going to say anymore. Then he turned and gave her a half-smile. "She was, to use the modern term, my significant other."

"Oh."

"She loved that designation. Said that's why she didn't want to get married. Then she wouldn't be significant anymore."

He stopped, seeming to take an intense interest in a hawk that was gliding in wide, lazy circles above them. Jenny put her curiosity on hold and followed the bird's movements until it suddenly dove out of sight. She didn't know if she should be happy for the hawk who had found his dinner, or sorry for whatever critter it had spotted.

When Steve started to speak again, it startled her.

"It seemed to amaze her that she could mean so much to someone that it made her significant," he said, still keeping his gaze averted.

"What happened?"

"She was an orphan. Spent most of her life being kicked around foster..." He stopped and turned to her again. "That isn't what you meant, is it?"

Jenny sat up. "Listen. This is none of my business. You don't have to—"

"It's okay. There's really not much else to say. She died three years ago."

"Oh."

Jenny felt like a verbal idiot. Was that all she could say? 'Oh?'

As the silence lengthened, she remembered what he'd said about running scared. Loss was a good enough motivation. She fully understood that.

Watching him scuff his boot in the dirt again, she wished her wits hadn't deserted her. It would be nice to be able to offer some word of comfort, of understanding. But she couldn't think of anything but those horrible platitudes people had tried to foist off on her.

Sometimes words were so totally pointless.

Steve ceased the aimless action of his foot and brushed a hand across his cheek. "Don't know what made me say all that."

Sensing that he was as disconcerted as she was, she went for the joke. "Some people say I'm easy."

"No." He turned and studied her for a long moment. "You're much too complicated to ever be considered easy."

Jenny swallowed. The intensity of his gaze held her, yet she couldn't fathom what was in the depths of those incredible eyes. Did she dare follow her instinct to lean into him? *Whoa, girl. Back off. He probably isn't even headed where your mind went.*

She stood again. "I should get home."

"I'm going to stay a little while."

Her shadow touched his face and clouded his expression. Should she offer to stay with him? Was he okay? Should she just go? It would be nice if she had a cue.

When one didn't come, she shrugged. "I'll call when I have something to report."

"Sure."

Walking back to her car, Jenny tried to figure out what had just happened. Or was it more what hadn't happened? At one point his look had appeared to be one of interest. Either that, or she'd lost all ability to gauge the opposite sex. And she was sure that the confidence he'd shared wasn't one he tossed out to every person he worked with. That had to mean something.

Then again, it had been a long time since she'd been in this awkward emotional dance between two people. She may have read it all wrong. If he harbored an interest, wouldn't he have made some move? If the electricity was real, not just something she imagined, certainly he would have felt it, too. Then again—

To keep her mind from wandering that path again, Jenny spent the hour it took to drive home trying to think of something that would ease the tension between her and Scott. If she could just buy some time, she could get through this without destroying the tenuous hold they had on their relationship.

Maybe a couple of nights at home would help. He'd seemed to appreciate it last time, especially when she made the apple pie. She could resort to bribery again if she had to.

When Jenny walked in the back door, she saw Alicia sitting at the kitchen counter, dipping Chips Ahoy in a tall glass of milk.

"Mmmmm. That looks good." Jenny dropped her purse on the counter and grabbed a glass out of the cabinet. "Can I join you?"

Alicia giggled. "That's silly."

"What's silly?"

"The way you asked."

Jenny smiled as she straddled a chair and set her glass on the table. She grabbed a cookie. "Did you make me proud at school today?"

"I guess."

"You guess? Don't you know?"

Alicia shrugged. "We didn't get any marks today."

"That's okay, Honey. I was just goofing around." Jenny finished her cookie and took another out of the bag. "Where's Scott?"

Alicia shrugged again and took a bite of a soggy cookie.

"Didn't he meet you after school and walk home with you?"

"Nope."

"Doesn't he usually?"

"Mostly. Sometimes he forgets. Or sometimes he's with Caitlin."

Jenny hoped that's all it was; simple adolescent forgetfulness and not some retaliation against her.

The jangle of the phone claimed her attention. Jenny hopped up and went to lift the receiver. She'd barely said 'hello' when Ralph's angry voice assaulted her.

"What the hell are you doing?"

"Eating cookies."

"Don't be a wiseass."

"Don't shout at me." Jenny saw Alicia look up with interest and wished she'd kept her voice lower.

"Scott called."

"Oh." Jenny turned and walked into the hallway, bracing for whatever onslaught was to come. She should have realized it was going to be bad when Ralph's opening gambit repeated Scott's accusation almost word for word.

"He told me you've been acting strange lately."

"Well, life is hardly normal now, is it?"

"Don't hand me that crap. You've been staying out half the night. Not working. Don't expect help from me when the bills pile up."

Only the knowledge that it would fuel his anger kept her from laughing out loud. "Don't worry, Ralph. We'll manage. We always have."

He either didn't pick up on the sarcasm or chose to ignore it. "How can I not worry? When will I get another call from Scott?"

"You won't."

"I'd better not."

"Or what?" Jenny fought to keep from yelling. Alicia didn't need to hear them fight.

"Let's just not let it get that far."

"Is that a threat?"

"No. I'll let the court do that. Remember. Custody can be revoked."

Long after he broke the connection the words roared through Jenny's mind like a spring flood rushing through a gully. Could that really happen? Would he dare? Not that any judge would easily give custody to Ralph. He didn't have an exemplary record as a caring father. But then he could make one hell of a case against her if he wanted to and Scott continued to complain. The system had snatched kids away from parents on less provocation than her brand of neglect.

She walked back to put the handset on the receiver and glanced at Alicia, who paused with a cookie in one hand. White drops of milk dripped off the cookie and splashed on the tabletop. "What's wrong, Mommy?"

"Nothing, Honey. That was Daddy. We just had to work something out."

"Didn't he want to talk to me?"

Jenny winced at the forlorn note in her daughter's voice. How long before she wouldn't even ask anymore? Jenny sighed. "He probably didn't realize you were home. The time is different where he lives."

Alicia dunked her cookie again and took another bite. Then she looked up again. "Next time, tell him I'm here. Then he'll talk to me."

"Sure." Jenny went to the sink so her daughter couldn't see the lie on her face. It seldom mattered if she told Ralph the kids were home. Most often he would make some excuse that he had to call them back, and most often that would never happen.

# SEVENTEEN

SQUINTING AGAINST THE LATE-AFTERNOON SUN, Chico stood at the edge of the pool and watched the Cuban flail against the water like a fish trying not to get caught. It reminded him of the time he'd tried to teach his cousin to swim. All the boy had accomplished was to stir the water in the creek so hard it had taken hours for the silt to settle. Some people were just not meant for the water.

"He's doing laps," Solly said. "Doesn't talk to anyone while he's doing laps."

Glad the Boss couldn't see how he struggled to keep a straight face, Chico waited for the wild churning of arms and legs to end. If Frank had any opinion about this sad excuse for exercise, he didn't voice it. But then Chico knew the other man hadn't climbed the corporate ladder by having opinions out loud. Maybe it would be in Chico's best interests to work harder on impassivity.

It was a moderate day for November but not warm enough for a swim, and Chico wondered why the Boss did this kind of workout when he had enough money to buy an entire gym.

The steam that billowed from the pool indicated it was a lot warmer in the water than out, but still, Chico wouldn't be swimming on a bet, sunshine or not.

The Cuban splashed to the ladder and pulled his lean body out of the water. Chico saw goose bumps erupt across the exposed skin that was streaming with moisture. Solly quickly stepped forward and handed over a large, plush towel.

"Good for the heart," the Cuban said, gesturing to the pool as he walked over to Frank and Chico. "You should try it."

Chico wasn't sure what kind of response was appropriate; certainly not some wiseass remark about getting a bigger payout so he could afford a fuckin' pool. But Frank kept his mouth shut, so Chico followed suit.

"What's so important you boys had to come all the way out here?"

"That woman, Connie. She's got what it takes," Frank said. "Came after Chico here with a goddamn gun."

"How come he's still walking?"

Chico blanched at the callousness of that comment, risking a quick glance at Frank. He touched the scar on his face in a gesture Chico had seen only once before, when Frank had been ordered to take out that mule who'd been seen talking to the cops. The twelve-year-old boy was rumored to be Frank's nephew.

Frank dropped his hand and offered a smile. "Guess she didn't want him dead. Said it was payback from us ripping her off. Did it real slick, too."

"And I need to know this because?" The Cuban draped the towel over his shoulders and held it closed like a robe as he walked toward a portable bar.

Frank followed, talking as he went. "Chico wants to use her to push even more merchandise in North Dallas. I think she's good for it."

The Boss glanced at Chico. "You trust her?"

He nodded, doing his best impression of impassive.

The other man opened a decanter of scotch and held it aloft, the question inherent in raised eyebrows. Frank shook his head, and again, Chico followed that lead. Not that he didn't want a drink. A good strong shot would calm the jitters in his stomach, but it would be suicide to betray any nervousness by accepting.

After pouring two fingers of amber liquid in a crystal glass, the Cuban took a swallow, then looked at Chico. "How much can she move?"

"She's been handling a few bags now for a while. Figures she could double that easy. Maybe about two g's worth."

"A week?"

"Yeah."

"Must be some pretty big parties."

"Not that many people. But they're all high rollers. And they party all weekend."

The Cuban finished his drink and poured another, then turned his gaze back to Chico. "You think you're ready to take the next step up my corporate ladder?"

Chico fought to keep from shifting his weight under the intense scrutiny. "Yeah, Boss."

"Yes, Sir."

The reprimand was issued softly, but it rang so loud in Chico's mind he had to swallow a surge of fear that rose like bile.

"Yes, Sir," he repeated when he found his voice.

The Cuban ambled over to an ornate wrought-iron patio table and sat in the shade provided by the umbrella. He didn't indicate that the other men should sit, and Chico shot another quick glance at Frank for a cue. The other man stood expressionless at the edge of the shade. Chico stayed with him.

"So," the Cuban said, directing his focus on Frank. "What little task should we have our boy do?"

Chico read the real message behind the ambiguous words, and this time he couldn't stop the slight shift of weight as the significance hit him. The Cuban was dangling the carrot, but Chico would have to pay one hell of an entry fee to join the race. Did he really want to?

Getting in this deep had never been part of his long-range career plan. He just wanted a couple of good years running enough pushers to make a nice nest egg. Then he'd be on the first plane heading for a destination at least a thousand miles from here.

"We got that little problem in Denton with Johnny," Frank said.

"Maybe Chico here can teach him a lesson."

Again the message clamored behind the harmless-sounding words, and Chico remembered the ill-fated chess game a few weeks ago. There was a new man running the Denton franchise, and nobody knew for sure where Lazano had ended up. Some thought he'd been shipped back to Cuba. Others speculated that he'd never survived the ocean crossing.

And now there was a problem with the new guy?

Chico didn't trust himself with words. He gave a slight nod.

"Take care of it." The Cuban waved a limp hand in Frank's direction.

"Yes, Sir."

The Cuban smiled at Chico. "See how nice and polite he is?"

Chico did his best to match the Boss's smile as a cold stone of dread settled in his stomach.

---

Jenny sat at her desk with the phone pressed to her ear. "I think that whole thing was a test," she said. "And I passed when I—"

"Don't even say it. As far as I'm concerned, that never happened."

Suppressing a laugh as she imagined Steve putting his hands over his ears, Jenny continued. "They're letting me move more stuff. I think I should go for the big score soon."

"Don't rush it," Steve said.

Noticing that Mitchell had walked into the back room, Jenny hunched over her desk and lowered her voice. "I can see the end of this looming. Let's just finish it up."

"Okay. I'll talk to the rest of the team. Don't do anything until you hear from me."

"Sure." Jenny hung up and turned to see Mitchell still standing there. His expression indicated he had more on his mind than just getting supplies.

"I'm worried about you, Jen."

"What's to worry about?" She tried to brush past him, but he stepped in front of her.

"This has gone way beyond grief."

Jenny moved back to the work table and picked up a bunch of zinnias and plucked broken stems, hoping if she just ignored him, he'd give it up. But she should have known better. Mitchell, for all his effeminate ways, was not one to back down.

"It's not like you have to confide in me about everything. But don't shut me out." He stood next to her and leaned one hip on the edge of the table. "Something weird has been going on with you. And that scene with Scott a couple of weeks ago was something else. You did an admirable job of blustering through, but you never did answer his questions."

Jenny concentrated on wrapping the orange and russet flowers in tissue.

"You've had an uncanny way of avoiding questions of late,

Jen." Mitchell's voice had lost the edge of challenge and softened with a touch of concern.

Feeling boxed in by his proximity and his worry, she sidled to her right. She needed to think. What could she possibly say that would satisfy him? An outright lie was not an option. She'd never been able to pull that off with even a casual acquaintance, let alone someone she'd worked with for years.

Quickly discounting the few fabricated scenarios that flashed through her mind, Jenny finally decided on a piece of the truth.

"You have to promise that what is said here stays here."

"Sounds pretty serious."

"It is." She took a step toward him. "And you can't tell anyone. Not even Jeffrey."

"We don't have secrets."

"You have to this time, Mitchell. Or I say nothing more."

He picked up a roll of green tape from the table and spun it slowly on his fingers as he seemed to debate his ability to comply. Finally, he gave a curt nod.

"I'm working for the police."

Shock brought Mitchell's head up. "You're shittin' me."

"What? Is it so inconceivable that I could?"

"No." He shrugged. "It's just not what I expected."

"It was easier to think I was involved with drug dealers?"

"You know better than that." The look he shot her raised a twinge of guilt for being so sarcastic. "So, what is it that you're doing for the cops?"

"That's the part I can't tell you." Jenny pushed scraps of stems, ribbon, and discarded blooms into a pile on the table. "But hopefully it will be over soon. Then everyone will know all the sordid details."

"You aren't doing anything dangerous?"

"Of course not." She concentrated on sweeping the pile of

debris into a trash can. If she didn't look at Mitchell, maybe she could get that lie past him.

"Were Scott's friends right when they said you were hanging with drug dealers?"

Jenny set the trash can down and faced Mitchell. "Please don't keep asking questions. I can't give you any more answers."

Watching an expression of frustration play across his face, Jenny knew the amount of restraint it took for him to stifle his curiosity. He was an intellectual sponge, always needing to soak up every detail about things. Ambiguity drove him nuts.

She laid a hand on his arm. "Just trust me on this, okay? Soon it will end and I can tell you everything."

Mitchell nodded and then turned to leave. Watching his stiff back as he walked through the doorway, Jenny sighed. Would she live to regret telling him? Or worse, would she not live to regret it?

But, God, how she hated the lying.

A long-forgotten quote floated through her mind. *Oh, what a tangled web we weave, when first we practice to deceive.* She'd never lied so much in her life. Nor made so many promises she wasn't sure she could keep; first Scott, then Carol, now Mitchell. There was no way she could guarantee that this would soon be over. And how long before Carol pressed her for more answers, and she had to give her another little piece of the truth?

How many pieces could she give out without being in danger?

---

Thanksgiving Day dawned bright and clear, and Jenny stood on the back porch with her coffee, watching the birds that had decided to winter here flutter around the bare branches of the elm tree. They filled the morning with their bird chatter, as if wanting to proclaim to the whole world what a glorious day this was shaping up to be.

Glad she had her bulky terrycloth robe to keep the chill wind at bay, she warmed her hands with the mug. The weather had cooperated last year, too. After everyone had stuffed themselves on turkey, mashed potatoes, yams, and six different flavors of pie, the boys had piled out of the house to play football in her mother's huge front yard.

The memory was so vivid Jenny could hear the shouts and laughter and taste the cinnamon sweetness of the pumpkin pie her mother had brought out to the porch for the cheering section.

Remembering pierced the armor she'd so carefully wrapped around her heart, and the pain of loss came rushing in like a rampaging river through a broken levee. For almost three months now she'd made a conscious decision every morning not to think of Michael. She'd ignored the urge to go into his room, which was still the way he'd left it that awful night. And she'd fought every intrusion of unwanted memory.

Not that she was trying to pretend he never existed.

She was still trying to pretend that he wasn't really dead.

A tear trickled down her cheek, and she raised a hand to wipe it away. *You cannot cry. Crying weakens. You need to be strong.*

The scrape of the door opening startled her, and she turned to see Scott, hair tangled and eyes still puffy with sleep. She offered him a faltering smile. "You're up early."

"Damn birds woke me up." He waved an arm toward the tree.

"They are happy, aren't they?"

"Glad somebody is."

Searching his face, Jenny wondered if the puffiness around

his eyes was from sleep or something else. She longed for the closeness they'd once had so she could ask him. Or did she dare anyway?

"You okay?"

He shrugged.

Jenny sighed and took a sip of coffee, which was now almost as cool as the breeze. Should she push Scott to talk some more or let it go? They'd been treading some fine line of civility for the past week, and she'd barely gotten him to agree to the plans her mother had made for dinner today. Perhaps it would be wiser not to do anything that would upset the delicate balance.

"I miss Michael."

The words were soft, barely a whisper, but the anguish in her son's voice screamed at her.

"Oh, Scott." Jenny put her coffee cup on the empty plant stand and opened her arms.

It was like an instant replay of that first morning when the grief had seemed to ebb and flow between them like currents of electricity. Scott cried in soft shudders of sobs, and Jenny ran her hand across his back in a gesture she hoped was soothing.

This very act of holding her son for the first time in weeks managed to take the edge off the lingering pain of her grief. Holding him felt so good, so right, she wished she could stay in the moment forever. No more lies. No more deceit. And no more walks down the dark side.

Scott pulled away first, using the tail of his rumpled t-shirt to wipe at his face.

"Scott, I—"

"It's okay, Mom." He glanced away, then sighed. "I'll go see if Alicia wants to watch the parades."

Jenny wondered if he was truly okay. Would anything ever be okay in their lives again? But she filed the questions away for another time. They just had to get through today whatever way they could. And if that meant pretending, well, they'd all gotten quite good at pretending.

She smiled at her son. "That would be nice. She'd like that."

He hesitated just a moment, almost as if he was debating saying something, then shrugged and turned to open the door.

After he left, Jenny turned her face to the warm touch of the sun. Maybe it could reach clear down to that horrible, cold, empty hole that had been gouged out of her heart.

# EIGHTEEN

AS THE WAITER cleared the dishes from the main course, Scott looked at his grandmother and asked, "Did Mom tell you she's hanging around with drug dealers?"

Jenny choked on her water, and her mother went so pale Jenny was afraid the older woman would have a heart attack. "Scott, please. Not here."

The waiter gave her a strange look before hurrying away, and Alicia tugged on the sleeve of Jenny's dress. "What does he mean, Mommy?"

"Nothing, Honey. It's nothing."

"Is that true?" Helen asked.

Jenny shot her son a look that she hoped would hold him in check. What had precipitated such an abrupt change since this morning? And what on earth was she going to say to her mother? Whatever it was, she'd better do it fast. Stalling was always the first indication of the lie coming.

"No, I am not 'hanging out' with druggies." Jenny tried to keep her tone light and dismissive. "Scott got this crazy idea because some friend of his saw me by the Dairy Queen one night. Drug dealers apparently show up around there. But how was I to know? I just wanted a hot-fudge sundae."

Scott stirred in his chair, and Jenny froze him with another look.

"Why on earth did they think you were with those hoodlums?"

"I don't know, Mother."

There was a moment of awkward silence, and Jenny couldn't hold eye contact with her mother. She glanced at her plate and tried to resume eating. Maybe it would all pass. God, please let it all pass.

"Don't fight anymore."

Jenny turned to Alicia, whose eyes were wide with confusion and fear. "I hate it when you and Scott are yelling."

"I know, Sweetie." Jenny touched her daughter's shoulder. "But it doesn't mean anything. Lots of people yell, but they still love each other."

Alicia didn't look convinced, so Jenny offered a weak smile. "Trust me. Everything's fine."

Scott stood so abruptly Jenny didn't have time to try to stop him. "Everything is not fine," he said, the tone hard and cutting. "You sit here acting like we're a normal happy family. Well, we're not. And I'm sick of pretending."

He threw his napkin on his plate, shoved his chair out of the way, and stormed out.

For a moment Jenny sat frozen. She didn't know what to say or what to do. People around them turned back to their food, offering a courtesy of feigned nonchalance. Alicia still looked like a rabbit caught in headlights. And her son was... God, she didn't know where he was going.

"I need to—"

"I know," Helen said. "Go. I'll take Alicia home with me."

Jenny turned to her daughter. "I know this is scary. But please believe me. It will be okay."

"Are you going to find Scott?"

"Yes."

"And make things okay with him?"

"Yes." Jenny hugged Alicia, wishing that she felt as confident as she talked. "You go with Grandma and I'll pick you up later."

Rising, Jenny glanced at her mother and murmured, "Thank you."

"When you finish, we need to talk."

Jenny nodded and hurried out. Damn. The last time her mother had used that tone of voice, Jenny had been sixteen and had snuck out of the house with Carol to meet some boys. She'd paid dearly for that indiscretion. No telling what would happen now.

Outside, Jenny saw no sign of her son. She checked the parking lot, but he wasn't by her car or her mother's. *Think. Where would he go?* He had some money. But how much? Enough for a cab?

Walking toward Preston Road, Jenny tried to figure out where Scott would even find a cab. Or what he would do if he couldn't. The thought that he might try to hitchhike sent a cold tremor through her, and she tried not to think of all those stories she'd heard about teens being abducted.

Traffic was light along the normally busy road, but that was no surprise. Most folks were home celebrating the day with family. But she did notice a small group of kids at the park on the next corner. Then she spotted the bus stop across the street. There, on the bench, was Scott, distinct in his red windbreaker.

Jenny let out a sigh of relief and crossed over. He didn't even look up when she approached, but she knew he was aware of her presence. "The bus doesn't go to Little Oak."

"It goes to Frisco. I can walk from there."

"It's ten miles."

"So?"

Still so rigid and unyielding, as if his body had been carved out of the same stone as the bench. And that surly tone. He was goading her, but she suppressed the knee-jerk reaction and sat down next to him. "Please let me take you home."

"I don't want to go anywhere with you."

Her first impulse was to slap him. Her second was to ask why he was treating her like the bad guy. But she knew why. She was acting like a bad guy, and there wasn't a damn thing she could do about it.

He shot her a quick look, then glanced away. "I'm going to call Dad. He said I could come live with him if I wanted to."

For a moment Jenny sat mute, crushed by Scott's words. Was he serious? He'd just up and leave? She felt a wrench deep inside, almost as if he was already gone. But that couldn't happen. She couldn't lose Scott, too.

And on a very practical level, she couldn't risk more trouble with Ralph. "When did he say that?" she asked.

"The last time I told him how weird you've been acting."

Jenny took a deep breath. "And how many times exactly have you called him?"

Scott shrugged, and she touched him on the knee. "Have you thought this through? Or are you just reacting?"

He didn't respond, so she continued. "Could you just wait? A week, maybe two?"

"Is that going to make a difference?"

"I don't know. Maybe."

Scott laughed, a harsh sound that was anything but pleasant. "You've been fucking up our lives for months, and it's all going to be okay next week?"

Resisting another urge to slap him, Jenny fought for control. "Don't talk to me that way."

"Or what? You going to send me to my room?" His eyes were cold and hard. "There isn't anything you could do to me that matters anymore."

The words stung, and the pain threatened to take her breath away. She gasped, then said, "Don't say things in anger that you'll regret."

Scott turned away, and into the dreadful silence came laughter from the kids across the street. Jenny watched them spin on the merry-go-round for a moment until a sudden memory of Michael and Scott in a similar park years ago slammed into her. Even as toddlers they'd had no fear of the merry-go-round. They'd scrambled up on the scuffed wooden platform and told her to push, faster and faster until she'd stumbled over clods of dirt. The laughter of all three of them had rung through the park when she'd ended up on her ass in the dirt.

Jenny wiped a trickle of moisture from her cheek, then laid her hand on Scott's knee again. "Do you really want to go live with your father?"

He shrugged.

"I mean, I won't stop you if you're sure. But it's been so long..."

She purposely let the sentence fade, and he finally spoke. "I just hate the way things are at home."

Jenny touched his face, forcing him to look at her. "I don't like it, either. But you're going to have to trust me on this. It's important."

"But you don't trust me enough to tell me what's going on. And I know something is."

"Not telling you wasn't my decision to make. Believe me."

A shadow of doubt clouded his eyes for a moment, then he sighed. "Two weeks?"

"I hope."

"Not a day longer."

"I hope not."

---

Chico leaned against the passenger door of Frank's Lexus, fingering the cool steel of the .38 Police Special in his jacket pocket. In a little while he was supposed to take that gun out and shoot a man. Could he do it?

Despite all the macho talk and swagger he put on with the best of them, at heart Chico squirmed if he thought too hard about where his steak originated. But somehow, he had the feeling that the answer to his mental question better come up 'yes.' Frank must've told him a hundred times how the Boss was counting on him. How important it was to the Boss to show this Johnny, and anyone else who was tempted to fuck with him, what the consequences were. Translation: if Chico fucked this up, he could kiss his ass goodbye.

The night grew darker as they left the busiest section of Denton behind and entered that section of Interstate 35 that didn't host a gas station and fast-food joint every hundred feet. The access road bordered a stand of trees that cast vague gray shadows against the black sky.

Some of those trees could have been there since the first settlers pushed down from the northern plains and claimed this little section of North Texas. And it was into those trees that Frank turned after exiting the freeway.

"Johnny thinks we're bringing him some stuff. I'll get a bag out of the trunk. We'll both take it to him, and that's when you pop him."

Chico remained quiet as Frank nosed the car down a narrow, rutted dirt road. It ended near a clearing where an old shed stood on three listing posts, scraps of wood and tin clinging precariously to rotting timbers. Their headlights shimmered on a sleek, dark Miata that stood in sharp contrast to the aging building.

Frank let his car roll to a stop, then killed the engine. A door opened on the Miata and Johnny stepped into the glow of the headlights. Chico fumbled with the handle of the door and tried not to think about what he had to do. Frank was already out and heading toward the trunk.

Johnny stayed by his car, and Frank called out to him. "The Boss says you should beef up your sales. We got some extra for you."

"New breed of students this year," Johnny said. "Most of them are just saying 'no.'"

Chico tried to let the feeble joke relax him as he stepped out and waited for Frank to come around from the rear of the car, but it didn't work. A trickle of cold sweat crawled down his spine, and his hand trembled on the butt of the gun in his jacket pocket.

"Come on," Frank said, stepping up beside him. "Time to rock and roll."

Following a few steps behind, Chico swallowed hard. As Frank handed the bag to Johnny, he glanced back. The moment seemed to freeze in time as Chico considered the hard set of Frank's face. The directive was unmistakably clear. Chico willed his heart to stop hammering in his chest. It pounded so loud in his head he was sure the other men could hear it. He needed to be calm. He needed to be clear. He needed to do the job he was brought here to do. Yet, he didn't move as Johnny took a step away from Frank and reached for his car door.

"Chico."

The word was less a question than a command, and knowing the consequences if he didn't, Chico tried to obey. But his brain seemed to have shut down. It still wouldn't give the command to his arm to move.

"I can't."

"For fuck's sake!." Frank drew a Glock out of his pocket and fired one shot. Johnny clutched his chest where the bullet had torn through his jacket and then his body. His blood oozed in a dark tide through his fingers. Then he slid down the side of his car, his gurgle of death the only sound to be heard.

For a moment Chico considered whether he could run. And where he could hide if he did. Then Frank took one step toward him, gun pointing slightly down. *Maybe he'll let me—*

The thought was cut short as Frank raised the barrel of the gun. "I'm real sorry about this," he said. "We never had no trouble. But it's my neck if I don't. You understand that, don't you?"

Chico almost wanted to laugh at the absurdity of that, but he knew the moment was beyond that. He nodded, then closed his eyes and said the prayers his mother always badgered him about. Did he even dare hope that God would rest his soul?

# NINETEEN

"AND YOUR MOM? She didn't, like, ground you for the rest of your life?"

Scott smiled at the incredulous expression on Caitlin's face. "I think she was too upset about dinner being ruined to think of it."

Caitlin shook her head. "I can't believe you did that."

"Sometimes I can't believe it, either. It's just like all these weeks of frustration just...erupted."

Scott looked over the railing separating the food court from the skating rink below, watching a girl cutting intricate figure-eights in the ice. She looked so carefree and absorbed in the moment. Unlike his state of mind, which seemed splintered in a million directions.

"What do you think your mom is doing?"

"Haven't a clue." He continued watching the skater for a moment, then looked at Caitlin. "But maybe I should find out."

"What do you mean?"

"I could follow her."

"You mean like some kind of private investigator?"

"You read too many mystery books."

She reached over and punched him on the arm. "Be serious."

"I am. Can you think of a better way to find out what's going on?"

Caitlin took a sip of her smoothie, then sighed. "What about Alicia? You can't drag her out late at night."

"You're right." Scott thought for a moment. "Think maybe you could watch her?"

"I don't know." She twisted the wrapper from her straw. "I have that stupid curfew on weeknights."

"That could pose a problem."

Speaking of which... Scott glanced at the crowd milling around the tables to make sure Caitlin's parents weren't nearby. They'd all come to the mall for Christmas shopping and split up a couple of hours ago; they could be back any time. It wouldn't do for them to catch the drift of this conversation, especially if he got the nerve to ask Caitlin what he'd like to.

But did he have a right to ask her to lie for him?

She touched his arm. "What are you thinking?"

"Just trying to figure a way."

If she sensed the evasiveness of his response, she didn't show it. Her wide, blue eyes were full of concern, not questions.

He took a deep breath. "Would you consider...uh...telling them you were sleeping over with Terry?"

"What?"

"I know. I shouldn't have asked."

"It's not like I've never lied to my folks." She offered him a sheepish grin. "But this is like, way complicated."

"Forget it. It was a stupid idea." Scott leaned back in his chair.

"Not so stupid." Caitlin finished her drink, then set the cup back on the table. "We'd have to figure out some logistics. Like is it a secret from Alicia? And where would I really spend the night?"

He glanced at her quickly. "You mean you'd really consider it?"

She intertwined her fingers with his. "It's not like I'm sneaking out to do something awful."

"Then you'd be okay if we can really pull it off?"

"There is one more big hurdle. We have to—"

"Figure out the morning thing."

"Yeah." She smiled. "I can hardly come traipsing out of your room."

Bright spots of pink touched her cheeks, and Scott felt the warmth of a flush cross his face as he realized that they were both thinking the same thing. He covered his embarrassment with a swallow of his cola, then he looked at her, offering a small smile. "You're right."

Her nod seemed to acknowledge the meaning behind his words, and he felt the slight tension ease as her blush faded. It's not like they hadn't explored their sexuality a bit in the few months they'd been together, but Caitlin had let him know right from the start just how far she was willing to go. And he was always conscious of the heartache Michael had shared with him after a girl had dumped him last year. Michael had said the hurt was deeper because it was the first girl he'd had sex with.

Scott could still hear the rest of his brother's words as if he were sitting here right now. "Don't let the other kids fool you. There's more to sex than just a good time."

At the time, Scott had told him he sounded like Mom, and Michael had said, "Maybe Mom's right about this one."

Even now, Scott had to stifle the urge to laugh. Up to that point there hadn't been much they'd ever thought their mother was right about, especially Michael. He'd argue with her about anything, and sometimes Scott had thought his brother would knock himself out to prove the sky wasn't really blue if she commented on what a pretty shade it was.

A sudden wave of sadness overrode his amusement, and he felt the sting of tears in his eyes. *Damn. When is that going to stop happening?*

He noticed a look of concern cross Caitlin's face, and he wondered, not for the first time, if she had some ability to read him. "It'll be okay," she said. "Give me a couple of days to figure something out."

Scott started to respond, and Caitlin held up a hand. "Shhh. Here's Mom."

He looked over to see Mrs. Bradshaw approaching, shopping bags in each hand. Mr. Bradshaw was behind her, parcels balanced precariously in his arms.

He set his burden down, then pulled two chairs to the corner of the table. Caitlin's mother sank into one of the chairs with a deep sigh. "I'm exhausted. How about you two? Finish your shopping?"

With a jab of guilt, Scott realized that they'd spent most of their time sitting here after picking up a couple of things at the Disney store for Caitlin's little brother. He glanced at Caitlin and saw her give her mother a smile.

"We sort of lost track of time," Caitlin said. "Guess you'll just have to bring me back."

Mrs. Bradshaw turned to her husband. "Kids. Can't count on them for anything."

Scott squirmed in the silence that followed that remark. It had sounded like teasing, delivered in that same exaggerated sarcastic tone his mother used to use; back when their life was normal. But at his house, laughter had always followed the comment, making sure there was never any doubt about intention.

Caitlin's smile withered, and her father averted his eyes, but Scott couldn't read the expression on her mother's face. He shook his head. Here all this time he'd thought Caitlin was exaggerating about her mother cutting her down. He'd even considered it a bit silly when she'd show up at school fighting off tears. But there was no mistake here today, and it wasn't fair. Whether Mrs. Bradshaw meant it or not, it was rotten to dig at someone that way.

With a sudden clarity, he realized that his mother had never done that. Not once. Sure, she pissed him off plenty, especially lately. But she'd never cut him off at the knees.

Thinking about her that way softened a bit of the anger he'd been clinging to for the past few weeks. Maybe he should quit hassling her about all this shit. Give her a break.

Caitlin touched his arm, drawing his attention. "We lost you there for a minute."

"Sorry."

"You ready to go?" Mrs. Bradshaw asked. "We've got to pick Joey up from his friend's house."

"Sure."

Amid the shuffle of gathering packages and tossing empty drink cups, Caitlin sidled up to him and slipped her arm around his waist. The gesture was warm and comforting.

---

"It's ruined." Alicia slapped the knife down, splattering white frosting across the counter.

"No. It's not, Honey." Jenny pushed the top half of the cake back up. "Get some toothpicks."

Alicia grabbed the little glass vase full of toothpicks and brought it over. "Can you fix it?"

"Sure." Jenny used several slivers of wood to secure the broken section of cake to the bottom layer, then carefully filled in the crack with frosting. "There. Good as new."

"Hardly." Alicia tried to press a glob of frosting back onto the side of the cake. It fell off again, taking a hunk of cake with it and scattering chocolate crumbs off the plate. "It's awful."

Alicia's chin quivered, and Jenny thought her heart would break. "You did splendid for your first time. It was ages before I could do sides at all."

"But I wanted it to be perfect for Michael."

A wave of tears poured out of Alicia's eyes, and Jenny pulled her into an embrace. "It doesn't have to be perfect. It's enough that you did it."

"For real?"

The words were barely intelligible amidst the hiccups of sobs, but the inherent hope didn't escape Jenny. "Yeah. For real." She blinked back the threat of tears. "Michael's probably up there saying, 'Way to go, Alicia.'"

The girl pulled back and looked at her mother. "You think?"

Jenny nodded and touched the tear that crawled down her daughter's cheek. "Now go get Scott so we can party."

After Alicia bounded out, Jenny set plates and silverware on the table. She was getting the glasses for soda when she saw Scott step into the doorway, jacket on and hands thrust deep in the pockets. "I'm supposed to meet Caitlin," he said. "We're going shopping again."

Forcing herself not to react to the hostile undercurrent in his voice, Jenny kept her response as calm as possible. "Stay just for a little while. It's Michael's birthday."

"What?" Scott's tone was harsh and he hunched his shoulders. "You thought I forgot?"

"No. None of us will ever forget."

He glanced away, and Jenny felt a stab of pain. None of them had had a proper time to grieve – if there was such a thing. She'd steeled her heart just to get through, and perhaps that was the worst thing she could've done for all of them. They should be coming together in shared mourning. Instead, she was off chasing pond scum, and God knows where the kids were channeling their feelings.

"Scott."

"What?"

Rancor underscored the word, and Jenny took a quick breath to hold back her anger. "Alicia's been looking forward to this all week. Could we just do it for her?"

"Whatever." He sat down at the table.

"You could take your coat off."

"Whatever." He rose and shrugged out of his jacket, then hung it on a peg by the back door, every movement dripping with repressed anger.

Jenny bit her lip so hard she could taste the salt of blood. *Let it be. He's entitled.*

"Look what I found." Alicia ran into the kitchen, her hands full of party hats and noisemakers.

"Great. Now we'll have a real party." Jenny forced a smile and glanced at Scott, willing him to put on a happy face for his sister.

"I'll call Caitlin and tell her I'll be late."

---

Later, in the darkness of her room, Jenny sat on the edge of her bed and rolled her shoulders to ease the tight knot that had plagued her all evening. Emotionally, it might have been easier to pretend that this was just another ordinary day. But just like her association with 'normal,' she was having a hard time remembering what 'ordinary' felt like.

She supposed it was good that they had spent time telling stories and remembering this evening, but she wished that doing something that was supposed to be good for them didn't have to leave her so emotionally battered. Her mother's therapist was right about this grief business being hard work.

And oddly enough, she discovered that she was out of tears for the night. So maybe that was the good part. And if they could get over this hurdle, maybe they could survive the next one, and the one after that.

Jenny almost laughed at the 'pie-in-the-sky' tone that thought had. Ralph had always told her she was too idealistic for her own good. Maybe he'd been right.

She shook off that thought and went into her bathroom, flicking the light on. Maybe she wouldn't feel so battered if she took a long hot soak.

Immersed in the steaming water a few minutes later, Jenny leaned her head against the back of the tub and closed her eyes. The faint aroma of lilac drifted on the steam, and Jenny could almost believe in spring. *Yes. This is definitely better.*

When her head slipped off the edge of the tub, Jenny came up in a spray of water. She hadn't even realized she'd gone to sleep. How long had it been? The water was warm, so it couldn't have been too long.

Then she had a flash of memory. Steve had been kissing her and... Wait a minute. It wasn't a true memory. It was a fragment of a dream. As other fragments presented themselves, she felt a flush of what she was sure wasn't total embarrassment. *Oh, God. I haven't had these kinds of erotic thoughts in...* She couldn't even remember the last time.

She quickly stepped out of the tub and wrapped herself in the bulk of her robe. She had to get a grip on this whole personal thing between her and Steve. In their last phone conversation, he had been all 'business as usual.' So she should keep it that way, too.

*Sounds good in theory, girl. But no way can it go backwards.*

"Oh, shut up."

# TWENTY

YESTERDAY, Jenny had spent an evening at home with the kids. After the tension of Michael's birthday the day before, she thought they all needed it, and, for the first time in forever, they had actually enjoyed a few hours together. It had been so pleasant; Jenny was tempted to just say 'screw it' and stay home forever. But she'd gathered her resolve, girded her loins — or ungirded them was more like it — and headed out to meet her friendly neighborhood drug dealer.

When she'd called Chico's cell phone, she'd been surprised when Leon answered, but since she didn't know what was considered polite in the drug business, she figured she wouldn't ask questions. But her current goose bumps were caused by more than the chill night air.

Leon stood just outside a circle of pale illumination cast by the security light at the edge of the deserted football stadium. He wore his usual baggy jeans and flannel parka, but something was different about his stance. Then Jenny realized what it was. He was still. No hip-hop jive tonight. His constant herky-jerky movements always made her think of a marionette, which somehow made him seem like less of a threat, but this absolute stillness was unnerving.

As she tried to chase away the prickle of fear, she realized her analogy wasn't so far off. Leon was somebody's puppet, except the puppet-master seemed to be missing. And who was that strange, silent man whose mere presence made her more afraid than she'd ever been in her life? It was the same man who'd been there when Chico had ripped her off.

*Where the hell is Chico? Or do I even want to know?*

Since she couldn't pretend not to notice his absence, Jenny tried to make her inquiry sound casual. "Where's my man?"

Leon opened his mouth, then glanced at the other man and quickly shut it.

"He's moved on."

He speaks. The melody of a long-forgotten hymn flashed through Jenny's mind, and she almost laughed at the incongruity of it. This man's voice was anything but sweet.

"Come on. Let's go for a ride."

*Oh, shit!*

Turning abruptly, the man headed toward a dark Lexus parked in the shadow of a tree. Leon shuffled after him, and Jenny had about two seconds to make a decision.

*Oh, shit!*

Leon opened the front passenger door and motioned for her to get it. Then he hopped in the back as the man started the engine. He glanced over at Jenny. "Fasten your belt."

*Oh, shit! He's gonna fucking kill me.*

*No, he's not,* a more reasonable internal voice said. *If he was going to kill you, why would he care about a fucking seat belt?*

Marginally reassured by that way of thinking, Jenny snapped the hook as the car eased out to the side street.

The man maintained his silence as he wove through the nearly deserted downtown streets, finally taking one that headed north. Then he turned east on Highway 360. Other than the hum of tires on asphalt, the only sound Jenny heard was soft rustles of fabric whenever Leon moved in the back seat. Now he seemed to be having trouble staying still, and she wondered if he shared her nervousness.

The man driving neither spoke nor looked at her, and Jenny wasn't sure if she should be relieved or not. His silence was anything but companionable, and she bit her lip to keep from filling the silence. That would never do.

The miles and the minutes clicked by, and after about forty of them, the man turned south on Interstate 75. It was a relief to be headed into a place with more traffic, and Jenny had a wild thought that maybe they were just going to drive in a huge circle. But to what purpose? Just so he could play this silent intimidation game?

*Well, it's working damn well.* She could swear if her heart beat any faster it would go into arrest. And her jersey top was drenched from her armpits down. She should never have gotten into this car.

"I've got a delivery."

Startled, Jenny glanced over at the man. He still didn't look at her, just kept his hands on the wheel and his eyes straight ahead. Weird. If she could ignore the ugly scar, he could be her old driver's ed teacher.

Before she could even speculate as to where that bizarre thought had come from, the man exited the freeway and turned into the entrance of an exclusive gated community. He pulled up to the security area and punched a code into the box. A few seconds later, the massive iron gate opened, and the car glided through.

After winding down a few tree-lined streets that were flanked by large homes with flawless landscaping showcased by solar lamps, the man pulled to stop in front of a two-story faux

Tudor. Pale lights illuminated a precise row of holly bushes along one side of the front, and a large ponderosa pine stood like a sentinel a few feet from the front entry.

The man dimmed the car lights, then glanced over his shoulder at Leon. "Take care of it."

Leon opened his door and slipped out. Jenny watched as he walked to the front door, rang the bell, then moved into the shadow of the tree. Seconds later, the door opened and a man quickly stepped out. For a moment he was clearly illuminated by the porch light, and Jenny drew in a breath.

George? Carol's George? Jenny didn't want to believe it, but there was no mistaking the identity of the man who stepped into the darkness to meet Leon. Shadowed by the tree, his face was no longer distinguishable, but the actions were unmistakable. She'd gone through the routine too many times recently not to recognize the exchange of money and drugs.

*Oh, shit! George is buying drugs?*

Jenny tried to still the whirr of thoughts spinning through her mind. What was she supposed to do now? Should she tell Carol? Would she even live long enough to decide? But wait. Maybe she was mistaken.

Even as that thought formed, Jenny knew that wasn't likely. When the man turned and passed through the light again, Jenny recognized the green silk shirt she'd helped Carol pick out for George's birthday last summer. The sales clerk had assured them it was one of a kind, and Carol hadn't seemed to mind shelling out the big bucks for it.

Still shocked by the recognition, Jenny was hardly aware of Leon sliding into the back seat and the car pulling away from the curb. But she was thankful for the quiet as they passed through the gate and turned right on the access road of the interstate. Not that the driver's silence helped her figure out what she was going to do. It was just that there was so much noise in her head, she was afraid any outside sound would cause some artery to blow.

Expecting him to backtrack the way they'd come; Jenny was surprised when he turned right again at Highway 121. Another delivery? Or just the long way back? And was there some purpose to this little ride-along?

"I'm Frank," the man said, his voice startling her. "You'll deal with me from now on."

He didn't look at her, so she wasn't sure if he even expected a response. A sudden wave of relief rushed over her. Obviously, he wasn't taking her off to some dark corner to kill her. She risked a quick glance at Leon, who gave her a brief flash of white teeth, then he turned away.

Twenty minutes later, they stopped almost in the exact spot where they'd started out. Frank opened his door and waved at her in a dismissive gesture. "Take off now."

He got out and closed his door before Jenny could respond. She fumbled with the release of the seatbelt, pushed her door open, and stumbled out. Rounding the front of the car, she felt the heat from the engine. Frank stood a few feet away, and she called out to him. "What about the arrangement I had with Chico?"

"We'll have to see."

Stepping closer, Jenny could see the impassiveness in his pale eyes, and she had this terrible dread that it was all slipping away. She couldn't imagine why Chico was no longer there, and maybe she was better off not even speculating. But she did know she'd invested way too much to lose it all now.

She took another step closer to Frank and spoke softly. "I've got a hundred grand for a buy. Either I do business with you, or somewhere else. Doesn't matter to me."

His expression didn't change, and Jenny resisted the temptation to swallow, willing the fear to stay down without that effort.

"I'll let you know."

She acknowledged with a brief nod. "Don't take too long. My people are anxious."

Walking away, Jenny could swear there were two warm spots on her back where his eyes followed her. She kept her back straight and willed her knees not to give out. She couldn't believe what she'd done. Pushing the sale like a freakin' used-car salesman. "Buy now. I might be gone tomorrow."

*This is nuts!*

When she was finally in the sanctuary of her own car, Jenny couldn't stop the tremors that shook her whole body like the aftershocks of an earthquake. She couldn't decide if she'd blown it back there, or if perhaps she'd earned another level of respect. Either way, she hoped she'd know soon. This whole thing was getting way too complicated. And now she had the added problem of what to do about George.

# TWENTY-ONE

JENNY WAS CLEANING up after supper with Alicia's help when the sound of the doorbell reverberated through the house.

"I'll get it." Alicia dropped the dishtowel on the counter and hopped off the stool.

"No. Let me," Jenny said. "We've already talked about you not answering the door after dark."

"Scott let me once."

Jenny wiped her wet hands on the towel Alicia had put down. *Wonder what else Scott allowed when I wasn't here?* "He shouldn't have done that," she said as she started out of the kitchen. "I'll talk to him."

Jenny pulled the front door open and tried to mask her surprise. "Mom?"

"I came to make sure everything's okay."

"Why wouldn't it be?"

"Oh, I don't know. Maybe the fact that I haven't heard from you since Thanksgiving—"

"I called."

"Yes. Once in three weeks. And Monday was Michael's birthday."

The tight lines around her mother's mouth told Jenny the woman was royally pissed. This was not going to be good. She stood aside and held the door open. "Come in."

Alicia spotted Helen the minute she stepped in and ran over. "Grandma!"

Thankful for the momentary respite as her mother hugged Alicia, Jenny closed the door and leaned against it. *Isn't this a pisser. I'm supposed to meet Steve in an hour. How in the hell am I going to do that with this incredibly angry woman in my living room?*

"Alicia. Why don't you take Grandma's coat and hang it up."

Helen slipped out of her Bayberry and handed it to the girl. Jenny stepped away from the door. "Can I get you anything?"

"Something warm would be nice. It's a bit chilly tonight."

*Boy, I'll say.* "I'll make tea."

Alicia ran back into the living room. "We had a party Monday. For Michael. And I made the cake."

"That's nice," Helen said. "Had I known, I would've come."

Jenny was glad the sarcasm was lost on her daughter. And she wasn't sure how to respond. This wasn't a normal tactic for her mother.

"We have cake left. You want some?" Alicia took her grandmother's hand.

Jenny risked a glance at her watch. Fifty-five minutes and counting.

"Is Scott home?" Helen asked.

"In his room." Jenny nodded toward the sound of rock music bumping down the hall. "Alicia, why don't you tell him Grandma is here."

The girl looked a little dubious about letting go of Helen.

"Go ahead," Jenny said. "I think Grandma can find her way."

Alicia moved toward the hallway, and Jenny motioned her mother to follow her into the kitchen. She put the kettle on to boil and pulled cups out of the cabinet. *If she doesn't say something soon, I may scream.*

The tension eased a notch when Scott walked in and gave his grandmother a quick hug. Then Helen managed a smile for Alicia. "Where's that cake you promised me?"

Jenny glanced at her watch again. *Oh, shit.*

"Am I keeping you from something?" If her tone were any cooler, icicles could've hung from it.

"Uh...no."

The whistle of the tea kettle saved Jenny from any further explanation, and she turned away from her mother's searching gaze. She poured the hot water over teabags in the cups while Alicia took the leftover cake to the table.

The mood shifted as Alicia babbled on about a friend at school who might take her horseback riding. When her mother actually smiled, Jenny thought it would be okay to excuse herself on a ruse of going to the restroom. She hurried into her bedroom, picked up the handset of the landline, and dialed Steve's cell number. He answered on the second ring.

"I can't meet you tonight."

"Jenny?"

"Yeah."

"What's wrong?"

"Nothing I can't handle. It's just that my mother stopped by."

"I thought she was one person who wasn't hassling you."

"She isn't. At least not yet."

"Listen, if this is getting too tough, just say the word. We can stop anytime."

Jenny paced the small confines of her bedroom. The offer was tempting. No more lies. No more aggravation. But no more hope for vindication, either. "No, Steve. I'm not ready to quit just yet."

"Okay. You want to try for tomorrow night?"

"Sure." Jenny heard footsteps outside her door, then a soft knock. "I've got to go."

Without waiting for Steve's reply, she replaced the telephone receiver, then called out, "Just a minute."

She ran into her bathroom, flushed the toilet and rinsed her hands. Then she went and opened the door, hoping her guilt over the charade wasn't written all over her face for Scott to see. He gave her an appraising look then said, "Grandma asked me to see if you're okay."

"Why wouldn't I be?"

He shrugged. "You've been gone a while."

"Tell her I'll be right out. I just have one more thing to do."

Scott hesitated a moment, then shrugged again and headed down the hall. Jenny leaned against the doorframe and took a few deep breaths to steady her emotions. If she had her game face on, maybe she could get through the rest of the visit without probing questions from her mother.

# TWENTY-TWO

JENNY PULLED into the parking lot at Billy Bob's, turned off her engine and doused her lights. It had been ages since she'd been here, but she wasn't surprised the lot was packed on a Wednesday evening. As one of the "must see" places in Fort Worth, it was always busy no matter the day of the week.

The front of the building was a blaze of Christmas lights, and a giant Santa and sleigh were mounted on the roof. *Man, I do not need another reminder that Christmas is swiftly approaching.*

Jenny stepped through the heavy wooden doors to see a crowd of people jamming the entry area. The wail of country music drifted in from the main dance area, and a haze of smoke hovered over the bar.

It took a minute for her to recognize Steve in his jeans, suede jacket, and white Stetson. Should'a known he'd be the guy in the white hat. A woman all in denim, wearing enough turquoise jewelry to open a boutique, stood next to him. As she talked, she gestured expansively and her face was so animated it could have been lit from inside.

Jenny watched for a moment until she recognized the feeling that stirred deep inside. *Cool it, girl. You have nothing to be jealous of.*

Steve glanced over and she gave a little wave. He said something to the woman, then approached with a smile.

"Thanks for rescuing me," Steve said.

"Rescue?" Jenny glanced at the woman.

"Yeah. I think she was here all through happy-hour, had a few snacks and was looking for dessert to take home."

"Do you mean...?

"Exactly." He took her arm and led her toward the bar area.

"We could always reschedule again if you'd like to accept her offer."

He stopped so suddenly, Jenny had to laugh.

"Not on your life," he said. "I told her you were my main squeeze."

Something serious flashed through his eyes for just a second, then the exaggerated smile returned. "Undercover work makes you a good liar."

"Guess that must take a few years to master."

"Yeah. It doesn't always come easy." He gestured to a small table near the entrance to the dance floor. "Why don't you snag that, and I'll get us drinks."

"I'll take a beer. Something dark."

Jenny took off her jacket and hung it across the back of a chair, then sat down and watched Steve weave through the crowd to the bar. She couldn't help but notice the fit of his jeans on an incredibly sexy butt and the way he carried himself with a fluid grace.

*And are you going to ask him home for dessert, too?* Jenny stifled a laugh. *Better not let him see you looking at him that way. This is business. Purely business.* She glanced over the dance floor where several couples were line dancing.

She took a deep breath to relax, but even the environment seemed charged with an edict to make her heart pound and her blood race. The music was loud, throbbing, and voices were raised to shrill levels in competition.

"I can't believe you suggested this place," she said when Steve came back, a longneck in one hand and a frosty mug in the other.

"It's perfect." He handed her the mug of beer and sat down. "No one can hear a word we say."

"I'm not sure I can hear a word we say."

He set his bottle down on the table. "I can fix that."

He stood, took the beer out of her hand and led her around the railing to the dance floor. Almost as if cued, the music segued into a slow number, but the volume dropped only slightly. He pulled her close enough that she could see a small cluster of whiskers just under his jaw that had been missed by his razor.

"This works," he said. "It has something to do with distance and proximity. But don't ask for details. I never was much good at science."

For the rest of the dance, Jenny again entertained the fantasy that this was a regular date — with a not-so-regular guy. She had to admit being this close reminded her of how many years had passed since last she'd been in someone's arms.

And they seemed to fit together so well, like two ends of the same piece of fabric.

The fantasy was shattered when Steve spoke. "Tell me again what happened the other night, detail by detail."

Unlike the condensed version she'd given him on the phone the night it happened, Jenny replayed her little adventure with Frank and Leon. And again, she edited out the fact that she'd recognized George. She still hadn't figured out what to do about that, but it didn't seem right to turn him in. Not yet, anyway. And there was the little problem of her loyalty to Carol to consider.

"They never explained what happened to Chico?"

"No."

"Hmmmm."

It was such a benign response, Jenny wished she could believe that it wasn't bothering him that Chico had gone missing. Hell, she wished it wasn't bothering her so much.

The music ended and Steve led her back to the table. He pulled his chair around and sat so close his knee brushed hers. "You okay about going ahead?"

"Yeah. If I didn't blow it the other day."

"I doubt it. They don't want to walk away from an easy hundred grand." Steve took a pull on his longneck, then set the bottle down. "Call them and say your people want the deal done in two days. See what reaction you get."

"And if they say 'no'?"

"We come up with a plan B."

Jenny fiddled with the edge of her napkin and tried to think of what an alternative plan could be. Something that wouldn't involve her? And would she like for the final scene to play without her? On one hand, it would be a relief to be out of this whole mess. Then again, it would be a huge disappointment not to be there for the big showdown.

Somewhere along the line, proving herself had become almost as important as getting the bad guys. Maybe it had something to do with that first look of skepticism on Chief Gonzales's face that was still crystal clear in her memory.

"Jenny?"

She looked over at Steve. "Sorry."

He smiled. "You were off somewhere."

"Bad habit, I guess. Comes with living alone for so long. I tend to go inward."

He hesitated a moment as if considering his next question. "How long have you been divorced?"

"Seven years." She took a swallow of her beer, acutely aware of his leg touching hers every time he shifted.

"Would you rather not talk about it?"

"It's okay." She shrugged. "Not much to talk about. My ex has pretty much been out of our lives since then."

Steve studied her for a moment, the dim lights turning his eyes almost black. "What's his reaction to all this?"

By 'all this' she assumed he meant her walk on the dark side. She smiled. "He's done some blustering. I think I told you."

Steve nodded.

"Then it was okay for several weeks until recently. He's put a little heat on me again."

"As in?"

Jenny took a sip of her beer, then set the mug down. "Apparently Scott has dumped on him a few times about Mom not being home much. Since Ralph doesn't know any other way, his response is to attack me."

Steve looked at her intently. "You talking physical?"

Jenny laughed. "Pretty hard to do long distance. No. Just threats to seek custody."

"You think he'd really do it?"

"I'm not sure." Jenny mopped a few drops of condensation off the side of her mug. "He's never been the devoted father. On the other hand, he'd do anything to hurt me."

"What about Scott?"

Good question. What about Scott? She couldn't remember the last time they'd managed to move beyond cool civility. She sighed, hoping for the truth in what she was going to say.

"I think I can handle him. He's just going through that horrible mid-teen time. Michael..." Her voice cracked, and she cleared her throat. "Michael did the same thing at that age. Eventually he grew out of it. And I made a deal with Scott to give me some time."

Steve seemed to take a minute to think about all that, then leaned back. "Maybe Ralph is all bluster."

Jenny wanted to grab the assurance, but the truth was, she wasn't sure about Ralph at all. And despite the temporary truce with Scott, she knew that could blow up any day.

As if sensing her inner anxiety, Steve touched her hand lightly. "If he's planning some legal action, that takes time. We could have this all wrapped up even before any papers are filed."

The words were comforting, but the touch was disconcerting: too much warmth tempting her. Jenny pulled her hand away. "Maybe we should be going."

She couldn't read the expression on Steve's face. Was it disappointment? Could it be that he noticed her now and then as a woman and not just the CI he was responsible for?

"Maybe we should have one more dance," he said. "People might wonder if we leave too soon."

He followed that comment with a smile, and Jenny couldn't resist. "You're the expert."

The fact that another slow tune was playing at just the right moment made her wonder if Steve had somehow arranged all this. Then she touched her mouth to hold back a laugh. How ludicrous to think he would have gone to that kind of trouble.

This time they didn't talk as they danced, allowing Jenny to savor the feel of him and the rhythm of the music. He danced as fluidly as he walked and held her just close enough that she could feel the warmth of his chest and smell the musk from his aftershave.

Halfway through the number she realized that they'd

somehow become closer. She didn't know if she'd stepped in to him or the other way around, but now she was aware of more about his body than was probably appropriate for their relationship.

She pulled back, and he stopped in the middle of the floor with the oddest expression. He studied her face for what seemed like an eternity, and she wondered what thoughts were spinning through his mind. Then he shifted his gaze. "Maybe you're right. We should go."

*Well. That was certainly abrupt.* She tried to figure out what might be driving him as he led them back to the table. Did he think she was coming on to him like that ditzy lady in the lounge? Or was he embarrassed about having a physical reaction to her? Perhaps worried about what she thought?

Not giving her time to ponder that for more than two seconds, he dropped some bills on the table. "I'll walk you out."

He was two steps ahead of her as she slipped into her jacket and followed, part of her still shell-shocked and another part getting angry. Talk about the bum's rush.

She finally managed to catch up to him just outside the door. She grabbed his arm. "What's wrong?"

"Nothing." He shrugged out of her grasp.

"It was only a dance."

He stopped but didn't turn around. "Yeah. But for a moment..."

He started walking again, and Jenny had to hustle to keep up. *For a moment... what?*

He stopped again. "Where's your car?"

"Over there." She pointed to a far corner where her Taurus reflected the lights strung around the perimeter of the lot. "I can find my own way."

She took a step forward and he touched her arm. "Listen. I'm sorry."

Turning, she met his gaze and wondered what exactly he was sorry for. The dance? That moment of awareness they had felt? The breach of professionalism?

He took off his hat and ran his fingers through his hair. "Sometimes I forget that you're..."

"What? A woman?"

"Oh, no. I don't ever forget that." He glanced at her quickly, then averted his gaze. "We can't afford to complicate things, Jenny."

Of course. He was right. But they couldn't undo what was done. And when her mind wasn't clouded with grief and anxiety, she recognized a comfort level that had settled between them that went beyond the ease of working together. It wasn't really chemistry, not the kind that had first drawn her to Ralph a hundred years ago, but something connected between them each time they met. She'd been aware of it even that very first time when he'd been so kind about Michael.

If only they could get past this minor little issue of professional ethics.

Suddenly he leaned forward and brushed her lips with his, the contact so light she wasn't sure for a moment that it was real. Then he kissed her again. This time there was no doubt, and Jenny responded with an intensity that surprised her.

When he pulled back, he held her gaze for an eternity, then lightly caressed her cheek. "This never happened."

Breathless, she could hardly speak. "Uh...right."

"Go on." He motioned toward her car. "I'll wait until you get in."

"Steve, we should—"

"We can't."

"—talk."

"Not now." He shoved his hands deep into the pockets of his jeans. "Go."

Jenny walked to her car, her mind whirling. What on earth had that all been about? And how was she supposed to act now? Pretend it didn't happen?

Just before getting in the car, she glanced back and saw him still standing there, backlit by the lights. The silhouette effect caught her up short, and she suddenly understood the appeal of all the cowboy heroes in the popular romance novels.

# TWENTY-THREE

STEVE KNOCKED on the door and heard Gonzales call, "Come in."

He stepped through the doorway, noticing a pronounced haggard look about the Chief, who was elbow-deep in papers strewn across his desk. The room smelled of stale coffee and sweat with a hint of onion from the take-out bag on top of the bulging trashcan.

"Sit down." Gonzales motioned to the visitor's chair and leaned back in his own.

Steve paused with a hand on the back of the chair. "You look like shit."

"Isn't that insubordination?"

Steve laughed. "Want me to get fresh coffee?"

"I'm fine. Sit."

He did, crossing his legs at the ankles and waiting. He knew his boss would get to the purpose of this impromptu meeting soon enough.

"Heard from Burroughs."

Steve didn't like the somber tone of that statement. "And?"

"Seems like this Chico guy wasn't the only one to go missing."

"Shit."

"My sentiments exactly." Gonzales took a swig of the sludge in his coffee mug, then made a face. "There's been another change of command in Denton."

"You mean since that first guy disappeared?"

"Yeah. And it's only been, what? A little over a month?"

Steve uncrossed his legs and sat forward. "What is Burroughs thinking?"

"He's not sure. There'd been problems in Denton for a while now. Has a pretty reliable snitch who said there'd been some skimming going on. But Burroughs thought that was only with the first guy. It was no surprise when he took a walk. Possibly to nowhere."

"The snitch say the skimming is still happening?"

"He doesn't know." Gonzales bounced a pencil on the edge of his desk in a rhythmic tap, tap, tap. "That whole operation out there seems to be too loose. Lots of distrust and quick tempers. No telling what's behind it."

Steve rubbed a hand across the stubble of late-afternoon beard and considered the implications of the unrest. Nothing that came to mind was good, especially not for their operation. There was a good chance Chico was dead. And probably those other dealers, too. How much risk did that create for Jenny?

"I'm worried about our lady." Gonzales putting words to the concerns made them unavoidable. "Maybe we should've paid attention to the bad karma from the get-go."

Every time the Chief referred to karma, Steve was seized with a wild impulse to laugh, but he knew better than to even entertain the thought. Gonzales was dead serious. His wife, a practicing Hindu, was big into the spiritual discipline of yoga, and through fifteen years of marriage a lot of it had rubbed off.

And as Steve had reminded Linda some time back, except for the terminology, it wasn't so different from the standard 'gut instinct' most cops operated on.

"It hasn't been all bad," Steve countered. "And we always worry when things go too smoothly."

"I'd take smooth over three guys disappearing like that." Gonzales leaned back in his chair. "Maybe we should pull the plug."

For a moment, Steve felt a surge of relief at the thought. It would be nice not to have to worry about Jenny anymore. At least not the worry associated with guns and drugs and unpredictable dealers. Then he could turn his attention to that personal thing that seemed to be trying to develop between them. He was still kicking himself for overstepping the bounds the other night.

"What are you thinking?" Gonzales asked.

Steve felt the warmth of a flush start on his neck, and he hoped his boss didn't notice. He mentally scrambled for something innocuous to say before the silence betrayed him. "Doing the pro and con list."

Gonzales studied him a moment, then asked, "Which side is winning?"

With sudden clarity, Steve realized there'd be no personal thing with Jenny if he didn't fight for her right to finish this. Not to mention the possible risks should she suddenly drop out of the business. This was a small town. They'd find her.

"We passed the point of no return a long time ago," Steve said. "There's no safety net either way."

"We could offer witness protection."

Steve didn't resist the laugh this time. "You got an hour? I could tell you all the reasons she won't go for that."

Gonzales didn't respond, so Steve continued. "We could at

least get her thoughts on it all. And input from Burroughs before we make a move."

"Okay. Set it up." Gonzales stood and stretched, and Steve heard the crunch of a couple of bones popping.

Recognizing all the signs of dismissal, Steve rose and adjusted the crease of his jeans. After stepping into the hall and closing the office door, he allowed the flicker of anxiety that had hovered at the edge of his consciousness for the last half hour to gain strength. He'd worried all along that Jenny was in way too deep and questioned his motives for championing her cause. And now there was no doubt that the line between professional and personal had blurred when he wasn't even looking.

But there was no undoing that, either.

He shook his head and strode down toward his office. Maybe he's the one who should consider a whole new identity in a whole new place.

# TWENTY-FOUR

AFTER LUNCH, Jenny settled at the little desk in the back room with her coffee and the accounts payable book. She thought Mitchell was busy in the front and was shocked when he walked in and grabbed the ledger out of her hands. She frowned. "What are you doing?"

"Have you shopped for Christmas?"

"What?"

"It's a simple question. I don't think it needs interpretation."

Jenny tried to grab the book back, but he held it away from her. "Let me finish the paperwork," he said. "I'll even make the deliveries. And you can go to the mall."

"Last time I checked, I was still the boss here."

He smiled. "Yeah. But I'm one of your best friends, so I can get away with a lot of shit."

She laughed. "But what if I don't want to go shopping?"

Mitchell touched her on the shoulder, a serious expression replacing his smile. "You need to go shopping. You have two other children, and Christmas is just three weeks away."

Turning so he couldn't see the pain in her eyes, Jenny tried to think of a good reason she couldn't leave, but whatever she thought of, he'd shoot down. He was good at that.

She sighed. *Damn. He's right, but I really don't want to do this.*

"Just go. Do what you can. It'll get easier after this first time."

"Promise?"

His expression told her that he'd love to do anything that would make life easier for her.

She stood and touched his cheek. "If you ever decide to switch sides, let me know."

He laughed and pushed her away.

---

The strings of colored lights at the Stonebriar Mall reminded Jenny of the lights at Billy Bob's and that last evening with Steve, and she was seized with a wild idea. She'd buy a present for him. She spent some time in a tobacco shop before realizing nothing there would be appropriate. Then she moved on to a store called His Place.

She fingered some golf towels, considered a boxed set of playing cards, finally realizing she had no idea what he might like.

"Shopping for your hubby?" a voice asked at her side.

She turned to see a short man with graying hair. He was a bit rotund, and his suit matched his hair. He offered a broad smile.

"What are his hobbies?" the man asked.

"Uh..." Short of being rude, Jenny wasn't sure how to extricate herself from his interest. She glanced at her watch. "Oh, my gosh. It's late. I need to go."

She rushed out of the store, glancing back once to see the man watching with a puzzled expression. She moved down the walkway, then sat on a bench, feeling like she was trapped on some unknown planet.

What on earth had she been thinking? Or not thinking might be more like it. How could she even have considered buying a present for Steve?

She took a deep breath and tried to focus on the reality of people bustling through the mall. They were loaded with packages, smiles, and good cheer. Would she ever get to that place again?

Fragments of Holiday music drifted from the overhead sound system, and she remembered a Christmas past when the boys were toddlers. Michael had asked her to play "Frosty the Snowman" so many times she'd almost worn out the tape.

It had been a good year. One when Ralph had even been a decent husband and father. Maybe the only one.

Jenny looked around at the lights twinkling in store windows, hoping that something would connect her to the good feelings of those early years, but she felt empty. Even the tree that stood in decorated glory at the end of the walkway left her flat.

She wasn't sure how long she sat there lost in some weird emotional place, but she finally shook herself free and stood up. *Just go buy one thing.*

The nearest store was a Gap Kids, so she walked in and browsed, not even sure if anything was registering in her numb mind. She was about to say screw it when she spotted a tan suede vest with silver horses etched into the fabric. Alicia would love it. *Okay, good. Pay for it and you're out of here. Maybe Mitchell is right and it'll be easier next time.*

At home, Jenny walked in the back door, relieved when she found the kitchen empty. She hurried to her room and looked for a place to hide the package with the vest. It had long been a tradition for the kids to hunt for Christmas presents, although she doubted that she had to worry about Scott. He seemed to have less holiday spirit than she did. But Alicia was doing her damnedest to put on a happy face. She might snoop just to have a connection to the tradition.

Rooting on the top shelf of her closet, Jenny's fingers touched the security box with the guns, and she shuddered. She should give them back, but truth be told, she was avoiding Carol. There was still that unresolved issue with George. Jenny wasn't sure she could be in the same room with her friend and not give something away. They'd been too good at reading each other for too long for subterfuge to work.

She stashed Alicia's present, then closed the closet door. She was halfway across the room when the phone rang. She turned and grabbed the receiver, sinking to the edge of her bed. "Hello."

"It's Steve. Can you come to the station tomorrow night?"

"What's up?"

"Can't talk about it right now. Can you make it?"

"Sure. What time?"

"About eight."

After making arrangements for Steve to meet her at the back entrance of the station tomorrow, Jenny hung up and went to the kitchen to figure out something good for dinner. She dug through the freezer and found a container of spaghetti sauce hiding behind frozen packages of vegetables of indeterminate ages.

She put the sauce in the microwave to defrost and started water to boil for pasta. Then she pulled out the makings for salad. Since she was staying home tonight, they could have a nice dinner and talk about what to do for Christmas.

That plan barely stayed in place through the main course,

then Scott said he'd already made plans with Caitlin for that evening. "You told me yesterday that you were staying home tonight, so I figured it was my turn to go out."

Jenny sighed. "I was hoping we could make plans for Christmas."

"You can plan without me. Just like you did at Thanksgiving."

This was said with an air of defiance, and Jenny clamped her mouth tight to keep from reacting. Alicia was looking at both of them with that "deer in the headlights" expression that was becoming all too familiar.

"Fine," Jenny said, forcing a smile. "Alicia and I will figure something out."

"Whatever." Scott pushed his chair out and stood up.

Any smidgen of Christmas spirit Jenny might have had walked out the door with Scott, but for Alicia's sake, she made an effort.

---

Caitlin glanced at her watch in the soft yellow glow of the porch light. "It's late. I should get in before Dad comes out to get me."

"Would he really?" Scott asked.

"No, silly. It was a joke."

Scott glanced off into the darkness beyond the ring of light, and she touched his arm. "What's wrong?"

He sighed instead of answering. What could he say? It was always the same old shit, and she was probably tired of hearing it. That's why he hadn't said much about how he'd been feeling since Michael's birthday as they'd walked up to the park and back. But, God! Sometimes he just wanted to scream.

"Is it that deal with your mom? Maybe we could still work

something out about watching Alicia. Let you get away to see what she's up to."

"That's okay. I'm not sure I even care anymore."

"Of course, you care."

"Don't tell me how I feel. You don't know how I feel."

The minute the words were out, Scott wished he could take them back. Caitlin shifted away from him, that same look of intense hurt on her face he'd seen that day at the mall. He reached out to touch her. "I'm sorry."

She brushed his hand away. "Sorry doesn't cut it anymore. I am so tired of your anger."

Scott shoved his hands in his jacket pockets to keep from hitting something. He'd never consider hitting her, but that tree looked mighty tempting.

"Maybe it would be best if I just left for a while."

"What do you mean?"

He took a quick glance at her, then looked away. "Been thinking again about going to my dad's."

"But what about me? Us? You're just going to run away from that, too?"

"I'm not running away from anything."

"No? Seems to me you've been running since Michael died."

This time he faced her square. "That's not fair."

"None of it's fair. But you've been slowly closing down for months. I don't even know what to say anymore."

"Seems to me you've had plenty to say."

"I can't believe you can be so..." She faltered a moment, as if searching for words. "You never used to be cruel."

"Then maybe it'd be a relief if I was gone."

Scott turned, but not before he saw another shadow of pain cross her face. It was almost strong enough to pull him back.

Almost.

*Damn you, Michael. Why did you have to go and die?*

That thought made him falter, and for one brief moment he considered turning around and seeking the comfort of Caitlin's arms. But the loud thud of the door slamming told him it was too late.

*God, maybe I am turning into some kind of bastard.*

He walked away from her house, and as he neared the corner where the streetlight was out, a cloud scuttled across the moon, casting him into an eerie darkness. He shuddered. *Serve me right if some maniac took me out.*

But even as the thought took shape, Scott knew he didn't mean it. He didn't want to die. He just wanted to stop hurting so bad. And stop being so angry. Caitlin was right. He had hardly displayed any emotion of late except this anger that bordered on rage.

The counselor at school kept telling him it would pass in time. What he'd like to know is when. Three fucking months seemed plenty long enough.

Maybe his idea of going out to California wasn't such a bad one after all. Get away from this place that had reminders around every corner. And since he'd probably just screwed everything royally with Caitlin, there wasn't much holding him here now.

*But I'll wait until after Christmas. Mom would kill me if I went before.*

*Ha. She's going to kill you anyway.*

# TWENTY-FIVE

JENNY DEBATED about parking at her shop and walking to the police station. It wasn't too far. But what if Mitchell drove by and thought she was there? If he stopped and then discovered the place empty, what would he do? She'd left so many of his questions unanswered. She didn't want to risk another.

The urge to laugh was strong, and she recognized the impulse for what it was: a release of nerves that had hovered like vultures since Steve had called. Why on earth had he risked so much by having her come to the station? If even one whiff of an association between her and the cops made it to the streets — then possibly to Frank — the whole deal would be blown. All those weeks of subterfuge for naught.

She finally opted to park in the lot to the rear of the old Catholic church that resembled a Quonset hut. Despite its unconventional appearance, everyone in town knew it was a church, and it might be the last place anyone would notice her car, especially if she pulled into the farthest corner of the lot where a huge, untrimmed oak stretched a long finger of branch over the concrete.

After checking the review mirror to make sure her hair was tucked into the baseball cap, she pulled the collar of her jacket up, donned sunglasses and stepped out of the car. Keeping to the backstreets, she hurried the few blocks to the police station.

To get to the back of the building she turned down the dark alley, pausing a moment to let her eyes adjust to the shadows. Senses on overdrive, she took a few tentative steps forward, then heard a loud clang and the rustle of scurrying feet. She froze. Even though she knew the sound was too small to be human, she wasn't thrilled at the prospect of meeting a rat big enough to make that much noise.

Another rattle, then she caught a flash of white — hopefully a cat — as it dashed by and disappeared around the corner.

She let out a breath in relief and walked toward the end of the alley where she could see a faint sliver of light. As she neared, she could just barely make out a figure standing by the door. She called out tentatively, "Steve?"

"Yeah. Come on." He opened the door wider and hustled her in. "Anyone see you?"

"Not unless you count the cat in the alley."

Steve smiled. "We have ways of taking care of that."

"You can let him go." She took off her sunglasses and slipped them into a jacket pocket. "I don't think he recognized me."

Her joke elicited another smile, and she realized that she'd taken to doing that a lot lately, wise-cracking to prompt the expression that softened the hardness in his eyes and created a hint of a dimple on one cheek. She knew she probably shouldn't. It was only setting herself up for disappointment. But the temptation was too strong to resist.

Walking into the conference room, Jenny picked up the unmistakable air of tension in the room. Burroughs, sitting at the head of the table, gave her a brief nod, and Gonzales motioned for her to sit in a chair across from him. Steve sat beside her. Nobody spoke for an agonizing moment, and Jenny studied the frown that creased the Chief's face. "What's wrong?"

He glanced toward Burroughs. "We located Chico," Burroughs said.

Something in his tone suggested that she wasn't going to like the next part.

"Some fishermen found his body early this morning in Lake Lewisville."

Jenny swallowed the lump that rose in her throat. Chico had seemed like such a decent guy — if drug dealers could be considered decent. Under his tough-guy performances, she had always suspected there was a kid who'd simply taken a wrong turn somewhere in his life, and perhaps even regretted it. When she'd looked into his eyes, she'd never seen the same hard edge that was in Frank's. She swallowed again. Maybe it was that core of decency that had been Chico's downfall.

"We think the two guys from Denton are probably floaters somewhere, too. And we're pretty sure why they were taken out. That place has reeked with internal trouble for a long time." Burroughs rubbed the back of his neck. "What we can't figure is why this Chico guy was whacked."

Gonzales poured a glass of water from the pitcher in the middle of the table and pushed it across to Jenny. "You have any ideas?"

On one hand it was nice to be asked for an opinion; almost made her feel like one of the guys. But it also made her realize how little she did know of this whole underworld of drugs. "To tell you the truth, I was so busy making sure I came across credible I wouldn't have spotted anything wrong even if I knew what to look for."

"Did you have a rapport with Chico?" Burroughs asked.

Jenny nodded and took a swallow of water.

"What about this other guy, Frank? You okay with him?"

"He gives me the creeps more than—"

"He try anything else since your midnight ride?" Gonzales asked.

"No. Been pretty much business as usual. But he's still the silent type. Leon does most of the talking."

"Has he said anything about the big buy?"

Jenny shook her head, and Gonzales wiped a hand across his cheek. Then he looked to Burroughs. "Think we ought to scrap the whole operation?"

"Do I have a vote?" Jenny asked before the other man even opened his mouth.

"This isn't a democracy," Gonzales said.

"I think she knows that," Steve said. "But she has a right to some input."

The support was unexpected, and Jenny shot him a quick glance, sending a silent message of thanks. Gonzales watched the exchange and sat silent for a moment.

"Steve's right," Burroughs said. "She's had the most contact and probably knows the temperature better than any of us."

"We still decide," Gonzales said.

After waiting for nods of acknowledgement, he gestured to Jenny to go ahead.

"I think I've earned their respect." She glanced quickly at Steve, hoping he wouldn't mention how exactly she'd done that. "Way I see it, the ride that night was a test. See if I'd scare off."

She was glad to see a nod of agreement from Burroughs. The nod gave her confidence. "So even though Frank doesn't say much, I think I'm still credible. I'd like to at least make the approach again."

Gonzales glanced from Steve to Burroughs, one eyebrow raised in question. Burroughs seemed to consider for a moment while he twirled a pen on the table, then he abruptly stopped the motion with the flat of his hand. "It's worth a try. We can always bail out later if we need to."

"What do you think?" Gonzales directed that question to Steve.

"She's got the most on the line," he said, nodding in Jenny's direction.

"That's true," Gonzales said. "And that's one reason I'm leery. She's not a professional, and how do we know revenge isn't clouding her reason?"

"Because I'm not doing it for revenge." Jenny could feel a distinct chill permeate the room after that statement, but she didn't care. She continued in the same controlled tone. "And you're a sorry son of a bitch if you don't know my motive by now."

The chill turned glacial as Gonzales sucked in a quick breath. Jenny held up one hand to deter what she knew was going to be an angry response. "If I only wanted revenge, I would have simply bought a gun and shot the bastards."

She ignored the slight rustle of movement she heard from Steve and focused on the Chief. As the seconds ticked by, the red in his face slowly gave way to the natural olive color. "You are one ballsy woman," he said. "But you do have a point."

Jenny didn't risk any more words.

"Still, any new wrinkle comes along, we shut down."

"That seems like a good plan," Burroughs said.

Gonzales kept his dark, cold eyes on Jenny. "We clear on that?"

She nodded.

# TWENTY-SIX

WHEN JENNY OPENED THE DOOR, she almost fainted. "Ralph? What are you doing here?"

"I came to see what's going on."

"What do you mean?"

"Carol called—"

"Carol? My friend?"

"Yeah. She got my number from Scott."

Jenny leaned her head against the edge of the door, her mind in a whirl. *Is every fuckin' thing spinning out of control?*

"Are you going to let me in?"

She nodded and stepped away from the door. When he entered, Alicia saw him and bounded up from the sofa. "Daddy!"

She threw herself at him, and Jenny stilled the wild beating of her heart. There had to be a way out. There just had to be.

Ralph put his bag down and drew Alicia into an embrace. "How's my girl?"

*How's my girl? He can just barge in here and act like it's just a friendly father visit?*

"This isn't a good time, Ralph."

He released Alicia and turned to her. "You're right. We'll talk after dinner."

"I've got plans."

"Oh? Something more important than the family?"

Jenny bit her lip hard. How dare he take that tone?

Forcing a calmness she didn't feel inside, Jenny turned to Alicia. "Why don't you hang up Daddy's coat."

Ralph shrugged out of his overcoat and handed it over. Alicia took it to the front closet then headed down the hall. "I'm going to tell Scott that Daddy's here."

Jenny faced Ralph, her voice a low hiss. "Don't think you can just come in here and take over. You haven't given a good goddamn for too many years to pull this shit."

"Let's save it for later. For the kids' sake."

"Of course. We're so concerned..." She let the rest of her thought fade as Scott walked in.

"Hello, Dad." He gave Ralph an awkward embrace, then stepped back. "I didn't believe Alicia when she said you were here."

"Guess I shocked everyone," Ralph said. "Took a few days off work. Thought it would be a nice surprise."

*Some surprise. But I'd hardly call it nice.* Jenny forced a tight smile.

"It's cool," Alicia said, snuggling up to the other side of her father. "I like surprises."

"So how is everything?"

Ralph directed the question to Scott, and in the few seconds it took for him to glance at her, then back to Ralph, Jenny held her breath.

After what seemed like forever, Scott shrugged. "Same ol' same ol'."

Jenny didn't miss the significant pause as Ralph studied

their son's face. Then he put on a broad smile. "How about I take you all out for dinner?"

"Goody. I want McDonald's," Alicia said.

"How about some place nicer?" Ralph turned to Jenny. "Is there a family restaurant in town?"

"There's Randy's Steakhouse on Main. Scott knows where it is."

"You're not coming?"

It was as much challenge as question, but Jenny held her temper. "No. You and the kids can have some time together. It'll be good."

His lips worked for a second. Like he was trying to find the right thing to say, then he nodded. "We'll talk later."

It seemed to take forever for Ralph and the kids to get out the door. Alicia decided that she wanted to dress up and scooted off to her room before Jenny could assure her she was fine in her jeans.

Jenny didn't want to be too obvious about checking her watch, but time was getting critical. She was supposed to meet Leon and Frank in half an hour. It would be a real hassle to try to leave first.

It was only five minutes, but it seemed like forever before Alicia reappeared. At first glance, she didn't look much different, but she'd traded rumpled jeans for ones with creases and a t-shirt for a peasant blouse, and her hair was freshly brushed.

"We won't be long," Ralph said as he herded the kids out the door.

Jenny almost told him to take his time but held it back. She smiled at Scott and Alicia. "Have fun."

After she saw the taillights of Ralph's rental car round the corner, Jenny ran to her room and changed into one of her "tart" outfits. On the way out she grabbed a jacket, locked the door and raced to her car.

One benefit of small-town living was it didn't take long to get from one place to another. Thank God. She drove to within a block of the high school, found a parking space, and got out. Walking toward the edge of the sport field she heard the hoot of an owl from the stand of trees that bordered the fence. The sound jangled nerves that were already stretched to a breaking point, and sweat pooled in the small of her back despite the cold night air.

A rustle of movement commanded her attention, and she saw Leon step out of the trees into the light provided by a moon that was almost full. Frank was a dark silhouette behind him.

"You're late," Leon said. "We were about to boogie."

"Well, I'm here now." Jenny fought to keep an air of nonchalance in her stance and her voice.

She dug in the pocket of her jeans and pulled out a hundred-dollar bill. Leon glanced at it, then at her. "Business drying up?"

"Just a little light this week. You know how it goes."

"Yeah." Leon took the money and passed her a bag.

After stashing it inside her jacket, Jenny turned to Frank, who hadn't moved during the entire exchange. "What's the word on my other deal?"

"What? We don't even get a little foreplay first?" Leon cast a quick glance at the other man as if seeking his approval for the clever line.

"Sorry," Jenny said. "It'd be different if we were someplace warm."

Frank stepped out of the shadows, and Jenny suppressed a shudder when the moonlight touched the ugly scar on his face. "Friday night."

She was about to ask, "Friday night, what?" when it hit her. *That's when we make the buy.* Despite a surge of excitement and apprehension, she kept her voice steady. "Sure."

"You'll have the money?"

"Yeah. Sure." Three days. That only gave them three days.

"Come here at eight. We'll take you to the stuff."

When Jenny got back to her car, her hands shook so bad she dropped the keys twice before she got the door open. Then she sat behind the wheel for a full minute, taking deep breaths to settle the rush of adrenaline. How were they going to pull this together in three days? And what on earth was she to do about Ralph?

A finger of icy air crawled up her leg and reminded her she wasn't going to solve any of those problems sitting here in a cold car. She brought the engine to life and drove home. If she was lucky, she'd have time to call Steve before Ralph and the kids got back. She had to tell him about the buy. And the complication of Ralph showing up.

As she expected, Steve was as juiced as she was about the buy, but he didn't share her doubts about pulling things together in time. "We're pros, remember?"

The little joke eased her tension, and they talked a bit about the logistics of setting up for Friday. Then he asked what he could do to help her handle the situation with Ralph.

"I don't know. I'm just not sure I can bullshit my way through."

"Maybe we should talk to him."

"I thought that was verboten."

"It is. And I'd rather not. But let me run it by the Chief. Call me later if you need to."

"Okay." Jenny kicked off the stiletto heels and rubbed her foot. She would be so glad when she didn't have to be 'Connie the tart.' "I'll see what I can do when Ralph gets back."

She heard the front door slam. "They're home. Gotta go."

Jenny hung up the phone, stripped off the sleazy clothes

and pulled on jeans and a sweatshirt. She took a swipe at the makeup with a tissue, then went out to the living room.

"You stayed home?" Scott's tone implied the question, but his expression held a hint of challenge.

Jenny considered just letting it go, but her perverse side took over before she could stop it. "I did run up to the store for juice. But I came straight home." Her tone carried a hard edge of sarcasm, and the minute she saw the look of confusion on Alicia's face, Jenny regretted taking Scott's bait. He said nothing, and for a moment they were all caught in a moment so fragile Jenny thought it might break if someone didn't say something. She went to Alicia and put an arm around her. "That was just way too hateful for me to say," she said. "I'm sorry." She directed the final comment to Scott. He gave her nothing in return, standing rigid with his hands deep in his pockets.

The silence was still painful, and Jenny mentally scrambled for something to lower the emotional temperature. Scott finally broke the mood, shifting and making a vague gesture down the hall. "I've got to call Caitlin." He moved toward the darkened hallway. "Thanks for dinner, Dad."

Jenny let out her breath in a soft whoosh as Scott disappeared into the shadows. Ralph sat down on the overstuffed chair across from the sofa, and Alicia balanced on the arm.

*It's like she's Velcroed to him.* Jenny fought a surge of resentment. It had been weeks since Alicia had snuggled with her. *And whose fault is that?*

*Oh, shut up.*

Noting the contented smile on Alicia's face, Jenny pushed the resentment aside. It wasn't productive. For her or her daughter. Better to just let the girl have this time and hope like hell she could go to sleep tonight with a smile.

"You want anything? Coffee?" Jenny asked Ralph.

"Got anything stronger?"

She had to think a minute. It had been so long since she'd entertained — the funeral definitely didn't count — she couldn't remember if she had anything besides cooking sherry. Wait. Carol had brought that bottle of Jack Daniels. "Strictly for medicinal purposes," she'd said. "Beats the hell out of sleepless nights." That had been before the funeral, and Jenny had stashed the bottle high above the refrigerator, too afraid to take the first dose.

She pulled herself away from the pain that memory caused. "I might be able to scare up some bourbon."

"I like it neat."

"I remember."

Jenny went into the kitchen and dragged the bottle down. She found a reasonably clean small drink glass and poured a couple of inches of amber liquid. She set the bottle down, then thought, what the hell, grabbed another glass and splashed some bourbon in it. Maybe some medicine would help the rest of the evening go down a little easier.

She stepped back into the living room in time to hear Alicia telling Ralph about the recent school trip to the Dallas Art Museum. He appeared to be listening with rapt attention. *Does that mean he really cares?*

She handed him his drink and nudged Alicia. "Time for bed, Punkin."

"Aw, Mom."

"Mom's right," Ralph said. "You've got school tomorrow."

The reasonableness of his tone took Jenny by surprise. She'd seldom known him to be reasonable. And back when they'd 'shared' responsibility for the kids, he'd seldom backed her in anything. There were times when she'd thought she was raising four kids.

Ralph hoisted Alicia off the arm of the chair. "You go get into your PJs, and I'll come look at your painting in a minute."

He sounded so domestic Jenny choked on a swallow of bourbon. *Who is this man sitting here and what has he done with the real Ralph?*

Or was this all part of some plan? Had he come here to take the kids? Was he trying to make it easier by winning them over first?

Jenny studied him, searching for a clue, some indication that he was merely acting. But there was nothing devious in his actions or expression as he kissed their daughter. Alicia came over to Jenny, and she gave her a quick hug before sending her down the hallway.

"Nice place," Ralph said, gesturing around the living room. "I don't think I told you that when I was here...before."

Jenny sat down on the sofa. "We were a little busy."

Ralph nodded, as if acknowledging the understatement of the year. "How've you been holding up?"

"So-so." Jenny dropped her gaze before he could see the swell of tears. "You?"

"I'm managing." He looked around again. "Sometimes it's so hard to believe it's real. I can go days without remembering, then, bam. It hits me."

"I don't have that luxury."

Ralph winced as if she'd slapped him and drained half his bourbon.

Jenny resisted the urge to continue to pummel him with all the angry, hateful things that came to mind. It would feel so good to just beat up on someone. But she realized he was already a crushed man. He'd lost a son he'd hardly known and had to live with regrets the rest of his life.

The only regret she had was that she'd never see Michael's future. The past had pretty much been okay between them.

"I'm sorry." Jenny tried a slight smile. "Sometimes my mouth opens before I've exercised any caution."

"Sometimes? That was one of—" He stopped, shook his head, then took a deep breath and faced her again. "Truce?"

She hesitated, not sure about giving up the anger quite yet. He'd just waltzed in here, playing doting father, and she should just step back? Let him...? She stopped that runaway-train thought process. If there was to be any hope of keeping Ralph from screwing this whole deal, she needed to be reasonable. She nodded. "I'll get us another drink."

Ralph handed his glass over, and Jenny stood, then walked into the kitchen. She poured generous amounts into each glass, then set the bottle down and glanced out the window above the sink. The bare branches of the elm stretched like black fingers into a moonlit sky, and against the inky silhouettes she could see parts of her face reflected in the glass. It was like looking at a bizarre Picasso painting.

The analogy prompted an urge to laugh, but other emotions were too strong to allow it. She still had to answer that all-important question Ralph had asked when she'd first opened the door. And she was still no closer to knowing what to say than she had been then. Should she just tell him the truth?

That was absurd. Of all the people she wanted to tell, Ralph was not even among the top ten.

The living room was empty when she stepped through the doorway. She set the drinks down on the coffee table and walked down the hall. She heard the god-awful screech of guitar from behind Scott's door. How she hated what some of those folks did to a fine instrument. She debated about knocking to see if he was okay, then realized he may be still talking to Caitlin. Although how they could converse in the midst of all that racket was a mystery.

Alicia's door was open, and Jenny rounded the doorway and stopped. The sight of Ralph sitting on the bed with Alicia snuggled next to him stole her breath away. The girl was turning pages in her painting tablet, sharing treasures she most often kept private.

The scene was so poignant, Jenny felt tears warm her eyes, yet her heart hardened at the thought of how hurt Alicia would be if Ralph's interest waned and things went back to the way they used to be.

Or could this truly be a new and improved version of the father who had been so sorely missing all these years?

Watching him caress their daughter's arm, Jenny hoped the latter was true. Otherwise she might have to kill the bastard.

Her husband and daughter looked up, and for a second Jenny was afraid she'd voiced that thought out loud. But Alicia smiled. She wouldn't be smiling if Jenny had said something so awful. "I'm showing Daddy my pictures."

"I see." Jenny stepped into the room. "But now it's time to go to bed. You can finish sharing your art another time."

She held Ralph's gaze in a silent plea for assurance that there would be another time. And soon.

After Alicia was tucked in, they went back to the living room. Jenny motioned to the drinks on the table, and Ralph took his and settled in the chair.

Silence reigned for what seemed like days, and Jenny could feel his eyes on her as she wandered through the room, adjusting a couch pillow, straightening a picture, sighing often.

"Could you light somewhere?" he asked. "You're making me tired just watching."

Jenny walked to the sofa and perched on the edge of one cushion. Maybe they could continue with small talk until they both fell asleep from sheer boredom. "How is work going?"

"Talk to me, Jen."

*God. He hasn't used that pet name since—* She stopped the thought, not wanting to remember those early years when she thought she'd been living every woman's fantasy. "We are talking."

"You know what I mean."

"What do you want me to say?"

"Whatever it is that prompted your friend to call me."

Jenny stood. "She shouldn't have done that."

"Too late now."

Jenny walked to the window and lifted the curtain to look out. Between the streetlamp on the corner and the moon, there was almost as much light outside as in. She counted the cars parked across the street. Somebody must be having a party. Then she turned and faced Ralph, waiting for his control to snap. Waiting for the old Ralph — the one who pushed and shouted and pressured her — to come back. But this new guy just sat, so still he could have been sewn to the fabric of the chair. That calm made her decision.

"I have to call someone," she said.

# TWENTY-SEVEN

RALPH DIDN'T SAY anything as they headed south on I-75, destination I-Hop in Plano where they'd meet Steve. It was so quiet in Ralph's rental car, Jenny could hear the tires hum on the concrete.

She'd been surprised when he hadn't protested her phone call or pushed for an explanation. She hadn't told him who she'd called or why, and he seemed to accept that this was the way it needed to be handled. He waited without a single question while she made arrangements for Scott to watch out for Alicia.

Now the silence was beginning to grate. Jenny glanced over, studying Ralph's profile. "You're different, somehow."

"We all are since..."

She waited a minute for him to finish, but he didn't. "Since Michael died," she said. "As painful as it is, it's better to say it aloud."

"Better for whom?"

The note of belligerence backed her off. It sounded too much like the old Ralph for comfort.

"Never mind." She turned to look out at the concrete and steel landscape streaming by.

When they got to the restaurant, Jenny spotted Steve in a U-shaped booth in a far corner. Good choice. It was fairly private, and it gave each of them their own space. "We're with him," she said to the young, blonde hostess before leading the way to the table.

"Ralph, this is Lieutenant Steve Morrity. Little Oak PD." She bit back an urge to laugh. *God, I sound like I'm on some cop show on TV*.

Steve stood and shook hands, then slid to the middle of the booth. Jenny stepped aside so Ralph could go in next. She took the opposite end of the bench. Good neutral setup.

Ralph glanced at Jenny, then back to Steve. "Why the cops? Is this about Michael's accident?"

"Loosely."

Again, Ralph studied the two of them for a moment. "And does it have something to do with this nonsense Jenny is mixed up in?"

"I'd hardly call it nonsense." Steve smiled into Ralph's glare, and Jenny noted the stark difference between the two men. The smile was nice. She cut her own off when she noticed Ralph giving her another speculative look.

Before he could voice the question that had raised one of his eyebrows, the waitress, a tall woman with almond-colored skin and a controlled mass of dreadlocks, stepped to the table, order pad ready. "What can I get you folks?"

"Coffee all around?" Steve glanced at Ralph and Jenny, who nodded.

"No dinner? Dessert?" A flash of white teeth accompanied the questions and Jenny realized this woman should be gracing the cover of a top women's magazine. Not pushing pancakes.

She also realized that the tightness in her stomach was triggered by hunger as well as nerves. But she didn't want to stall things by placing an order. "Maybe later."

The waitress brought back tall glasses of water, cups, and a thermal pot that she set in the middle of the table. "I'll leave you folks to visit," she said. "Just holler when you're ready for dessert."

Steve poured for all of them.

Watching the bluish sheen of acid swirl on top of the coffee in her cup, Jenny's stomach rebelled, so she softened the coffee with a touch of cream and sugar.

Ralph did the same, then set his spoon down and faced Steve. "Tell me what's been going on with Jenny."

"She's been working with us," Steve said.

That stopped Ralph in the middle of taking a swallow of coffee. He shot a quick glance at Jenny, then turned his attention back to Steve, who continued, "Part of a drug task force."

Ralph's cup clunked against the table. "You're shitting me."

Steve shook his head. Ralph looked over at Jenny, eyes wide with amazement.

"Guilty as charged," she said.

He sat back as if the revelation was too heavy to bear. "And just what is it you're doing? Baking cookies for the guys?"

Jenny was almost glad to hear the old needling tone in his voice. She'd been growing weary of the 'nice' Ralph. Something about his recent actions had been ringing false, like watching a performance by the kid who got the part in the school play because he was the only one to audition. She bit her lip to keep from saying something nasty.

Steve looked at Ralph for a moment, seeming to take his measure. "She's been a valuable asset to the team. Haven't seen a single cookie."

It pleased Jenny to see Ralph back down. He fiddled with his spoon, twirling it in circles on the Formica tabletop.

Steve continued. "We've been working a little over two months now. She's made inroads into the local drug business, and we're about to take down the big guy."

Now Ralph looked at her again, his expression vacillating between disbelief and something she couldn't quite name. She tried to see the moment from his point of view. It had to be mind-boggling.

He finally found his voice. "This is unbelievable."

"What?" she said. "You didn't think the little woman had it in her?"

"There are lots of things I don't know about you, Jen."

"Because you—" She shook her head, not wanting to engage in this verbal battle in front of Steve. She took a sip of coffee, which had cooled to perhaps a degree above tepid.

"Did you even give a damn about the danger? The kids?"

"Hold on, there." Steve grabbed Ralph's arm, but Ralph shrugged out of the touch.

"It's all right, Steve."

He looked at Jenny. "You sure?"

She nodded.

Ralph glanced at her, then at Steve. "How could you let her?"

He smiled. "She's a force to be reckoned with."

"You think this is a joke?"

"Do I look like someone who would joke about something like this?"

Jenny leaned forward and touched Ralph's hand before hostilities broke out. "This is something I wanted to do. Something I needed to do. They're selling drugs at the school, for God's sake."

"Couldn't you just step back and let the cops do their job?"

"That's part of the problem, Ralph. Everyone expects the

cops to handle it. But it's too big for that. It's like pissing into the wind."

Jenny saw Steve smile again, and she hoped the tension would ease all around. Ralph shot a glance from her to Steve, then back again. "What is this? Fucking *Comedy Central*?"

"Ralph." She waited until the flush of anger receded from his face. "You need to keep your voice down."

"What I need..." He leaned so close she could feel his breath on her face. "Is my ex-wife to stop putting my kids in danger."

"So now you're suddenly worried about—"

"Cease fire." Steve waved a napkin between them.

"Don't tell me—"

Steve grabbed Ralph's arm, pulling him against the backrest. "I will tell you," Steve said. "And you'll bloody well listen. There is no way you are screwing up this deal for us. You hear me? No way."

"Everything okay here, folks?"

Jenny looked up to see the waitress, concern furrowing her perfect forehead and dark eyes carefully assessing the group. Jenny forced a smile. "We're fine."

The waitress shot a speculative look to the men, then back to Jenny. "You want that dessert now?"

Despite the rumble in her stomach, Jenny shook her head, mentally urging the woman to just walk away. After another hesitation, she did, but Jenny knew the woman would be back if Ralph didn't ratchet his emotions down several notches.

For a moment it was like nobody knew what to say. Jenny reached for her coffee cup, then reconsidered and took a sip of water. Then she looked at her ex-husband, who had his arms folded across his chest. "I understand your concern, Ralph."

"Then it won't be that hard to step aside, will it?"

His words hung in the air like autumn leaves stopped in mid-flight, his posture daring her to accept his challenge.

"That's not even a possibility," she said.

Ralph shook his head. "Fucking drug deals. My ex. The mother of my children is making fucking drug deals."

"Why don't we get you a microphone?" Steve said.

"You stay out of it. This is between me and Jenny."

"Not exclusively. There's a whole lot of folks that have been busting their asses to get this guy."

"And have they put their families at risk?"

"The only risk here has been telling you."

Ralph opened his mouth, then shut it as if words were stuck inside and couldn't get out. Steve poured more coffee, took a sip and then set his cup down. "I'm serious," he said. "We're working her as a confidential informant. You know what that is?"

"I've seen my share of cop shows on TV."

Jenny caught the undercurrent of sarcasm, but either Steve didn't, or he chose to ignore it.

"Then you understand. She has this whole other identity with the dealers. No way can they connect her with the kids."

"He's right," Jenny said, hoping she could add ammunition to Steve's assurance. "They don't know my real name. Or where I live. I've never even let them see the car."

"What? Based on this nice little speech I'm supposed to sit back and—"

"No," Steve said. "You'll keep your mouth shut because we chose to trust you with this information."

Ralph picked up his spoon again and made circles in the puddle of condensation from his water glass. Jenny watched, wondering if he would respond to the invitation to do the principled thing. Ralph might have been delinquent as a husband and father, but he lived by some machismo code of duty. A man stood for justice. Had Steve somehow figured that out in this brief encounter? That he could appeal to some sense of honor?

"It's only for a few more days," Steve said.

"Is that true?" Ralph directed the question at Jenny.

She nodded.

"When exactly?"

"That's a piece of information you can't have," Steve said.

"And what do I do between now and this unspecified date?"

Jenny winced at the goading tone in his voice. "What do you think? Go back home. Go to work."

"No way in hell. I'm not leaving. I'll stay out at the house. Be there in case—"

Jenny touched his arm. "Nothing's going to happen."

He pulled away. "And you can guarantee that?"

"Nothing in life is certain, Ralph. We both know it." She waited a moment for the message to sink in. "Just go—"

"And what? Pretend that my ex is not risking her life? And maybe our kids?"

"We've got her covered," Steve said.

"That's supposed to make me feel better?" Ralph sneered, and Jenny wasn't sure if his outrage was really about her safety and the kids, or about him. Somehow everything always ended up being about him.

Steve took a swallow of coffee, then carefully set his mug down. "We have enough personnel working with us to take out a small country. And don't discount her," he nodded at Jenny. "She's an amazing woman."

The words were almost like a caress, and Jenny swallowed hard. If they weren't in the middle of this ludicrous debate, she might even take a minute to figure out just what he meant by amazing.

Ralph gave them another speculative look. "You two got something going besides work?"

The question was absurd, yet so close to a truth she'd entertained on more than one occasion Jenny gulped again. She saw a faint stain of red on Steve's neck, but otherwise he didn't react.

"Don't be ridiculous, Ralph." Jenny gave him a moment to bring his mind back around.

Steve made a production of pouring more coffee. Jenny appreciated the distraction but couldn't imagine drinking any more. Ralph took a swallow, then looked up, chin raised in defiance. "I'm not going back."

"Staying at the house is not an option."

"I have a right to spend time with the kids," Ralph said. "Therefore, it's up to you. We can do this hard, or we can do it easy."

When he got that edge in his voice, Jenny knew it was fruitless to continue the battle. Not if she wanted to emerge somewhat intact. She sighed. "You're right. I can't fight you on that."

She took a sip of the coffee, setting off a roil of protest from her empty stomach. "But you can't stay at the house. It just wouldn't work."

"The kids might like having—"

"I said no, Ralph." She thought for a moment. There had to be a way to satisfy him without increasing any of the risks. Then it hit her. "Maybe you can take them away for a few days. Until the weekend."

He looked like she'd sucker-punched him. "Are you serious?"

His question gave her pause. Was she? She'd never spent more than a day without the kids in the years since the divorce. And she'd never let them go with Ralph on the rare occasions he'd requested it. No way would she allow them to fly halfway across the country and then maybe get hurt.

But it was different now. Hell, everything was different now. And maybe it would even be good for the kids. She sighed. "Yeah. I guess I am."

# TWENTY-EIGHT

"I GET to go away with Daddy?" Alicia dumped her backpack on the floor and sat down at the kitchen table. "For three whole days?"

"Yes." Jenny poured orange juice and set a glass in from of her daughter. "We talked about it last night."

"What about me?" Scott grabbed the box of Cheerios off the counter and slid into a chair.

"You can go, too. It won't hurt either of you to miss a couple of days of school."

"I can't skip now. Got an English paper due Friday and exams coming up next week." Scott poured a tan stream of cereal into the bowl and topped it off with milk.

Jenny set the juice pitcher down. "We didn't think of that."

"You're the one that was all over me about my grades." Scott picked up the Cheerios that had escaped over the edge of the bowl and ate them dry.

"Don't be smart with me."

"Finish your paper today," Alicia said. "Mom could take it in for you tomorrow."

Jenny thought of all the things she had to do the next day. Show up at work for a few hours. Meet with the task force. Give Carol hell for calling Ralph. There just might be time somewhere in there to go by the school and be nice to Miss Brenda Ames of the pinched lips. "I guess I could do that," she said.

"Won't work," Scott said, talking around a mouthful of food. "Paper's not even started. Besides that—" He stopped to shovel another spoonful of cereal into his mouth. "I'm not sure I want to go off with Dad for a few days."

Jenny caught her coffee cup before it crashed on the counter. "What about ...? Thanksgiving? What you said?"

She hadn't intended the sharp edge to her voice, but it had snuck in anyway. She tried for a smile to dispel the shadow of alarm that crossed Alicia's face. "What's the matter, Mom?"

"Nothing, Honey."

"But you've got that look. You both do." Alicia flung her napkin down and pushed away from the table with such force the juice glass tumbled over, spreading a pale orange puddle across the dark wood. "That's the way it starts. Angry faces. Then all the yelling."

Jenny moved toward Alicia, but Scott was quicker. He grabbed his sister and held her. "We're not going to yell. Are we, Mom?"

"No." She grabbed a handful of paper napkins and dropped them in the middle of the spilled juice, then sat down in Alicia's chair.

Alicia disengaged herself from Scott and came over. Jenny pulled her onto her lap and pushed a wisp of blonde hair off the girl's damp cheek. "You can go with Dad by yourself," she said. "It'll be fun."

"But I've never been to a cabin before. What if I don't like it?"

"You will," Scott said. "Trust me. I've been there. They have this great lodge. With all kinds of games and a big-screen TV. And the best part ... You know what the best part is?"

Alicia shook her head.

"They have horses."

"Really?" Excitement replaced tears in those incredible eyes. "Can I ride one?"

Jenny didn't have the heart to tell her that Ralph was terrified of horses. "I'm sure that can be arranged."

After the kids left for school, Jenny cleared the rest of the breakfast mess, then called Ralph at the motel. He sounded groggy when he answered. Probably still operating on California time. "You want me to call back later?" she asked.

"No. What's up?"

She gave him an edited version of the morning with the kids, and he seemed genuinely disappointed about Scott not being able to come.

After settling the specifics of picking up Alicia, Jenny remembered the excitement about the horses. "I told her you'd take her horseback riding."

"Why'd you do that? You know I—"

"I did it because this is the first time I've seen her excited in months. Surely you can get past your fear for a couple of hours."

"Okay. Okay. Whatever."

"Go back to sleep, Ralph."

Jenny hung up the phone and grabbed her purse and jacket. Mitchell always worried when she was late.

———

"These bleachers are freezing." Caitlin stood, took off her long crimson scarf and made a pad out of it, then sat back down. "Tell me again why we're out here and not someplace warm."

Scott put his arm around her and pulled her close. "I like the privacy out here."

Caitlin motioned to the groundskeeper who was clearing dead leaves that the wind had plastered to the boards behind the goalposts. "Not totally."

"He's cool. He won't bother us."

She unwrapped a chocolate snack cake and offered him half. "You looked upset this morning. Something happen?"

Scott devoured the cake in two bites. "You could say that. My dad showed up last night."

"Really?"

Scott nodded. "And he seemed really pissed at my mom."

"About what?" Caitlin brushed crumbs off the front of her jacket.

"I don't know."

"Did you call him again?"

"I haven't talked to him in two weeks. That's when I told him everything was cool. You know. When Mom and I had that little talk, and she asked me to chill for a while."

"Then why did he come?"

Scott shrugged.

Caitlin nudged him with her elbow. "He had to have a reason."

"This morning the reason turned out to be a trip to my grandparents' cabin." He paused for a moment, then continued. "But I don't think that was the reason last night."

"Why not?"

"Because of the way he acted." Scott laughed. "He looked so much like me when I get in Mom's face, I couldn't believe it."

A gust of wind tossed Caitlin's hair, and she snuggled closer. "When is this trip?"

"Today. He's picking Alicia up after school."

"Just Alicia?"

Scott nodded. "I begged off."

"Thought you wanted to get away from here. From your Mom."

"I did. I do. I think." He paused and watched the groundskeeper haul a large black trash bag toward the other side of the field. "Although I'm not always sure about that."

Scott sighed and turned to Caitlin. "But I also figured sticking around would solve my other problem."

"What problem?"

"Following Mom without having to worry about Alicia."

"I told you I'd watch her."

"I know. But this is better. No complications for you."

Caitlin was quiet for so long, Scott wondered if he'd upset her somehow. He didn't mean to. Ever. But sometimes she had the weirdest reaction to things. Got mad when he least expected it.

"You could've consulted me before deciding what's best for me."

*Oh, God. Here it comes.* Scott took a deep breath. "Think about it, Caitlin. It's not like it would be a simple thing to sneak out, especially that next-morning complication."

She sighed and wadded up the cake wrapper, then stuffed it in her jacket pocket. "You could have just asked me first."

"Okay. Next time I'll ask."

Again, a silence strained between them. Scott scuffed at the edge of the bleacher with the toe of his sneaker, wondering if he'd be better off just keeping his mouth shut. Don't pile any more fuel on a potential flare-up.

Caitlin leaned back, resting her elbows on the metal rung

behind them. When she spoke, it was without a trace of anger. "What are you going to do if you find out it's true? What you suspect?"

He let out a soft sigh of relief. "I don't know."

"What if you get caught?"

"Cha. I won't do anything."

She sat up. "Maybe I should come with you. Just in case."

"In case what? I'm going to watch her. That's all."

"And what? You're going to make yourself invisible so they can't see you back?"

Her tone rankled, and Scott checked his rising anger. "Forget it. I don't want to have to worry about you."

"Like I won't worry?"

He blew out a breath in exasperation. "It's not the same."

"It's absolutely the same." Caitlin looked away quickly. "Honestly, sometimes you just don't get it."

"Get what?"

She stood and grabbed her scarf in one swift move, flinging it around her neck. "Anything." She stomped toward the ground, each footstep making the metal ring in the cold air.

Scott called after her. "Hey, I'm sorry."

There was the briefest of hesitations in her stride, then she pushed on, her scarf trailing behind in a red stream.

*What the hell was that all about?* But even as the question formed, Scott was pretty sure he knew the answer. Not that he liked the answer. Maybe Caitlin did overreact because of the way her mother treated her. Like an imbecile who wasn't capable of the simplest responsibility. But that didn't give him the right to act like her feelings weren't as important as his.

"Caitlin. Wait." He scrambled off the bleachers, but she was already across the field. "I said I'm sorry. What do you want?"

She turned to face him. "Sometimes sorry's not enough."

He stopped and watched her disappear through the entrance. Well, the hell with her. If she didn't understand, then too bad.

He tried to maintain that justification, but even as the words reverberated through his head, he knew they were all wrong. He was acting like an ass. Almost like he had to provoke her just to mess things up. Tears threatened, and he swiped angrily at his face. *No fucking way am I going to cry.*

---

Jenny rapped on the door so hard one of her knuckles split in the cold air. She sucked on the blood while she waited for Carol to answer. When she did, her face registered a mixture of surprise and wariness. "I didn't expect—"

"I'm sure you didn't." Jenny pushed past her friend, then turned to face her in the spacious foyer. "I can't believe you called Ralph."

"I was worried." Carol let the door close, cutting off the outside light, but made no move toward the large living area where the afternoon sun streamed through tall windows.

"Calling me would have been cheaper."

"You haven't exactly been accessible of late." Carol pushed past her and walked through the living room into the kitchen.

Jenny followed. "I answer my goddamn phone."

Her friend turned and faced her, leaning one hip against the counter. "Really? The last three times I called the house one of the kids answered. And your cell always goes to voice-mail. Do you even check your voicemail?"

Jenny swallowed, trying not to be the first to break eye contact. "Sorry. I don't, but I go to work every day. You can catch me there."

Carol didn't respond, and for a moment Jenny forgot she'd come here to confront her friend. "What's up, Carol?"

"There's talk."

"What kind of talk?" Even as she asked the question, Jenny wasn't sure she wanted to hear the answer.

"That you're hanging with the wrong kind of—" Carol stopped abruptly and shook her head. "Jeez. Listen to me. That's something I should be saying to George's kids. Not to my best friend."

Jenny had to stifle a manic urge to laugh. *Should I tell her about George*? "We've already had this conversation, Carol. I've told you as much as I can. You'll just have to trust me."

"I was trying to. Until Millie told me her granddaughter saw you out on the street the other night with some lowlife scumbags. At first, she wasn't sure it was you. Didn't recognize you. But she was curious and followed. Saw you get into your car."

Carol averted her gaze. "You do have to admit your car is very distinctive."

The words hit Jenny like a blast of winter sleet, and for a moment she was afraid to move. To speak. *How the hell do I get out of this one*? "It's not what it appears."

"Then pray tell, what is it?"

Jenny walked over to look out the kitchen window. Carol's pool shimmered in the afternoon sunlight, and a few orange oak leaves skittered across the water, driven by the harsh wind. *Why didn't I just wait until tomorrow like I'd planned? Or better yet, just skip coming over here at all?* She took a deep breath and faced her friend. "You know I can't."

"Then I guess this discussion's over." Carol turned and started walking toward the front door.

Jenny didn't move. How dare Carol just dismiss her like an unwanted salesperson? "We've always trusted each other,

Carol. And we had this discussion before. And no matter what you thought, I never dreamed you'd rat me out."

That stopped Carol in mid-stride.

"Yeah. It's about Ralph." Jenny took a step forward. "For God's sake, Carol. He could take my kids. Did you even consider that?"

Carol didn't say anything for what seemed like forever. She walked to the door, opened it, then slammed it shut again, turning to face Jenny again. "Did you bring my guns back?"

It took a moment for her to adjust to the sharp turn. "What?"

Carol crossed her arms across her stomach. "My guns."

"You've thoroughly fucked up my life, and you're worried about your guns."

"No, Jenny. I really couldn't give a rat's ass about my guns. I'm worried about you."

A sentiment in those words almost broke her, but Jenny quickly averted her gaze and took a deep breath. "I'm okay."

"Are you?" Carol reached out to touch her arm, but Jenny pulled away. The gesture would be her undoing. She knew it would. She ached to tell her friend everything. About the bad guys. About Steve. About how scared she was when she thought about what was going to happen on Friday. About how much more afraid she was that she'd alienated everyone she loved beyond a point of no return.

But she couldn't do that. Not now. Somehow, she had to get out of this conversation. Then hold her raw emotions together for just a few more days. She pushed past Carol and opened the door.

When she was outside, she turned back for just a moment. "I'm sorry. It's... That's all I can say. I'm sorry."

Jenny made it home in time to throw some things in a duffel for Alicia before Ralph showed up. A few minutes later, Alicia bounded through the door, dumped her book bag in the middle of the living room and ran down the hall.

"Hey," Jenny called. Alicia stopped. Jenny nudged the bag with her toe. "Take this to your room."

With an Oscar-caliber show of theatrics, the girl came back and slung the bag over her shoulder.

"Nice move," Ralph said.

"If I didn't stay on top of them, they'd move their beds out here."

Jenny heard the back door open, and a moment later Scott walked into the living room. He mumbled greetings then started toward his room. Something in his slouch, more pronounced than usual, set off an internal alarm. Now what? Could things get more complicated?

Jenny took a step toward him. "Something wrong, Scott?"

"Nope." He didn't pause in his forward progress.

"It's not too late to come with us," Ralph said.

This time Scott did stop and glance over his shoulder. "Wish I could, but..."

He finished the sentence with a shrug, then continued on, almost colliding with Alicia as she came running out of her room. "I'm ready," she said.

In the few minutes it took to bundle Alicia and her things in the car, Ralph didn't speak, and Jenny was just as glad. There wasn't anything else that needed to be said. But he did turn to her before sliding in the driver's seat. "You be careful."

Just like Carol's sentiment, this one touched her deep inside. *I've spent all this time trying to be tough, and I'm just a marshmallow.* She managed a smile and a nod. "See you Sunday."

Jenny stood in the driveway and watched the car pull out, returning Alicia's farewell wave. Scott stood in the doorway, then turned to go back in the house as she approached. He'd disappeared down the hall by the time she stepped into the living room. So much for an evening of quality time together.

He did honor her with his presence for dinner, though it could hardly be called a pleasant social experience since he wolfed the pepper steak like a man who'd been deprived of food for a month. When he was finished, he wiped the tomato sauce from his lips with a napkin, then pushed away from the table. "Better get to work on that paper."

It was the only thing he'd said to her since she'd called him to dinner, the words rendered doubly irritating because they begged no response. A simple declaration that was benign on the surface. But something told her it wasn't so temperate below. She thought about calling him back to clear his dishes, then said, "The hell with it." She didn't need more of his surly mood. She needed a long, hot bath and maybe fifty drinks before she could even think about sleeping tonight.

# TWENTY-NINE

JENNY'S STOMACH twisted as she surveyed the room, which as full of so many cops they could have manned an entire season of all the *Law & Order* shows. It didn't help that sleep had eluded her well into the witching hour, and she'd needed way too much coffee to get through the morning at work. Thank goodness Mitchell hadn't pressed her about why she was leaving early this afternoon. If he had, she doubted she had the emotional stamina to support the lie of the teacher conference.

Steve drew her toward the table, making introductions as they passed various people. No way would she remember names, but she would remember how able they all looked, the women as much as the men. Another coup for women's lib.

She recognized Linda and Burroughs and gave them each a nod as Steve pulled out a vacant chair for her. Gonzales stood at the head of the table and motioned toward a bucket that held cans of soda and bottles of water under a blanket of ice. "Help yourself."

Jenny grabbed water and swore her stomach relaxed at the

prospect of no more coffee. When this was over, she might give it up entirely. Then again...

"Okay," Gonzales said. "Let's get up to speed."

He shuffled the stack papers in front of him. "Operation Sting commences tonight at 1800 hours." He paused and looked at the Sheriff. "Tubbs, have your men in place one hour prior."

The beefy man nodded, and Gonzales motioned to Burroughs. "The bugs in and working?"

Burroughs nodded. "Coming through loud and clear."

Jenny remembered asking Burroughs about this when he'd first mentioned it as part of the plan weeks ago. She wondered why they didn't just use the bugs to gather evidence and skip the sting entirely. To his credit, he hadn't laughed, giving her a brief overview of what constitutes admissible evidence.

"And your men are sure the curtains along that glass wall are not closed at night?" Gonzales asked.

Burroughs nodded. "They've watched for two months. Barring some fluke that we can't prepare for, we should be able to see in just fine."

Gonzales turned to Jenny. "That's our backup in case the bugs fail for some reason. If we lose the audio, we'll come in as soon as we see the exchange being made."

She nodded.

Gonzales motioned to Steve. "You got communications set up?"

Steve rose and stepped over to a dry-erase board displaying a rough sketch of a map. He marked the spot where Jenny was meeting the perps that night. "There are only two main roads out of town that lead to this intersection of 720 and 423. We'll have men here and here." He paused to put an x at several places. "I'll be here with Linda." Again, he made a mark. "We're using the old 'car broken down' ruse, but hey, whatever works. We'll all be in touch via transmitters. Including the county and federal guys who will be up in the tree line beyond the perimeter of the property."

"What about the outside guards?"

Gonzales directed that question to Burroughs, who said, "We'll take them out as soon as the subject enters the premises."

Jenny winced, and Burroughs shook his head. "It's not what you think," he said. "We've got stun guns."

Jenny nodded to acknowledge the explanation, but she still found the idea distasteful. Burroughs was so casual about it. Like he was talking about picking up his dry cleaning on the way home from work.

"Okay." Now Gonzales turned his attention to her. "You ready for this?"

She swallowed hard and then nodded, not trusting her voice to make coherent words. Gonzales reached into a satchel and pulled out a two-inch thick parcel wrapped in brown paper. He slid it across the table to her. "Here's the money."

Jenny just looked at the package for a moment, shocked at the size. Was that really a hundred thousand dollars? Steve nudged her. "Go ahead. You've got to touch it sometime."

The comment drew a few chuckles as Jenny took the money. She couldn't wait to get it into the safe at the shop.

After running through an approximate timetable for later that night, Gonzales rapped his knuckles on the table. "When it's over, I'll come in with the cavalry and clean up the mess you make."

His attempt at humor raised a few chuckles, but Jenny didn't join in. She was too busy telling her stomach not to reject the half a bottle of water she'd consumed.

Steve touched her arm on the way out. "Holding up okay?"

Despite the doubts spinning through her head, and the anxiety tying her stomach in knots, she nodded.

"Things okay at home?"

"For the time being. Ralph left with Alicia yesterday. Scott should be no problem."

Jenny paused by the back door, a small part of her reluctant to take the next step. Steve jingled some coins in his pocket, avoiding her gaze, then he looked at her. "Don't take any risks. Just follow the plan."

"Yes, sir." She gave him a mock salute.

"I'm serious. We stick to the plan and nobody gets hurt."

For a second she almost asked him about the guards. Wouldn't being 'taken out' hurt just a bit? But she pushed the impulse aside. This wasn't the time for an ethics discussion.

Instead, she gave him a small smile of reassurance. Then she tucked the parcel of money into her briefcase and donned sunglasses and a wide-brimmed hat. "I'll be glad when I can just be me again."

"Soon," he said. "Soon."

Jenny played the words like a mantra as she slipped out the back door of the station. Only a few more hours and the whole mess would be over.

The mid-afternoon sun slanted through the trees, almost as if assigned to justify her costume. Or was that just a flighty turn of mind? She shook the silly thought aside and walked the few blocks to where she'd parked her car. She didn't see any sign of Leon or Frank. But then she didn't expect to at this time of the afternoon. Leon would be across town plying his trade closer to the school. And Frank? She had no idea what Frank did during the daytime. Maybe he never even came out of whatever hole he lived in.

Jenny tossed the hat and sunglasses into the back seat, then slid behind the wheel and dropped the briefcase on the passenger seat. She started the engine and locked all the doors. The thought of something happening to the money made her palms damp with sweat.

At the shop, she hurried in the front door, a gust of wind blowing in on her heels. Mitchell was just coming out of the back and he stopped. "Didn't expect you back today."

"Just have a few things to take care of. You can go ahead and make those deliveries. I'll lock up."

Mitchell picked up an arrangement of white and red mums. "How'd the conference go?"

For a moment Jenny was blank. What conference? Then she remembered the excuse. "Uh, it was fine."

She avoided his eyes as she walked through the split in the counter.

"Something wrong, Jen?"

"No." She tried a smile.

"I don't mean to pry," Mitchell said. "But I remember you were worried about Scott's grades."

"He's doing fine now. Actually, this conference was for Alicia. We, uh, went over the work she's missing."

"Oh."

Jenny was afraid that her face was going to crack under the effort to keep the smile. But she had to admire that quick bit of improvising. It seemed to satisfy Mitchell, and he headed toward the front door with the flowers.

"I'll bring the other one out for you." Jenny grabbed a small arrangement of pink roses and baby's breath and followed Mitchell. If he noticed her lugging the briefcase along, he didn't say anything. He secured the arrangements in the containers in the delivery van and drove off.

Jenny went back in. Locked all the doors and stashed the money in the safe. She felt much better after the lock clicked in place when she spun the dial.

Now all she had to do was muddle through supper with Scott and get out of the house without too much protest.

---

A chill permeated the shop, and Jenny shivered. She always hated coming here after dark to take care of some forgotten business. Why did it seem to only smell like a funeral parlor at night? Did the darkness do something to the flowers?

It was worse tonight because she couldn't even turn on a light.

Using a penlight to illuminate the dial, Jenny worked the combination on her safe and opened it. Inside, the wrapped stacks of hundred-dollar bills rested on the clutter of papers. She pulled out the money and stuffed it into a large money-belt strapped to her waist. Then she hefted the small gun she'd managed to avoid returning to Carol and again considered the wisdom of taking it. "Stick to the plan." That's what Steve had said, and he'd explode if he knew she wasn't. But then he didn't, did he? And she wouldn't feel so vulnerable if she had the gun along.

Ending the mental debate, she shoved the weapon under her waistband behind the belt. There was something to be said for skin-tight jeans. The gun fit snug between denim and skin and was covered by the money belt.

She shrugged into her leather jacket, leaving it open to reveal the tank top that was so tight it didn't even have a wrinkle. Could she count on that being enough of a distraction that they'd miss the gun when they searched her? She didn't even want to think about the consequences if it was discovered.

Making her way through the gloom to the door, Jenny slipped out, locked up, and headed toward her car. She had her hand on the door handle when she heard a rustle of movement in the trees beside the shop. She whirled. Was someone hiding in the shadows?

She couldn't see anyone, but she reached for her gun. *No fucking way am I going to be robbed.*

Another rustle of movement and she pulled the weapon free. Then Scott stepped out of the shadow.

"Jeez." Jenny shoved the gun behind the money belt, hoping Scott missed it in the darkness. "What the hell are you doing here?"

"What are you doing, Mom?"

How had he found her? Was this some kind of sign? Was God trying to tell her something with all these complications?

Probably not. Why would God bother with a person who'd long ago given up on believing?

But still she couldn't formulate a response and faced her son in this bizarre standoff for more minutes than she could afford to spend. She had to get him out of the way. "Scott. You have to go home. Now."

He crossed his arms across his chest. "No way. You talk. Then maybe I'll leave."

Jenny didn't know whether to hit him or laugh. He was trying so hard to be a tough guy, but compared to the real tough guys, his stance was almost a cartoon.

She glanced at her watch. There wasn't time to laugh or to talk. "Just go," she said in what she hoped was her firmest 'mom' voice. "I'll explain it all tomorrow."

Scott didn't move, but she was running out of time. She turned and headed toward her car.

Now he moved, stepping toward her. "Talk to me. Or I'll just follow you."

Jenny reached to open her car door, then paused. His threat was without substance. How could he even think he could follow on foot? It was ludicrous. But then, he'd been resourceful enough to find her here. And she certainly didn't want him wandering through town and stumbling on her meet.

She checked her watch again. Shit! How late could she be before Frank and Leon gave up on her?

"Okay. This is the deal, Scott. I'm going to give you the condensed version of what's going on. There's not time for more. No questions. No discussion until I come home later. Agreed?"

After what seemed like forever, he nodded.

"Part of what you've suspected is true. I have been meeting with drug dealers."

He opened his mouth to speak, and Jenny held up her hand to stop him. "I have exactly ten minutes before the whole deal implodes. So, shut up."

He did.

"I'm working with the cops to bring down a major distributor, and it's happening tonight."

She stepped closer. "I need for you to go home. Stay there. And you can say whatever you need to when I get back. I'm doing this for Michael."

That stopped him for a beat, then he asked, "Is it dangerous?"

Her first instinct was to reassure him. But her gut told her he wouldn't buy one more lie. "Yes."

"Then I'm going with—"

She stopped him with a wave of her hand. "You. Are. Going. Home."

"But what if you—"

She touched his lips. "I won't. I'll come home tonight."

It seemed to take forever, but he finally nodded. She squeezed his arm. "Later."

He didn't move, but time was wasting. She ran to the car, jumped in and started it. As she pulled out of the parking lot, she could see him still standing there. *Please, God, let me keep my promise.* Then she laughed. *Like He's really listening to you.*

Jenny pushed the speed limit to the max as she drove across town, but at least she didn't have to worry about a speeding ticket. The cops were all occupied elsewhere. But she did have some concern for other traffic and pedestrians.

She checked her watch again. Five minutes after eight. Would they wait? Perspiration trickled down her back as she parked several blocks from the meeting place. Then she got out, locked the car and hoofed it to the abandoned strip mall.

Relief flooded her when she saw figures at the end of the block. At first, she thought it was just Frank and Leon, but then she saw another man lounging against the side of the old laundromat. She hadn't expected a third man. Who was he, and why was he here?

For a moment panic seized her. Was this the main man? Were they going to do the deal here and not at the ranch?

Then the man stepped out of the shadows, and she realized he wasn't 'the man.' Burroughs had said the ringleader was Cuban. This guy was so white he almost glowed in the pale illumination from the streetlamp.

Jenny put a little sashay into her walk as she closed the distance and graced the men with a smile. Leon smiled back, but the Day-Glo man didn't. Neither did Frank.

"You're late," he said.

"I'm here now." Jenny fought to keep the smile in place and not dissolve under the intensity of his gaze. His expression didn't change. Just a flicker of something in his eyes that told her nothing.

*I'm screwed.*

The moment seemed to stretch forever, then a hint of a smile touched his lips. She let out her breath and tried not to drop in a faint. Then he made a vague hand gesture. "You got the money?"

Jenny opened her jacket to reveal the money belt. She didn't miss the hesitation as his eyes traveled down her chest to her waist. A shudder followed the path his eyes had taken, but she ignored it. *Just play the game. That's all it is.*

"What else you got there?"

She took off the jacket, letting him see there was no room for anything between the tank top and her. Frank motioned to the Day-Glo man with a nod and he stepped over. Another shudder passed through her as he patted her down, lingering a little too long on the insides of her thighs.

Swallowing some bile, she glared at him. "Don't worry. That doesn't bother me a bit."

The man took a half step back. "She's clean."

"Check the belt."

Jenny put one arm across her stomach. "Been ripped off once. Not going to happen again." She raised her chin. "You get to count the money when I see the goods."

They faced each other in silence, then Frank gestured to the other man. "Look, but don't touch."

Jenny unzipped the belt and held it open so he could clearly see the money. She held her breath for the entire time it took him to step close and glance inside. *If he touches it and feels the gun, I'm dead.*

His expression reflected a desire to disobey Frank, and she forced herself not to look away in panic. "Nice stack," he said.

A mixture of relief and revulsion washed over her as he again let his eyes linger on her breasts.

"Pick your dick up off the ground and let's move." Frank stepped away from the building and headed toward the corner.

Jenny pulled her jacket closed and followed Leon and the other man. Frank stopped at a black Lexus and opened the door on the driver's side. "Get in the back with Leon," he said to Jenny, then turned to the other man. "You ride shotgun."

After they were settled, Frank started the car and eased into the street. Traffic was no problem. A battered white pickup was the only vehicle in sight, and it turned off a block before it reached them.

Main Street looked lonely in its emptiness as they drove slowly east. Jenny found some security in knowing that the deputies posted at the intersection of Main and the loop to 720 couldn't miss the car.

The other little niggle of worry she pushed back into the recesses of her mind. She had to trust that Scott had obeyed her and gone home.

# THIRTY

STEVE HUNCHED by the rear tire of the car that was pulled to the side of Highway 720; a spare rested on the ground next to him. Linda sat in the passenger seat, playing the role of the patient wife. With the lug-wrench in hand, the charade of a flat tire was complete. Traffic was so light they'd been here close to an hour and only had to wave off one car whose driver slowed to offer help.

"Anything yet?" The question crackled through his two-way radio, but he recognized the voice of Burroughs, who was stationed with two of his men near the gate of the ranch.

Steve clicked back. "Nothing."

A few minutes later another voice came over the radio. "Coming your way. Black Lexus."

"Roger."

Steve stared into the darkness until a glow of headlights approached from the Loop. He keyed his connection to Burroughs. "I think we have action."

The light grew brighter as a vehicle approached and paused at the stop sign. The glare from the lights prevented

Steve from seeing what kind of car it was, but an instinct told him this was it. That instinct was proven right as the car crossed 720 and slid past him like some great dark beast, heading down the road in the direction of the ranch.

Steve activated his radio. "We have contact. ETA fifteen minutes."

"Roger."

As soon as the car was far enough down the other road, Steve quickly threw the spare tire and tools into the yawning cavern of the trunk and slammed it closed. Then he slid into the driver's seat and started the engine. "Ready to rock and roll?"

Linda snapped her seatbelt closed. "Let's go."

---

As the car turned off the highway onto the sweeping gravel drive, the ornate iron gates swung open and they passed under the large metal arch. Jenny wondered if Frank had some kind of remote that had opened the gates. She also wondered where the DEA guys were, but she kept her eyes straight ahead, lest some move on her part create suspicion.

The car rolled slowly down the drive, the crunch of tires on stone abnormally loud in the still night. But maybe it just sounded that way because all her nerves were on high alert.

Finally, they pulled into the half circle in front of the house and stopped. When Frank turned off the engine, the silence was so complete Jenny could hear the rasp of her own breathing. Frank tapped the horn twice and turned on the interior light. Not expecting the flash of light, Jenny was momentarily blinded. What the...?

She focused on the window facing the house, hoping some of her night vision would return. In the dimness, she saw what looked like two men step out on the porch and flank the door. They each held something dark in their hands that she suspected were guns. A third man, taller than the others, walked to the car. When he was close enough, their eyes met briefly, and Jenny was surprised to see an expression colder and harder than Frank's. *I'm gonna fuckin' die.*

A chill swept through her as the man headed around the back of the car. She shuddered and clutched her jacket tight across her chest.

Leon shifted beside her. "You cold?"

The concern for her comfort was so out of place, Jenny almost broke into manic laughter. It also made her take a second look at Leon. At that moment he looked like any ordinary young man, not some evil monster corrupting society. She wondered if he'd been in school with Michael. He was almost young enough. Could have even played football with him.

Something hardened in his eyes, and that image of innocent youth vanished. Jenny shook her head in response to his question, then turned to face forward.

*Don't forget for one minute that he's one of the bad guys.*

She heard a light tap on the window next to Frank. He rolled his window down, and there was a whispered exchange. Then Frank motioned to the Day-Glo man to get out. He did and opened Jenny's door. "Come."

She slid out, and he put a hand on her arm. "Wait."

Frank and Leon and the third man formed a human triangle around Jenny and the Day-Glo man and started walking toward the steps to the house.

Jenny repressed a shudder as they neared the two men by the door. Except for the slight movement of eyes sweeping the area, they could have been statues. The tall man at the point of the triangle opened both of the heavy, wooden doors, then stepped in and motioned the others to follow.

Under any other circumstances, Jenny would have gawked like some tourist as they walked through an entry hall that could have graced a museum. The paintings on the wall were probably the originals of some that Jenny had only seen pictures of, and they passed a Louis XIV marble-inlaid table that was probably worth more than her house.

The man gestured toward an arched doorway that opened into a spacious room that had one wall entirely of glass. As advertised in the briefing, the curtain had been pulled all the way back, allowing Jenny a glimpse of a pale blue illumination she guessed was from a swimming pool. Otherwise, the glass was as black as the night sky beyond the patio. She hoped the feds could see in better than she could see out.

She glanced around, noting that the room was sparsely furnished. One corner hosted a portable bar cordoned off with a serving counter. The wall opposite the windows had floor-to-ceiling shelves of random sizes, and she caught a quick glimpse of museum-quality sculptures. A small table with a marble chess set sat in front of that wall, two chairs positioned for players. A few other occasional chairs were scattered throughout, but the focal point was a dark table in the middle of the room that was nearly as large as the Oriental rug it rested on. There was a doorway slightly to the left of the table and a large sideboard directly behind it.

A man sat in a chair perfectly centered at one side of the table. He had thick black hair and wore a stony expression with his silk shirt and gold chains. Jenny figured him for the Cuban. Had to be. Even seated, he commanded the room without movement or sound.

Two men flanked him. Much like the men who'd guarded the front door, they neither moved nor appeared to even breathe, and for a wild moment Jenny wondered if they cloned guards here.

The Cuban motioned her forward. "You the little lady who wants to do business?"

Afraid her voice would come out in a squeak, Jenny nodded.

"You have the money?"

She opened her jacket and tapped the money belt. "In here."

"Show me."

She unzipped one section and pulled a few bills partway out so the denomination was clearly visible. "They're all the same. Crisp new bills." she said. "Now I see the goods."

When she'd practiced that line a hundred and one times with Burroughs coaching, it had felt strained. Today it felt okay, and she hated to think that it did because she was getting used to this. She'd sworn she'd never get used to this business of drugs.

The Cuban nodded to the guard on his left. The man stepped back to the sideboard, picked up an old-fashioned wooden roll-top breadbox, and carried it over. After placing it on the table, careful not to scratch the gleaming wood, he opened the box and pulled out a plastic bag filled with white powder.

Tapping the box, the Cuban flashed a smile. "The bread of life. Clever, no?"

A chorus of chuckles followed, and Jenny wondered what was supposed to be funny.

"What? You don't have a sense of humor?"

The words had been mild, but the hard glint in obsidian eyes sent a chill skittering down her spine. The tension was so thick in the room she could've spread it on toast and eaten it. She remembered what Burroughs had said about deals going sour over the silliest details.

She forced the flicker of a smile. "I thought the fun started after the business was done."

For a moment, the Cuban didn't react, and Jenny tensed. If weapons were drawn, would she even have a chance? Then he surprised her by laughing. "I like this *chica*," he said. "She no pussy."

He glanced at the other men who obliged with more hollow chuckles. Then he pulled out an ornate silver pocket knife, made a small slit in the bag and pushed it closer to Jenny. "Premium stuff."

She stepped to the table and dipped into it with the tip of a finger the way Burroughs had taught her. During the training she'd balked about this part, but he'd assured her that one little dab would not an addict make.

After touching the powder to her tongue, Jenny nodded at the Cuban. He motioned to the man on his left who pulled three more bags out of the breadbox. "You slide the money to me," the Cuban said, "and he gives you the rest."

Managing to still the tremble of her fingers, Jenny took the money out of the leather pouch and stacked it on the table. She hoped like hell the guys in the white hats were in place and were listening to this. They hadn't rehearsed what she should do if they didn't come busting in when the exchange was being made.

---

Steve hunkered with Linda and the two DEA guys in a high stand of grass about twenty yards from the edge of the driveway. As soon as they got the signal from the deputies on the west side of the house, they were to take out the men on the porch.

Well, the feds would take them out, Steve decided. He could interrogate the hell out of a suspect and brawl with the best of them, but he could barely shoot well enough to keep his badge. That's why he carried a Magnum. Hard to miss with a piece like that, but it also announced to the entire world that a shot had been fired. Linda beat him at the range all the time, but even so, they'd agreed to leave the outside shooting to the snipers and their special weapons. They'd get their chance inside the house.

"Now." A hushed voice spoke over the radio. The feds stood in unison and popped off shots, probably before their presence even registered to the men by the front door. Silencers muted the sound to a dull thump, and Steve and Linda were up running the moment the guards slumped in dark heaps on the porch.

The feds ran with them, and the men launched their bodies at the double door, the lock giving under the impact. When the doors slammed into the walls Linda dashed in and took the first cover position as the men rushed forward.

---

As the sound of the crash reverberated through the great room, the men froze for the briefest of moments, then the Cuban rose, pushing his chair back so hard it toppled. "You bitch."

The man next to him reached inside his coat, and Jenny dropped to the floor, rolling between two chairs and under the table. Steve had told her to look for the safest spot, and this seemed to be it. Then again, maybe not. She could see Frank and Leon running toward the table, expressions of grim determination hardening on their faces. She felt a spasm in her bladder.

*Oh, shit. I'm dead. And I'm going to wet myself.*

Would she even have a chance if she pulled her weapon?

She reached behind the money belt and touched the smooth butt of the gun, then hesitated when a voice called out, "Grab the merchandise."

She heard a rustle of movement, then saw feet and legs scurry around the far end of the table and disappear. *Where are the rest of them?*

"What about the broad?"

"Denny'll take care of her."

As she heard more movement behind her, another spasm tore through her bladder. *God. Please don't let me wet myself.*

She shook off the crazy thought and looked over her shoulder. Nobody there. Must have gone through that doorway.

*Okay. That's good.*

*Unless Denny is one of those other guards.*

*Where did they go?*

Scraping her cheek on the rough pile of the carpeting, she twisted again to face forward and saw the men move quickly toward the doorway, drawing weapons as they ran. Despite the fact that they were heading away from her, Jenny still felt the chill of vulnerability. One of them could cover the door and the other simply turn and shoot her.

Should she stay put or try to find better cover? But where?

Trying to still the incessant drumbeat of her heart, she looked around. Could she make it to that corner bar? If she could get behind that half-wall...

A sudden burst of gunfire thundered through the room and answered that question. Unadulterated fear flattened her to the floor. Did that mean the good guys had made it in?

She inched forward to get a better view.

Not a white hat in sight.

"Give it up," a voice called. "The place is surrounded."

Was it Steve? It sounded like Steve. The two men pumped more bullets down the hall, and Jenny realized they had the officers pinned. For a moment, she wanted to give in to the little girl deep inside that was trembling and calling for her mother to come rescue her. Then she realized that nobody was going to rescue her. If she wanted out of this mess, she'd damn well better do something.

Inching forward, she eased the gun out of her waistband and checked the positions of the men. Which one?

*It doesn't matter. As soon as you fire, you've got about three seconds to get off another shot.*

Taking a deep breath and letting it out slowly the way the gunsmith had told her, Jenny cradled the weapon and sighted down the barrel. Then her resolve faltered and the gun wavered. If she did this, she would never be the same again.

*If you don't do this, you'll be dead.*

She steadied her arm and pointed the gun at the back of the man on the left. She wanted to close her eyes. Desperately needed to close her eyes so she wouldn't watch herself kill a man, but shooting blind was not a wise option.

The report almost deafened her, and in that near soundless void, she saw the man slump to the floor. Bile rose in her throat, and she swallowed as the other man turned, gun coming around in an arc.

He fired on the swing, and Jenny felt the vibration of the bullet hitting the table edge above her head. She quickly returned fire, but panic obliterated what she'd learned, and her shot went wide.

For a fraction of a second, all she saw was the barrel of his gun pointed directly at her, then she caught a flash of movement in the doorway. A man...Steve? She couldn't be sure. The figure was a blur as he rolled several times before landing on his stomach, a very large gun jerking in his hand.

Now the other gun was no longer pointed at her.

# THIRTY-ONE

THE DEAD MAN slid down the wall, leaving a wet trail of red on the pristine white paint like a macabre work of Impressionistic art. Steve scanned the rest of the room. Another man lay unmoving on the other side of the doorway. Had they gotten that one in that earlier exchange? And what about Jenny? Where was she? Had they taken her hostage?

Then he saw her. Under the table. Not moving.

*Oh, my God.*

He quickly checked the rest of the room to make sure all the perps were down, or gone, then went to the prone figure. When he saw her eyes, wide with some kind of emotion that seemed deeper than fear, he touched her cheek, "Jenny?"

She blinked, but didn't answer, her hands clutched so tightly around the butt of a gun the tendons stood out. *What the—?*

He followed the angle the barrel was pointing, and dread kicked him in the stomach. She'd shot the other guard? Where the hell had she gotten the gun? *Of all the stupid—*

The recrimination died as he realized she was still frozen in place. He placed his large hand over hers. It was like touching ice. "Give me the gun, Jenny."

Still she didn't move.

"Are you hurt?"

"Inside."

Alarm gripped him. Where? There wasn't any blood—

Her fingers relaxed under his, not all at once, but slowly, like ice melting on a hot summer day. After a moment, he took the gun from her.

"I killed him." Pain replaced the look of abject terror in her eyes. "I killed him."

Momentarily Steve flashed back to his first use of deadly force. The memory was never easy to revisit and damned hard to forget. Linda was sure that difficulty contributed to his poor performance at the range. He was sure she was full of shit.

He touched Jenny's arm. "You have to come out of there."

"I know."

Still, she didn't move for several moments.

"Jenny," he said. "Come on. It's okay."

Eyes still wide with shock, Jenny scooted forward and allowed Steve to help her to stand. A great trembling seized her, and she faltered on weak legs. Steve supported her with one arm around her waist. "Do you want to sit down?"

"I need to get out of here."

"Sure."

Still holding her steady, Steve started toward the doorway. Jenny took a deep breath to hold back a wave of nausea as they stepped closer to the hall, her eyes riveted on the dead man and the smear of blood on the wall.

"You okay in there?" The voice was familiar. Burroughs?

"Yeah," Steve called out. "Just us good guys left."

Jenny didn't know if he'd injected that note of levity for her benefit or his. But it didn't work. She wasn't sure if anything would lift the weight of guilt and release the fists of iron that gripped her mind and her body.

Rounding the corner, she saw Burroughs and two other officers in flak jackets. She recognized Linda, who quickly stepped over, a look of concern creasing her forehead. "You hurt?"

"No." Jenny was surprised she could even get that one word out past the constriction in her throat. She had the horrible feeling that if she relaxed, the bile would come pouring out and she'd never stop retching.

"She's just shaken up," Steve said. "This being her first firefight and all."

Again, there was a note of levity in his voice, and a small part of Jenny wanted to respond to it. She was sure he was trying to ease the trauma, and she should be grateful. What she wanted, however, was numbness. No feelings.

Linda walked with them as they went outside where the night sky blazed with the red, yellow, and blue lights of county sheriff's cars, city patrol cars, and emergency vehicles. Linda spoke words that fell on deaf ears as Jenny focused on the flurry of activity in the vast yard. Paramedics tended to the wounded and loaded gurneys into ambulances, which then screamed their way out onto the highway that led to the nearest hospital. Police officers led handcuffed men to patrol cars and pushed them into back seats the way Jenny had seen so many times on television. But in real life the process was much rougher.

*Good. They deserve it.* She didn't even chastise herself for the hateful thought. They deserved much worse.

Steve stepped back and let Linda steer Jenny around the back of one of the patrol cars. There they came face to face with the Cuban. His look of pure hatred tore through her like a laser, and Jenny stopped, unable to move. Unable to look away.

Linda motioned to Steve to take Jenny's arm, then broke off to help the sheriff's deputy put the Cuban in the back of the car. Steve put his other hand at the small of Jenny's back and pushed her toward his car.

Gonzales stepped forward and intercepted them. He glanced at Steve, then held Jenny's gaze for a long moment. "Good job."

She stumbled for a response. What does one say at a time like this? Finally, she ducked her head in a semblance of a nod and let the pressure of Steve's hand move her down to the end of the long driveway.

Away from the lights and activity, the night took on a pastoral quality as moonlight filtered through a bank of clouds and the wind soughed through a small stand of pines. If she just focused on that, perhaps she could convince herself that none of those horrible things had happened in that house. But it didn't work. Her heart sat like a stone in her chest as she slid into Steve's car and fastened the seatbelt.

He pulled out onto the gray ribbon of highway, and Jenny concentrated on the hum of the tires, wishing for an emotional void. *Don't think. Don't remember.* But she couldn't stop her mind from playing that moment over and over again like an endless loop of film.

And what was she supposed to say to Scott when she got home? "Hi. It's Mom. I just shot somebody."

Steve gave her a quick glance. "You going to be okay?"

She wanted to laugh. "What is *okay* after this?"

"It'll come."

*Yeah. Right.*

He reached over and touched her hand, and she started to pull away.

"Don't," he said.

So, she didn't. He curled his fingers around hers and cradled them in warmth. She looked out the side window. She didn't want him to see her cry.

They rode the rest of the way in silence. A silence that was neither comforting nor discomforting. Just was.

Then Steve pulled to a stop next to her car. She slipped her hand out of his and grabbed the door handle. Steve looked over at her. "Want me to come with you?"

She considered for a moment, then shook her head and opened her door. His voice stopped her from stepping out. "You know you had to do it."

She sighed without looking at him. "Yeah. I know."

"Do you?"

She didn't answer. Couldn't answer.

Steve reached over and touched her shoulder. "Please let me help you."

She turned, tears ravaging her face. He started to pull her close, and she held him off with a hand to his chest. "No, Steve. Not now."

"When? When can I help you?"

She looked at his face, almost as ravaged as hers. What would it hurt to just lean into his offer and let whatever happens happen? But that impulse was so clichéd. So... revolting at this moment.

"I need to get home, Steve. Scott is waiting. Worrying. I need to go home."

"Sure." He released her and wiped a hand across his chin. "We'll give you some time. A few days. Then we need to debrief."

"Okay. Let me know when."

He nodded, and she slid out of his car and walked over to hers. He stayed until she buckled herself in before flicking his lights once and pulling out.

If not for Scott waiting at home, Jenny would have considered just staying there for however long it took for the fog to leave her mind and the weight to leave her heart. But she couldn't leave him hanging and anxious.

She put the key in the ignition and brought the engine to life. She drove home slowly, using every mental trick she could think of to banish the horrid events from her mind lest Scott look into her eyes and see the images.

As soon as Jenny pulled into the driveway, Scott ran down the front walk, a blur of motion in the shadows. Had he sat out on the porch the whole time?

He was at the car in a flash. "Mom? God... I was so worried."

She got out and slammed her door closed. "It's okay. I'm here now."

Before she could take a step, he grabbed her into an embrace so intense it was like he would never let her go again.

"What happened?" He took a step back and faced her. "Tell me everything."

"Can we go in first?"

"Sure."

Inside, Jenny tried to focus on all the things that were normal. Her muddy gardening shoes by the back door. A sale flyer from Brookshire's on the kitchen table. Crumbs on the counter. Hadn't she wiped it after making dinner earlier?

God. That seemed like a lifetime ago. She couldn't even remember what she'd made. How could she have forgotten something so simple and not be able to forget what she wanted to?

"Want some tea?"

Scott's question pulled her out of the confusion. She faced him. "You're going to make tea?"

"I'm capable, you know."

She wanted to say something funny back. Then maybe they could both laugh and dispel this terrible tension, but a sudden weakness hit her knees. If she didn't sit down, she was going to fall. She pulled a chair away from the table. "Tea would be good."

He put the kettle on the stove and pulled two mugs out of a cabinet. Then he stood for a moment, as if lost. "Uh, where are the tea bags?"

Again, she wished she had enough strength to laugh. She pointed to the squared-off metal container on the counter. "In the canister marked 'tea.'"

While Scott putzed at the stove, Jenny sifted through the details of the past few hours, deciding which ones to share with him. There was no question about what she wasn't going to talk about. She waited until he brought the mugs of steaming tea over and sat down. "So," he said. "Was it like on TV?"

*If only. On TV, people don't really die.*

Jenny ignored his question and took a sip of the amber liquid, letting the warmth slide down her throat and make a dent, however small, in that cold spot deep inside.

"Come on, Mom. You promised."

"Okay." She set her cup down. "But what I'm going say has to stay here."

"I can't tell Caitlin?"

She shook her head. "We can't risk it. If anyone connects me to what happened tonight, it could be dangerous for anyone associated with us."

"But you said it would be over." He slumped back in his chair, a flare of anger in his eyes. "Was that just a lie to appease me?"

"I didn't lie, Scott," Jenny reached across to touch his arm, but he jerked it away. "My work with the police is over. It ended tonight."

He crossed his arms over his chest and held that defensive

posture a few beats before giving her a quick glance. "What exactly did you do?"

She told him. Everything from beginning to end, only omitting the facts about George, the guns, and that unspeakable action she'd taken tonight. She noticed that as she talked, he relaxed and leaned his elbows on the table.

When she finished, he looked at her for a long moment, then said. "That is like, totally sweet."

"I take it that's good?"

"Well, cha."

Jenny took another swallow of tea, which was now tepid. Scott fiddled with a spoon, turning it over and over. "One thing I don't understand," he said. "If you got the bad guys, what's the danger?"

"These local drug rings are connected. Clear back to cartels in other countries." She paused to make sure she chose words that wouldn't alarm him. "They don't take kindly to having their business disrupted."

Scott's eyes widened. "You mean they could come after us?"

"Only if they know who *us* is." Jenny leaned forward. "Which is why you can't talk about it. Everyone who knows has the potential to pass the information to the wrong person."

"Does Dad know?"

Jenny nodded. "He threatened to take you away."

"On the trip?"

"I mean forever."

Scott shook his head, then stood abruptly. "I need cookies."

He went to a cabinet and pulled out a package of Oreo's. "Now I need milk."

Jenny watched him get a glass, then juggle the milk carton, the cookie bag, and the glass to the table. It was so reminiscent of a ten-year-old Scott turning to food when emotions got high, she smiled.

"Want one?" He pushed the package toward her, and she took a cookie out. He twisted his open and licked the frosting. Once more she was transported back to another time when Michael and Scott had held contests to see who could separate the cookie pieces the fastest without smearing the white stuff. Now they're doing commercials about that.

Scott ate three more cookies, downed a glass of milk, then leaned back and looked at her. "My mom, the drug buster. It's so..."

"What? Hard to believe?"

He shrugged, and she leaned over to touch his arm. "That's okay. There were plenty of times I wasn't believing it myself."

He laughed at that; the sound so ordinary that the heaviness in her chest shifted.

"Are you going to do it again?"

"God, no!"

"That's good." He closed the bag of cookies with a series of intricate folds. "I'd like to have my regular mom back."

Jenny's impulse was to hug him. Touch him. Say something that would mark this moment, but she sensed he didn't want that.

He stood. "Better put these up."

"Yeah. We should both get to bed." Jenny rose, grabbed the cups, and took them to the sink.

When he brought his glass over, he stood close enough that their arms touched. She leaned into him for a moment, and he didn't move away. It wasn't an embrace, but it was good enough.

# THIRTY-TWO

SATURDAY WAS A BLUR. Jenny tried some of the normal things; starting with going in to the shop for a few hours, but she couldn't concentrate on the anniversary bouquet she was trying to arrange. After she'd cut three roses too short and had to scrap them, Mitchell suggested he finish before she destroyed the entire inventory.

"Thanks. I don't know what's wrong with me today."

He gave her a look that suggested he didn't believe her, and she longed to tell him the truth. But she couldn't. She knew that. Ditto for her mother. She'd downplayed the issue last night with Scott, but the danger was real. If she was ever connected to the raid out at the ranch... She shuddered, not able to complete the thought.

She watched Mitchell finish off the arrangement with sprigs of baby's breath and fronds of ferns. The pink miniature roses nestled against the greenery like children leaning into the strength of a mother. "It's lovely," she said.

He smiled. "Thanks. Now why don't you go home and let me finish up here?"

She thought about arguing. Even thought about trying to make a joke of it. Was he trying to take over the store? But she was too tired for either. Making a silent promise that she would give him the biggest raise she could afford in January, she grabbed her purse and jacket and left.

The house was empty when she got home, and she had a moment of panic before she remembered Scott had gone to soccer practice. *It's over now. Stop imagining the worst.*

She spent a few minutes putting away the groceries she'd stopped for and realized if she didn't find a bed soon, she'd collapse. She could sleep for an hour or so and still have time to fix a decent dinner.

---

"Mom?"

Jenny pulled out of the depths of sleep and saw Scott standing in the doorway of her bedroom. The light from the hall slanted through the opening; otherwise it was dark as pitch in her room. "What time is it?"

"Seven."

"Oh, my gosh. I didn't mean to sleep so long." She swung her legs over the edge of the bed. "I bought stuff to make enchiladas for dinner."

"That's okay, Mom. I fixed scrambled eggs. There's some left if you want."

What she wanted was to go back to sleep, but she made herself stand up and walk to the kitchen. The eggs were decent, and Scott had even made a pot of coffee. "You're getting downright domestic," she said.

He smiled and sat with her while she ate. After she wiped the last of the eggs with a piece of toast, he stood to clear the plates. "Can I go to Caitlin's after I do the dishes?"

"What's gotten into you? I'm not complaining, mind you. But you haven't been this nice to me since that Christmas you wanted the mountain bike."

"Mom! Can I go?"

Jenny nodded. "Just remember what I said last night."

"I know. I know. I won't say a word."

A little edge of teenage defiance had crept into his voice and Jenny laughed. "Now, that's the Scott I know and love so well."

After Scott left, Jenny took a cup of coffee and tried to settle on the couch to watch TV, but nothing interested her. Restlessness pushed her to her feet, and she went to the front window. A light rain dotted the glass like tears.

She turned away, contemplated the idea of doing some heavy-duty cleaning to work off the tension, then decided it would be more productive to go talk to her friend. If she put it off for long, she'd chicken out and never tell Carol. And she couldn't do that. The woman deserved to know what had been going on. And she especially needed to know about George. *If only I can find a way to tell her that doesn't destroy us forever.*

---

Jenny made her way through the fine drizzle and took refuge on Carol's front porch. Porch was hardly a fitting word to describe the sweeping veranda that went across the front and down one side of the old house. It harkened back to another era when the porch was an extension of the living area, and Jenny was always a little jealous every time she came over.

Taking a deep breath, she knocked on the door, hoping her friend was home — alone. She could've called. Probably should have. But they hadn't exactly been on speaking terms of late, and she couldn't be sure that Carol wouldn't just hang up.

Seconds ticked by and became minutes before the front light flicked on, almost blinding Jenny. After a few more long seconds, the door opened and Carol stood there, wearing burgundy warm-ups and a white turtleneck. The picture of suburban domestic bliss.

"It's freezing out here," Jenny said.

"You can always go home."

"Please, Carol. We need to talk."

"Ah. Now she has time to talk."

The sarcastic tone almost drove Jenny off the porch. *Screw it. She's acting like a child.* But Jenny's heart had never let her turn away from a hurt child, even if that child lived in the body of a forty-something woman.

She pulled the door wider and brushed past Carol, then headed toward the kitchen. "Since you won't play hostess, I will. Want some coffee?"

Not waiting for an answer, Jenny shrugged out of her quilted jacket and slung it across the back of a chair. Then she filled the kettle with water and fired up the stove.

"I've got cognac."

Jenny turned to see Carol in the doorway. "Sounds good."

Carol went to a cabinet and pulled out a bottle. Jenny grabbed a couple of mugs and the jar of instant. *Okay, two sentences without rancor. Maybe we can do this without any collateral damage. Except for the part about George. That may be a deal breaker.*

Jenny heard the faint rumble of the water starting to boil just a moment before the kettle whistled. She turned off the burner and poured the steaming water over the brown crystals in the mugs. Then she carried the cups to the table. Carol joined her, topping off each mug with a generous shot of amber liquid.

Jenny reached for the sugar bowl, trying to figure a good

place to start a conversation. "Did you watch the news last night?"

Carol frowned. "What?"

"Did you watch the news? Local?"

"Yeah. Why?"

Jenny stirred her coffee, the clink of the spoon the only sound in the room for a long moment.

Carol frowned. "Was there something signi—?" She stopped, seemed to consider for a moment, then gave Jenny a searching look. "That ... that drug bust. That's what you've been doing?"

Jenny nodded.

The reality seemed to push Carol back in her chair. She was so still, Jenny wondered if the woman had stopped breathing. She leaned forward and touched her hand. "Carol?"

She took a deep, gasping breath. "How? What—?"

Jenny gave her a more condensed version of what she'd told Scott last night. When she was finished, Carol stared at her with wide, wondering eyes, then shook her head. "Wow. You really did do the Wonder Woman gig."

Jenny smiled. "Yup. Superhero Jenny."

The banter felt good. So good that she considered just skipping the part about George. Maybe that situation could work itself out without her interference.

Carol grabbed the decanter of cognac and splashed a bit more in her cup. "I'm still having such a hard time getting my mind around it all."

"Me, too." Jenny reached for the bottle to add more to her coffee. "But you do understand you can't tell anyone."

"Not even George?"

*Oh, God. Definitely not George.* "No one. Period. I'm only telling you because I put you through so much hell. And you are one of the few people I know who will actually respect the need for discretion."

Carol took another swallow of her drink. "You could've told me sooner."

"It wasn't allowed."

"I can keep a secret."

A hint of petulance accompanied that statement, and Jenny sighed. "It wasn't about friendship, or trust. It was about safety."

Carol pushed her mug in a slow circle on the table. Jenny reached across and stopped the movement. "That was the worst part. Hiding it. Lying to everyone. I hated it."

After another long moment Carol looked up with a half-smile. "Did you wear the steel bra?"

It took a second for Jenny to make the connection, then she burst out laughing. "Couldn't find one small enough."

"I still can't believe you did that." Carol picked up her mug. "I mean, I believe you. You don't lie—"

Carol stopped, and Jenny filled in the blank. "Only when I have to."

Relief brushed over her like a warm summer breeze when Carol chuckled again before asking, "Were you scared?"

"Shitless."

Carol fiddled with her cup again, tilting it one way, then another. Jenny wondered what she was thinking but hesitated to ask. She didn't want to invite more recriminations. Then Carol released the cup and stood. "I'm hungry." She walked to the refrigerator. "Does chocolate fudge ripple go with cognac?"

"Chocolate goes with everything."

Carol dished out two heaping bowls of ice cream and brought them back. "I guess I shouldn't be mad at you. At least it's all over now."

Jenny almost choked. This was the point of no return.

Either she would tell Carol now about George or let her friend charge blindly into God knows what. "Not exactly," she said.

"What do you mean, 'not exactly?'"

"It's not all over." Jenny took a breath. "I found out something about George."

Carol looked up. "What?"

Jenny hedged, studying the little stream of ice-cream that ran down the side of her bowl. "It's not good."

"What?" A touch of alarm widened Carol's eyes. "You don't mean about this drug mess?"

Again, Jenny hesitated for just a breath, then said, "We made a delivery to his house one night."

'No." Carol stood and pushed away from the table with such force her bowl slid off the end and crashed in a mess of broken pottery and brown globs of ice cream.

Jenny jumped up to grab a rag.

Carol glared. "Don't touch my ice cream."

Still not sure that telling had been the right thing to do, Jenny watched her friend's face contort as she seemed to process the facts. "Maybe he was away," Carol finally said in a soft whisper. "Somebody else was at his house."

As much as she hated to, Jenny knew she had to dispel that hope. "He stepped into the light. I saw him."

"No. Don't say that." Carol leaned against the wall and shook her head. "It can't be true."

Jenny crossed the space between them in two quick strides, but when she reached out to Carol, the woman held her back with a raised palm. They stood for a moment, eyes locked, then Carol closed hers and moaned.

Not sure if physical contact would send her friend skittering away, Jenny risked a touch on her arm. Carol didn't move. Her breathing had turned into gasping sobs.

Slowly, Jenny slipped an arm around the woman. "Before,

when I said the deceit was the worst part? I lied." She stroked the soft flannel on her friend's back. "This is the worst part."

The tears ran in rivers down Carol's cheeks, pooling momentarily in the hollow of her laugh lines, then spilling over. She turned into Jenny and clung to her. Now it was like sophomore year of college. That time when some jerk had walked out on Carol. Now, as before, Jenny didn't know what words might ease the hurt.

When the sobs abated, Carol pulled back and swiped at the moisture on her cheeks. "What am I going to do?"

"I don't know."

"Did you turn him in?"

Jenny shook her head.

"Why not?" Carol dug in a pocket and pulled out a crumpled tissue.

"God knows, I thought about it." Jenny shrugged. "But I just couldn't."

Carol dabbed at her nose. "What about now?"

"Eventually I'll have to tell. Unless someone rolls on him first."

After the words were out, Jenny bit back a laugh. *Jeez, no more* Law & Order *reruns for you.* She guided her friend to a chair, then sat down next to her. "But you need a chance to work things out first."

"You don't feel some moral imperative to clean him up, too?"

It was part question and part challenge, and Jenny wasn't sure how to respond. She could laugh, which might diffuse the tension. Or she could throw out some snippy remark that would make Carol good and mad. Would anger help make her strong?

Jenny touched her friend on the arm. "My imperative is over. Yours is just beginning."

---

When Jenny got back home, Scott met her at the back door. "Thought you were staying home now that your secret life is over."

"And I thought you weren't going to nag me anymore."

"You're right." He smiled. "Where were you?"

"I went to visit Carol." Jenny hung her coat on the peg by the door and entered the kitchen. "You want some hot chocolate? We haven't really had a chance to talk since the other night."

"I'd rather have coffee."

Jenny stopped and considered this son who more closely resembled a man than a boy. "When did you start drinking coffee?"

"It's not official yet. Still testing it out."

Thankful that he didn't take the opportunity to wound her with a reminder that had she been around more the past few months, she might have witnessed the beginning of the testing, Jenny got out the makings for a pot of decaf.

When it was brewed and they'd both laced mugs liberally with milk and sugar, Jenny took a warming swallow and sat down at the table. Scott sat across from her and stirred his coffee in slow, steady swirls. "I didn't tell you. But Dad called me last week."

"Then you knew he was coming?"

"No. He wanted to know if I still wanted to come out to California."

Jenny held her breath, wondering if she even wanted to know what Scott's response had been. And wondering why the hell Ralph hadn't said anything to her. Not even sure what to anticipate, she watched her son take the spoon out of his mug and set it on the table. Then he took a long swallow before meeting her gaze. "I told him no."

"Oh." *He told him 'no.' And that was before he knew the truth.* "Pretty big decision you made there."

"Yeah. But packing's such a drag."

A swell of emotion stung her eyes with tears, and she had to blink to hold them back.

"Dad said the offer was good any time."

She caught just the flash of a grin before he covered by taking another drink.

"And how long do you intend to hold me hostage to that threat?"

Scott set his mug down and this time didn't try to hide the smile. "I figure it's good at least 'til graduation."

# THIRTY-THREE

SUNDAY MORNING DAWNED bright and clear; the rain having been chased away in the night like an unwelcome guest. For a blessed moment, Jenny was able to forget and feel nothing but refreshing peace. Then the memories flooded back.

A picture of the dead man sliding down the wall flashed through her mind and brought a sudden chill. Then she remembered what Linda had told her that awful night. That it would be like this for a while. The burst of memory and the icy hand grabbing her heart. It would never go away, but the grip would lessen in time.

And like Steve, Linda had told her to fight the waves of guilt. "Otherwise they'll tear you apart. You did what you had to do. Nobody can fault you. So just keep telling yourself that."

Jenny played the words through her mind like a mantra. *You did what you had to do. There was no alternative.*

Maybe she could believe that someday. But not today.

She threw the covers off and padded into her bathroom. She couldn't face her reflection in the mirror. Proof positive that she was a guilty, guilty person. Then a goofy thought skittered across her mind. Well, goofy for her. She wasn't a church-going person, but the impulse was strong. Maybe she could find forgiveness in a holy place.

Yeah. Right. The building would probably fall down. She brushed her teeth, splashed water on her face and headed into the main part of the house.

In the early morning quiet, the emptiness of the house was profound. There was a note on the kitchen table from Scott. He'd gone for an early morning run.

Jenny microwaved some leftover coffee and considered her options. For the sake of the other people who might want to pray, she probably shouldn't risk going to church. In her estimation cooking was the next best thing, so she scarfed down a quick bowl of cereal, then pulled out the ingredients to make a pot of hamburger soup.

---

Jenny lifted the lid, and the pungent aroma of bay leaves rode the steam from the large kettle. She stirred the soup, noting that she'd made enough to feed a homeless shelter for a day. That's the way it usually turned out. She thought she was just putting a little bit of this and a little bit of that in it, but all those little bits added up. She'd have to clear space in the freezer for some of it. *Oh, darn. That means eating the rest of the ice cream for a snack.*

For a moment she considered calling Scott in to help her, but when she hefted the carton there didn't seem to be much weight to it. She grabbed a spoon and had just pulled the lid off when she heard the front door open and Alicia called out, "Mom. Mom."

Jenny set the ice cream on the counter and stepped into the living room. "No need to shout. I'm right here."

"It was so cool." Alicia dropped her duffle bag on the floor. "We rode horses. Both days. And Daddy wasn't even scared."

"I just didn't show it," Ralph said with the self-deprecating grin that had won her heart so many years ago. "How about you? How was your, uh... weekend?"

"It was fine."

Ralph's expression said he wanted to hear more, but Jenny nodded toward Alicia. He got the message.

"Can you stay?" Jenny asked. "Have dinner before you go to the airport?"

"I should probably just go. You never know how long it will take to go through security."

"I keep forgetting. I haven't had the pleasure of airline travel since nine-eleven." Jenny turned to Alicia. "Scott's in his room. Go tell him Dad's here."

The girl started toward the hall, and Ralph called out, "Come back here and pick up your gear."

As Alicia complied, Jenny tried not to let her amazement show. "That was very thoughtful. Thanks."

Ralph shrugged. "The cabin's too small to sling a bunch of junk around. We worked on being neat while we were there."

Jenny remembered the ice cream she'd left in the kitchen and pictured a mess dribbling off the counter. "I'll be right back."

After stowing the ice cream back in the freezer, Jenny returned to the living room as Scott and Ralph were saying an awkward goodbye. Then Ralph picked up Alicia and hugged her tight. "I'll call soon."

"Okay, Daddy."

Ralph put the girl down and turned toward the front door.

"I'll walk you to your car," Jenny said.

Ralph opened the door and they stepped out. Then he waved one more time to the kids before starting down the front steps. He paused at the bottom and looked up at her. "Is it too late?"

"For what?"

"To try. With Scott and Alicia?"

The shock was so great, Jenny was afraid her knees would buckle. She grabbed the banister on the porch.

"I know I wasn't..." Ralph's voice faded as if he couldn't put words to his failings.

*If that's what he meant. About being a lousy father. Or am I—*

"Losing Michael..." Again, he faltered.

Conflicting emotions threatened to tear her in half. Anger that he still had so much trouble saying anything significant, and anger at her impulse to help him out. That's the way it had always been. But she could also feel his pain... and something else. Almost a desperation that underscored his words. Maybe she should lead with her heart on this one. Do it for the kids.

"Scott and Alicia would love to have you in their lives."

He turned away quickly, fumbling for his keys. "I'll call. Make arrangements."

Was she mistaken, or was that the sound of a sob she heard as he opened the door?

He got in the car, brought it to life, then pulled away without looking back.

If that wasn't the surprise of all time. Motionless, she watched the taillights fade into the darkness. The shock was still so strong, she wasn't even sure how she felt. She should be happy for the kids. But what if it was just another empty promise?

That thought stirred the embers of her anger, and she realized that she was furious that it had taken this long, taken losing their son to bring Ralph to this epiphany.

And she still wasn't sure she could trust him.

But the alternative — refusing to let him — wasn't such a good thing for a lot of reasons. Mostly for the sake of the kids. They deserved to know and love a father.

---

Jenny and Scott were in the kitchen. They'd finally gotten around to the ice cream, which luckily was more than enough for three small bowls, and Alicia had just finished hers and gone to brush her teeth.

Scott stirred his spoon around his empty bowl. "Dad seemed kind of… I don't know. Different."

Before Jenny had a chance to respond, the doorbell pealed. She checked the clock on the wall. Almost nine-thirty. A little late for company.

"Want me to get it?" Scott asked.

"No." Jenny stood and pushed her chair back.

She walked into the dim interior of the living room and turned a lamp on before going to the front door. She opened it to see Steve standing just at the edge of the illumination. He wore a Dallas Cowboys jacket and had his hands thrust deep in the pockets of his jeans. The jeans had a very nice crease down the front of both legs.

He glanced away, then back, and she wondered what had brought him here.

"Is something wrong?" she asked.

"No, I—"

"Who is that?" Jenny hadn't realized that Scott had followed until he spoke. She shot him a quick glance, then looked back at Steve, hoping he could read the question in her eyes. He nodded.

"This is Steve Morrity." She faced Scott. "He's one of the officers I worked with."

Then she turned to Steve. "This is my son, Scott."

Steve reached around her and shook the boy's hand. "Can I borrow your mom for a minute?"

"Has something happened?" Jenny asked.

"No. This isn't official."

*That means it's personal.* She allowed a brief flight of fantasy involving knights and steeds and wondrous places like Camelot to play in her mind. Then she centered herself on reality. A reality that included a son and daughter who were sick of her being gone all the time. Not to mention the distinct possibility that a relationship with Steve simply wouldn't work.

"It's late."

"Of course. I should've thought." Steve took a step back. "Just thought we could talk for a bit."

*Do I dare?*

*If you don't, you'll never know.*

"I'll just be a minute." Jenny stepped back into the house and grabbed the jacket she'd dropped on the back of the couch. When she walked past Scott, she caught a hint of a smile on his face. "What?" she said.

"Nothing." He followed her to the door. "You're gonna owe me big time for this."

Jenny went down the steps and joined Steve on the front walk. He motioned toward Scott, who was closing the door. "Is he upset?"

"No. He's actually being pretty cool about it all."

Following her down the sidewalk, Steve mentally scrambled for a conversation opener. "Nice night."

"A little cool." Jenny tucked her hands into the sleeves of her jacket.

"You want to go back?"

"No. I'm fine." She stopped walking and leaned against the

trunk of a towering oak. "But if you'd just get to the point, we can both go in and get warm."

"I was hoping, maybe..." Steve pushed at an acorn with the toe of his brown leather boot, then glanced at her quickly. "Was I reading the signals right?"

He looked so much like an awkward teenage boy, Jenny had to stifle the urge to laugh. "What signals are you referring to?"

"Uh, at the club. When we were dancing. And afterward. I felt..."

"Yes?"

He chuckled. "You're enjoying the hell out of this, aren't you?"

She felt a twinge of chagrin. "Don't know what's gotten into me. I've had Scott on a string all day."

Steve took her hand and pulled her away from the tree. "It's been pretty close to a circus at the station, too. But that's pretty common after a big case breaks. That incredible relief that it's over and we're all safe makes us act a little crazy."

They walked for a few minutes with only the distant rumble of traffic on the highway filling the silence. Then Steve cleared his throat. "I still don't know where all the professional lines are drawn and how permanent they are. But certainly until after the trial. Which I sincerely hope will be plenty damn soon. So maybe we'll have to wait. But I was hoping we could see each other."

Jenny stood for a moment in awe at the length of his statement. Several sentences all strung together. Almost a full paragraph. Other than that day at Connemara, this was the most he had spoken at one time since she'd met him.

Part of her wanted to respond to the charm of the moment. He was as nervous as a teenager a month before prom, and that was incredibly endearing. Another part of her was afraid to let go of her reserve. They were both damaged goods, and it would take a lot of work to make them whole again. Was she up to it? Was he? Could they both let go of the past enough to do that?

"I don't think I'm going to like an answer it's taking this long to come up with."

As the moon broke out of some cloud cover, Jenny watched the light play across the planes of his face. He looked worried.

Reaching up, she touched the tight line next to his mouth. "It's too soon for answers. My life is an emotional wreck, and I wouldn't want you to become one of the casualties."

"I see."

He quickly turned his face away.

"Awfully quick to cave in, aren't you?"

He swung back around, and she smiled. "As they say in some self-help programs, could we take it one day at a time?"

He looked at her for a long moment, then matched her smile. "We could do that."

"Good." She took his arm and turned back toward her house. "Let's start with relieving any fears Scott may have about you dragging me off on some new undercover operation."

# EPILOGUE

A FULL MOON slanted silver rays through the branches of bare trees, and Jenny felt like she was being led by a beacon. This was one night that Scott hadn't objected to her going out. In fact, he'd almost pushed her out the door. What a relief the past few days had been. With the exception of that one big hole in their home, things had been as close to normal as she could remember.

It was also a relief to be out minus the skimpy clothes and miles of chains. Why did so many druggies wear chains when they were so friggin' cold?

She parked on the side street and walked toward Main. She didn't want to drive these streets. She wanted to stroll and savor the fact that the dealers were gone. Maybe more would take their place eventually. At least that's what Burroughs had said. The big-city gangs would try to come back and set up business again. But for now, people could go to the Dairy Queen and simply enjoy an ice cream without worrying about what was going on in the parking lot.

After getting a chocolate cone, Jenny wandered down

several streets without a purpose in mind and was surprised when she realized she was next to the cemetery. The ice cream soured in her stomach, and she threw the rest of the cone into the bushes. Some critter might enjoy the treat.

Then she entered the cemetery. The wind was stronger here, and she had to pull her coat tight against the chill.

Following a path that she would remember the rest of her life, Jenny wound her way through the narrow lanes until she came to the spot where Michael was buried. The mound of earth was still raw and bare, and she played the beam of the flashlight across the headstone. Michael Jasik BELOVED SON. Her tears blurred the dates, and she looked away quickly.

*Just go. What are you doing here anyway?*

She swiped at the wetness on her cheeks and faced the rounded hump of dirt. "I killed a man the other night."

She waited, feeling foolish for the pause. Did she expect a response? Some heavenly word of absolution? She slumped to her knees on a patch of winter grass at the edge of the grave. Dampness seeped through her jeans, but she didn't have the strength to stand up again.

"Next to losing you, it was the worst thing that ever happened in my life."

Feeling a tightness grip her stomach, she listened to the wind soughing through the trees, like some distant lullaby that was somehow soothing. "I didn't tell Scott. Or Alicia. I don't know if I ever will."

She fingered the coarse, brown turf. "And I don't even know why I'm telling you this. Hell, I don't even know if you can hear me. Why is it that people come to gravesides and talk?" She sat back on her heels and looked around. "Do spirits hang around waiting for loved ones to come?"

She returned her gaze to the grave. "Or is everything that was you gone from this earth?"

A new flood of tears choked her for a moment, and she took a deep, heaving breath. Somewhere close a cricket chirped, and from further away came the baying of a hound. Normal, everyday sounds in a moment that was anything but normal.

Leaning forward, she picked up a handful of the loose dirt, drawing the pungent aroma deep. She liked the rich, earthy smell of loam. Always had. "I wonder what it's like. Heaven." She let the soil drizzle slowly through her fingers. "Probably not like it's usually depicted."

A fluttering in a nearby tree sent a jolt of panic through her, and she turned to see an owl lift off from a drooping branch. "Was it something I said?"

She laughed, then. Not something she'd ever thought she'd do at Michael's grave. But the act seemed to free something up in her and allow her to say what she'd come here for. "I don't know if that man is up there with you. If the preachers are right, he went straight to hell. Which is probably where he deserves to be. But maybe..."

A sense of absurdity almost drove her out of there.

*What in the hell are you trying to prove?*

*I don't know. I just...*

In a desperate effort to center herself, she touched the hard, cold granite of Michael's headstone. "If he's there. If you see him. Could you...Could you tell him I'm sorry? I just didn't want to die."

Dear reader,

We hope you enjoyed reading *One Small Victory*. Please take a moment to leave a review, even if it's a short one. Your opinion is important to us.

The story continues in *Perfect Love*. To read the first chapter for free, please head to:

https://www.nextchapter.pub/books/one-perfect-love

Discover more books by Maryann Miller at

https://www.nextchapter.pub/authors/maryann-miller

Want to know when one of our books is free or discounted? Join the newsletter at

http://eepurl.com/bqqB3H

Best regards,

Maryann Miller and the Next Chapter Team

# ABOUT THE AUTHOR

Maryann Miller is an award-winning author of numerous books, screenplays, and stage plays. She started her professional career as a journalist, writing columns, feature stories, and short fiction for regional and national publications. This is her second book to be published by Next Chapter. *Evelyn Evolving: A Story of Real Life*, was released in May 2019, and celebrates the strength of her mother's life. In addition to women's novels and short stories, she has written a number of mysteries, including the critically-acclaimed Seasons Mystery Series that features two women homicide detectives. Think "Lethal Weapon" set in Dallas with female leads. The first two books in the series, *Open Season* and *Stalking Season* have received starred reviews from Publisher's Weekly, Kirkus, and Library Journal. *Stalking Season* was chosen for the John E. Weaver Excellence in Reading award for Police Procedural Mysteries.

Other awards Miller has received for her writing are the Page Edwards Short Story Award, the New York Library Best Books for Teens Award, first place in the screenwriting competition at the Houston Writer's Conference, placing as a semi-finalist at Sundance, and placing as a semi-finalist in the Chesterfield Screenwriting Competition. She was named The Trails Country Treasure by the Winnsboro Center for the Arts, and Woman of the Year in by the Winnsboro Area Chamber of Commerce.

Miller can be found at her Amazon Author Page her Website on Twitter and Facebook and Goodreads She is a contributor to The Blood-Red Pencil blog on writing and editing.

One Small Victory
ISBN: 978-4-86750-071-2

Published by
Next Chapter
1-60-20 Minami-Otsuka
170-0005 Toshima-Ku, Tokyo
+818035793528

4th June 2021

Lightning Source UK Ltd.
Milton Keynes UK
UKHW011322180621
385747UK00001B/110